ALSO BY SUSAN HUBBARD

The Society of S
Blue Money
Walking on Ice

The Year of Disappearances

Susan Hubbard

Simon & Schuster

NEW YORK   LONDON   TORONTO   SYDNEY

SIMON & SCHUSTER
Rockefeller Center
1230 Avenue of the Americas
New York, NY 10020

Copyright © 2008 by Blue Garage Co.

First Simon & Schuster hardcover edition May 2008

SIMON & SCHUSTER and colophon are registered trademarks of Simon & Schuster, Inc.

Designed by Paul Dippolito

Manufactured in the United States of America

1   3   5   7   9   10   8   6   4   2

For information about special discounts for bulk purchases, please contact Simon & Schuster Special Sales at 1-800-456-6798 or business@simonandschuster.com.

Library of Congress Cataloging-in-Publication Data
Hubbard, Susan.
The year of disappearances: a novel / Susan Hubbard.
    p.   cm.
1. Vampires—Fiction. 2. Murder—Fiction. I. Title.

PS3558.U215I53 2008
813'.54—dc22
2007045259

ISBN-13: 978-1-4165-5271-0
ISBN-10:   1-4165-5271-5

To the ones who never come back

It is a frightening thought that man also has a shadow side to him, consisting not just of little weaknesses and foibles, but of a positively demonic dynamism. The individual seldom knows anything of this; to him, as an individual, it is incredible that he should ever in any circumstances go beyond himself. But let these harmless creatures form a mass, and there emerges a raging monster; and each individual is only one tiny cell in the monster's body, so that for better or worse he must accompany it on its bloody rampages and even assist it to the utmost. Having a dark suspicion of these grim possibilities, man turns a blind eye to the shadow-side of human nature.

—CARL JUNG, *ON THE PSYCHOLOGY OF THE UNCONSCIOUS* (1912)

So much of nature has been ruined. Spirits of trees and rocks are displaced and haunt humans because they have nowhere else to go. No wonder the country is a mess.

—KIM MYUNG-SOON, A KOREAN MUDANG (SHAMAN), QUOTED IN *THE NEW YORK TIMES*, JULY 7, 2007, P. A3

The Year of Disappearances

Preface

Someone is standing in my bedroom doorway, watching me sleep, then watching my eyes open. In the dim light I can't see who stands there, looking at me.

But a moment later I am with the watcher, closing the door and moving down the corridor, toward my father's room. We don't open the door, but we know he's sleeping inside.

We smell the smoke. As we move toward the kitchen, the smoke becomes a presence, a gray mass spiraling down the corridor. Wan light spills from the kitchen, and now we see the fire—white flames shooting through gray whorls—and the shadowy forms of two men. At first they look as if they're embracing, but their embrace is really a struggle. They're fighting for something we can't see.

Then I am myself again.

The watcher leaves, followed by one of the men. They pause outside to lock the front door. I hear the click of the lock and lurch away, trying not to breathe. I'm on my hands and knees, crawling from the fire. I keep my mouth shut, but the smoke is already in me, burning my lungs. Then come words: *Help me,* trapped and strangled in my throat before they can be spoken.

As I wake from the dream, I hear guttural keening—a primordial noise that predates language—rising within me.

My mother's voice comes out of the dark. "Ariella? What's wrong?"

She sits on the edge of my bed, lifts and cradles me in her arms. "Tell me."

Why do we tell our dreams to those we love? Dreams are unintelligible even to the dreamer. The act of telling is a vain attempt to decode the indecipherable, to instill significance where likely there's none.

I tell my mother the dream.

"You were back in Sarasota," she says. Her voice is measured and calm. "On the night of the fire."

"Who were they?" I ask.

She knows I mean the shadow figures. "I don't know."

"Who locked the door?"

"I don't know." My mother holds me closer. "You had a bad dream, Ariella. It's over now."

Was it a dream? I wonder. *Is it over?*

∞

A few days before my fourteenth birthday, I awoke in a glass coffin, a chamber used for oxygen therapy to treat smoke inhalation. On another floor of the hospital, my father recovered inside a similar device.

The third person rescued by the Sarasota firefighters was Malcolm Lynch, an old friend of my father's. The emergency medical technicians reported finding a driver's license in his wallet. But when their van reached the hospital, the stretcher was empty.

The investigators said the fire had been caused by ethyl ether, a highly flammable liquid. They found an empty canister in the kitchen, but they weren't able to trace its source.

Those are facts that others have told me. When I think about the fire, my recollections come out of order. I remember waking up in the hospital. Then I recall the day before the fire—Malcolm, a tall blond man in a tailored suit, stood in the living room, telling my father without apology that he'd killed my best friend.

The experience of the fire itself? I don't know if what I recall is a memory, or only a bad dream.

~ ONE ~

In My Mother's House

Chapter One

*I*t was the year of disappearances. The honeybees were the first to go.

The stacks of old white cabinets kept near the herb gardens were eerily still. Normally the air around them shimmered with hundreds of bees moving from hives to flowers and back again, and as I approached, a scout or two would fly out to meet me, hover over my forehead, their buzz barely audible above the others' collective hum. The bees knew me and could smell that I wasn't afraid. Sometimes I closed my eyes and stretched out my hands, felt the air around me throb with the vibrations of tiny wings, even felt the brush of wings against the hairs on my forearm. I'd never been stung.

But that day in August, no scout approached me. The air was quiet except for the faint shuffling of saw palmetto leaves down by the river. When I drew closer to the hives, I saw a dozen or so bees, walking in erratic circles. Others lay on the ground, dead.

I lifted the cover of a hive and pulled out a frame. Instead of fuzzy worker bees moving purposefully over golden combs, a few bees crawled haphazardly along the cells, as if it hurt them to move. Some were missing wings. The honey looked dark and smelled pungent, more sour than sweet. I saw no sign of the queen.

∞

In July, a hurricane had blasted through Florida's Citrus County, leaving behind twisted trees and broken houses. My mother's house was one of several in Homosassa Springs to lose its roof. A companion tornado took out walls and windows, along with the stables, a guesthouse, and most of the gardens. We'd lost furniture, clothing, and books, but somehow the kitchen survived intact, and none of us had been harmed.

Now a blue tarpaulin shrouded what remained of our home. When I woke in the morning and looked up at the wrinkled plastic overhead, my first sense was of displacement—where was I?—then of being in storage, under wraps, waiting for life to begin again.

Every morning brought the harsh sounds of reconstruction. My mother worked alongside a hired crew clearing away debris and making repairs to the house's frame. To complement the machines and hammers, the workers played a portable radio; they preferred an oldies channel that mixed pop with heavy metal, so most days I awoke to the sound of Iron Maiden or Steely Dan or Led Zeppelin (eternally playing "Stairway to Heaven").

The morning that I found the dying bees, a deejay was talking about Iron Butterfly ("The soul-daddies of metalheads everywhere!") as I walked back to the house. The kitchen table was strewn with sketches and blueprints, and a bowl of oatmeal had been set next to a note from my mother: "Ari, Blueberries in the fridge. We're pouring concrete out back!— M."

I had to tell her about the bees, but I hesitated. I wasn't ready to bring her more bad news.

My mother's handwriting slanted right, full of loops and twists and optimism—nothing like the way my father wrote, in small, vertical lines close to calligraphy in their consistent precision. Comparing the two was easy—a letter from him lay half-visible beneath one of the sketches. The envelope had been torn open with my mother's characteristic impatience, and the postmark read *Ballinskelligs, Eire*.

Is it wrong to read another's mail? Yes, I'd consider it an invasion of privacy. Nonetheless I felt tempted. Would Mãe (the Portuguese word for "mother," and the name she preferred me to call her) really mind? After all, she'd left the letter in plain sight.

She knew how much I missed my father. He'd been gone only ten days, but he'd taken with him my sense of belonging—either to him or to her. They hadn't lived together since I was born, and I'd managed to reunite them briefly. Then came the hurricane, and the fire that nearly killed my father and me. Since then, I sometimes felt that I belonged nowhere at all.

After he recovered, my father couldn't wait to leave the life he'd so carefully constructed, so that he could design a new one in its place.

I didn't read the letter. Instead I put blueberries on my lukewarm oatmeal and sprinkled both with Sangfroid, the freeze-dried tonic I take three times a day, same as my parents.

I didn't share my father's talent for engineering change. I savored the brief periods when things seemed to stay the same, even while I realized that all around us, things were evolving or devolving, the living ones moving inevitably toward their own extinction or rebirth.

My hair, in a long braid, fell into my cereal bowl. I sighed and went to the sink to rinse both clean. Then I went to find my mother.

∞

Mãe stood in the shade of a mangrove tree, talking to two of the builders. Her long auburn hair trailed out of a bun she'd pushed under a canvas hat with a wide brim. Her sunglasses were large and dark. She wore a faded blue chambray shirt and jeans with holes in both knees.

For me she epitomized elegance. The men clearly were mesmerized by her.

To clarify: they hadn't literally been hypnotized. Although she was quite capable of that, too. Both my parents and I had special talents. They used theirs sparingly.

Mãe stopped talking and turned to me. "I thought you were down at the hives."

"I was," I said. "But you'd better come see for yourself."

She gave me a quick look of concern, then excused herself and followed me down the path that led to the hives. They'd been moved to shelter before the hurricane and returned to their old site only a week ago.

My mother took off her sunglasses and moved from hive to hive, lifting covers, pulling out trays. "Poor things," she kept saying. "Poor things."

"They were all right last week." I'd helped unload the hives from the truck and set them back in place.

"I've been neglecting them." Mãe stared down at the tray in her hand. Dark honey and unfertilized eggs that looked like grains of rice were scattered in the hexagonal cells, but not a single bee was there. "I've been so busy with the house." She slid the tray gently back into the cabinet and looked up at me, her eyes the same dark blue as mine. "We've lost bees before, but never so many."

"Maybe the hurricane made them sick?"

"Possibly." She didn't sound convinced. "I'll make some calls to-night, check in with the other beekeepers." Her jaw clenched, as it tended to do when she worried. "Right now, I have to get back. The builders are on a tight schedule."

"Can I do something?"

"Why don't you see what you can find out on the Internet? Search for *dead bees*." Her voice sounded wry, and she tried to smile. "See if this is happening elsewhere." She pushed her sunglasses back on and turned away from the hives.

As we walked to the house, she suddenly put an arm around me and squeezed my shoulders.

"It's okay." I felt clumsy, trying to comfort her. "We'll put everything back together again."

∞

I like solving problems. My father taught me the art of analysis—of defining a problem, then delving into its history and context, then restating it, and taking these steps again and again until the true essence of the problem emerged and could be addressed creatively and scientifically. Often, when you considered all the possible solutions, you realized that the real problem wasn't the one you'd begun with. The real problem often lay elsewhere—sometimes hidden, sometimes right in front of you, in plain sight.

But problem-solving worked better when we had Internet access. On that day, as on many others, the connection failed.

"I'll do some research at the library," I told Mãe. "Maybe stop for a swim on the way back." I stuffed a towel into my backpack.

"It's a long walk for such a hot day." She looked at my cutoff jeans and tank top, wondering if I'd put on enough sunblock.

I took the bottle out of my backpack, poured sunscreen into my palm, and for the second time that day spread it across my face, neck, arms, and legs. I checked the mirror. As usual, my reflection wavered; with intense concentration I could make it clarify, but only for a few seconds at a time. Those few seconds were enough to make out my long hair, stubborn chin, and the streak of white on my nose. I rubbed the sunblock into my skin.

"Be back by one for lunch," she said. "I'm making gazpacho."

Grace, the blue-gray cat my mother had adopted years ago, followed me down the dusty path to the gate. We kept the gate locked. I let myself out and shut the gate carefully. Grace, as usual, stayed behind. I blew her a kiss before I went on.

Near the intersection where the dirt road became a paved street, I stopped to watch two dragonflies—one perched on the road itself, the other hovering several feet above it. Both had translucent wings; the one on the ground had light blue patches on its thorax and head, while the one in the air was black except for the vivid blue tip of its tail. I focused on the one on the road, on the intricate, yet delicate, etching of its wings. Suddenly the hoverer dove at the percher—and the odd thing, the thing that mystified me, was that the percher didn't move, but let the other bombard it.

"Shoo!" I waved my hands at the attacker. I thought the other dragonfly must be injured, but after a second it flew off after the first.

As I walked into town, I wondered, *Were they enemies or friends?*

∞

Homosassa Springs was a sleepy place on the Gulf Coast of Florida, next door to the town of Homosassa. I never could figure out where one ended and the other began. Most of the locals referred to both as "Sassa." The area was popular with fishermen, manatee lovers, and vampires.

I passed the supermarket and the gas station, the restaurant (Murray's) that we never went to and the other one (Flo's Place) favored by vampires—and there were quite a few of us, attracted as much by the area's mineral springs as by its promise of anonymity. I waved at the post office in case the postmistress might be looking out the tinted window. She was one of us.

At the library—a small brick building overhung by live oaks trailing Spanish moss—I used a computer to search for *dragonflies*. The most intriguing thing I learned: dragonflies are capable of motion camouflage, a predatory technique that makes them appear to be stationary even when they're in motion. The predator dragonfly (called the *shadower* in the article I read) moves in a way that produces the image of an unmoving object on the retina of its prey, the *shadowee*—who might be food or a prospective mate. The camouflage works so long as the shadower keeps himself positioned between a fixed point in the landscape and his target. The shadowee sees the shadower as part of the background, right up until the moment it strikes.

The concept fascinated me. If dragonflies could camouflage themselves by the way they moved, could we?

Then I remembered what I'd come for, and I began to search for *honeybees disappear*. (I didn't think *dead bees* would prove as productive.)

Yes, the phenomenon was happening elsewhere, across the United States and in parts of Europe. Some of the articles I read called it a crisis, others an epidemic. Bees were simply flying away from their hives and never returning. The few left behind were found dead, crippled, or diseased. Researchers weren't sure whether to blame pesticides, mites, or "stress" caused by environmental factors. Some beekeepers blamed all three.

I printed out three articles to take home.

Before I left the library, I browsed through the fiction and nonfiction shelves, finding nothing much of interest that I hadn't already read. Then I glanced through the stacks of periodicals. My father never had subscribed to newspapers, and the only periodical I knew well was *The Poe Journal*, devoted to literary and biographic scholarship about Edgar Allan Poe. My father said he found solace in reading about Poe.

More to my liking were general interest magazines devoted to fashion and entertainment. I'd been home-schooled, and I grew up without TV or movies, except for brief exposures to both at a friend's house. Reading about popular culture had become a guilty pleasure of mine. My father would have dismissed this sort of reading as a waste of time. Why take an interest in temporal, inconsequential matters?

But American culture struck me as a roiling mass of contradictions, and I intended to familiarize myself with at least some of them. Why couldn't film stars stay in love (or keep their underwear on)? Why were the athletes so likely to take drugs? Why were the political candidates so anemic looking?

And why were vampires so invisible?

As usual, I left the library with more questions than I'd had when I walked in.

∞

The post office served as the hub of Sassa, the place where you'd run into the whole town(s) if you lingered long enough.

Two girls about my age leaned against the building. Like me, they wore cutoff jeans and tank tops that showed the straps of bathing suits underneath. Their eyes were invisible behind oversized sunglasses, but I knew they were appraising me.

The tall one with shoulder-length dark hair tilted her head to survey me from head to toe. The other girl had golden ringlets that framed her face, which had a doll's tiny features, and a rose tattoo on her right wrist. Her glances were more discreet.

But the dark-haired one looked more interesting, to me. The way she stood, the way she wore her clothes, made her look older, sophisticated, cool.

For a second I thought about stopping to talk to them. Maybe they were new in town, like me. I hadn't had a friend my age for a long time.

A beige-colored van idled in the post office parking lot. The driver's window was rolled down. The driver was a big man with a shaved head and fleshy lips. Even though he wore sunglasses, I knew his eyes were fixed on the girls.

By the time a girl turns fourteen, she's accustomed to men staring. But this man showed more than casual interest. He'd turned his thick torso to face the window, and he leaned forward, his mouth half-open.

Another thing about the man: he wasn't human. But he wasn't a vampire—I could sense that even from fifty feet away, even if I couldn't tell you then how I knew. He was another kind of *other*.

The two girls watched me, not him. I slid off my own sunglasses and let them see the direction of my eyes. I jerked my head in the direction of the van, to be sure they got the message.

That's when the driver saw me. When he took off his sunglasses, I flinched. His eyes were entirely white; they had no pupils. He must have seen my reaction, because suddenly the van jerked backward out of the handicapped parking space.

Before he drove away, he smiled at me—and the worst part was, I recognized the smile. I'd seen him earlier that summer, crossing a street in Sarasota, a day or so before the fire and the hurricane. Then, and now, I had a feeling hard to describe, a combination of revulsion and paralysis and fear, dark and swirling in me. I felt I'd encountered evil.

The dark-haired girl said, "Relax. He's only a perv." Her voice was low pitched and close to a monotone.

I wish she'd known then how wrong she was.

She said, "I'm Autumn." The most expressive part of her face was the dark sunglasses.

"You must have a birthday coming soon," I said.

"My birthday's in May." She kicked the wall behind her with her flip-flop. "My mother just had to name me after her *favorite season*." The sarcasm in her voice made *favorite season* a deep shade of red, bordering on purple. But I sensed she didn't share my ability to see words in color.

"My name's Ari." I turned toward the blond girl.

"Mysty." She was able to talk and chew gum at the same time. "Spelled with a *Y*." She pronounced *spelled* like *spayled*.

Autumn said, "Two *wahs*."

I looked at them, and they looked at me. "I'm going swimming," I said after several seconds of mutual scrutiny. "Want to come?"

Mysty yawned, but she thought, *Why not?*

Autumn said, "Whatever." I couldn't hear what she was thinking.

Listening to others' thoughts is one of the compensations of being a vampire. But it calls for concentration, and it works much better with some minds than with others.

∞

After a brief swim in the river—the shallow water felt too warm to be refreshing—we sat on an old dock to dry off. I'd brought an oversized towel with me, which had plenty of room for the three of us. Autumn and Mysty lay back on the towel to sunbathe while I reapplied thick coats of sunblock. They talked as if they'd known each other forever, but from their thoughts I knew better.

Autumn's family, the Springers, had lived in Sassa for more than twenty years, and Mysty was a relative newcomer, like me; she'd arrived four months ago. Both of them were far wiser than I was in the ways of the world.

"Seein' Chip tonight?" Mysty asked, her voice lazy.

"He says he has to work." Autumn's voice was dismissive.

"You put all that stuff on, you'll never get a tan."

It took me a second to realize that Mysty was talking to me. "I never tan," I said. "I'm susceptible to burning."

Autumn said, "I'm susceptible to burning," in a higher-pitched version of my voice. "What the hell is *susceptible*?" she said in her own voice, low and hoarse.

Mysty flipped onto her stomach. "Lordy, give me a cigarette," she said.

Autumn took a battered pack of Salems out of her jeans pocket. She wriggled out a cigarette and threw it in Mysty's direction. Then she threw a second one at me. I picked the cigarette up and looked at it.

Autumn sat up, a cigarette stuck to her lip, and fished a matchbook out of another pocket. She lit Mysty's cigarette. Mysty cupped her small hands around the match, even though there was no wind.

Autumn turned to me. "No, hold it like this," she said. She opened the fingers of her right hand into wide vees and inserted the cigarette between her index and middle fingers. "How old are you, anyhow?"

"Fourteen," I said.

"And you never smoked?"

Mysty watched us, smoking. She didn't need instruction.

"Make your fingers relax." Autumn's brown hair wasn't nearly as long as mine, I thought. Mine reached my waist.

"Dang it, you look like you're holding a pen. Here, watch."

She removed the unlit cigarette from her mouth and held it in her left hand, her fingers loose, almost limp. With her right thumb she slid open the cover of the matchbook and folded a single match so the head of it just reached the emery strip. Then she swept the match head against the strip with her thumb. The match flared on the first try and she lit the cigarette, taking a deep drag. She blew smoke in my face and handed the cigarette to me.

"Don't you try to light a match that way," she said. "Sometimes the whole book goes up. You can really burn yourself."

I brought the cigarette to my lips and sucked tentatively. The smoke scorched my mouth and throat; I felt as if I were back in the smoke-filled condominium on the night of the fire. I coughed so hard I thought I might faint.

Their laughter sounded like artificial coughs. *They must have practiced that laugh,* I thought. Autumn laughed so hard her sunglasses fell off, and I saw her eyes—dark brown, elongated, with a weary expression and a flicker of something in her left eye that caught my eye, glimmered, then blazed.

She put the glasses on again.

I handed her the cigarette and reached for the water bottle in my backpack. The water helped, but afterward my throat still felt raw. I knew I'd never get the hang of smoking. Yet I vowed to prove some other way that I was worthy of their friendship. They knew things that I didn't know.

But they didn't strike me as particularly good company. Mysty's thoughts were a jumble of cattiness *(Autumn's half as cool as she thinks she is)*, greed *(Just let Autumn try to steal my fries at lunch)*, and self-doubt *(Am I fatter than Autumn?)*. When I tried to tune in to Autumn's thoughts, all I heard was static. Listening for even a few minutes made me tired.

Sounding bored, Autumn said her brother Jesse had a car and could drive us to the mall sometime. I didn't know where the mall was. But I said why not. I gave her the number of my cell phone.

∞

I walked home slowly, carrying my backpack, feeling the weight of my damp hair heavy on my shoulders, breathing in the world around me— the cicadas, the tall grasses, the songs of the mockingbirds, the hard blue sky. The landscape pulsed heat and humidity and smelled of sun-baked weeds. Since the hurricane and the fire, details of the natural world announced themselves to me more loudly, vividly, than before. Before, I'd noticed, but I'd taken them somewhat for granted, I'm afraid.

Then my skin began to tingle. I stopped moving. Something was watching me.

I made a slow turn to the left, then to the right, seeing nothing but bushes and trees. Finally I spun around. The road behind me was empty. I told myself the sun was making my skin sensitive. But I knew better.

I walked on, slowly, measuring the intensity of my reaction with every step. Gradually my skin calmed again. Whatever had been watching me had moved on.

After the gate, the dirt path to the house curved to the right, and Grace bounded down to meet me. We came around the final curve and there stood the house, only its front limestone wall intact. A savory smell came from the kitchen, one of my mother's astonishing soups—garlic, cucumbers, basil, and tomatoes, as well as red wine vinegar and lashings of Sangfroid crystals and the tonic that kept us from drinking human blood.

Yes, we still had the urge to drink blood. I couldn't tell you which appetite was stronger, which one propelled me home.

∞

At lunch I handed my mother the pages I'd printed. Only the two of us sat at the table. Her friend Dashay, who co-owned the property, and Dashay's boyfriend, Bennett, were in Jamaica to attend a funeral. They'd be back in a week.

"So much speculation," she said, after she'd read them. She said she'd called the state agricultural office a few minutes before I'd come home, and left a message on their voice mail.

I told Mãe about the girls I'd met at the post office.

"What are their last names?" she asked.

I didn't remember.

"What do their parents do?"

"That never came up," I said. Did she think I cared about such things?

I was going to tell her about the man in the van when she pushed her chair back from the table. Her shirt was stained (with tomato juice or tonic?), her auburn hair had fallen down completely, and her eyes had the worried cast that made them seem darker. But her skin glowed as if it were made of pearl dust. She was as beautiful as ever.

She smiled, as if she appreciated the compliment. "I'm glad you found some friends," she said. "It's lonely without Dashay and the horses." *And the bees. And Raphael,* she thought.

Yes, I missed Dashay. And I missed the bees, and the horses, too. They'd stay at a friend's farm in Kissimmee until our own stables were rebuilt.

And yes, I missed Raphael. I missed my father most of all.

∞

Some voices have undernotes of rusty hinges. Others hint of water gurgling down slow drains. But most vampires' speech is melodic, measured, sometimes as lyrical as a song. I guess it's because our sense of hearing is so acute. We can hear our own voices, and most mortals don't pay attention to their own.

After lunch I'd taken a nap. I must have been asleep for hours, because when I opened my eyes, the light in the room had turned blue-gray. The wrinkled ceiling overhead reminded me of the underbelly of an ocean floor. From outside, voices drifted in, fluid and fluent as music. My mother's voice counterpointed that of her best friend, Dashay.

I pushed my hair away from my face and sat up. Their voices floated through my open window.

They sat outside in what remained of the moon garden. Once, pale night-blooming flowers had filled the circular borders behind the benches. But the hurricane left bare roots, broken stems, and piles of leaves and debris. The benches, upended against the house during the storm, now were set face to face. The sun must have just slipped beneath the horizon, because the sky had turned indigo—not blue, not quite violet, but a color in between. *The color of secrets,* I thought.

My mother, facing me, sat slumped in her chair, listening.

Is it wrong to eavesdrop? Of course. But if you'd seen the unhappiness on my mother's face, you wouldn't have been able to resist. I did resist listening to their thoughts.

Dashay's words poured out in clusters so fast that they ran into each other, and she spoke with an accent and lilt I'd heard only hints of before.

"Then I told them, I told them no, how can you be so quick to judge, but they do not listen, they are all against me, they tell me to go, and then I look for Bennett, I go after him, I look all through the trees, but he's not there, he's not there." Her shoulders were shaking.

I didn't want to hear any more. Bennett had been Dashay's true love, or so I'd thought. He was a tall man with broad shoulders and a beautiful smile. I'd watched them dance one moonlit night in our garden, turning and dipping, their hands clasped, and I'd thought, *Someday, I want to have what they have.*

I didn't want to hear any more, but I couldn't stay away. From the house's west side, still unfinished and open, I could see Dashay's face.

She was crying. I'd read the expression that tears "well," but I'd never seen it happen before; tears continually reached the lower brims of her eyes and overflowed, streamed down her face. Her white skirt was streaked gray with tears. And she said words I didn't understand: "Duppy get the blame, but man feel the pain."

My mother left her bench and bent over Dashay, wrapped her arms around her, pulled her out of the chair. They stood, holding each other in the ruined garden. The sky turned from indigo to midnight blue to black.

I turned away, surprised (but not for the first time) that I felt jealous of their friendship.

∞

The next morning, I awoke with the sense that everything was normal. The blue plastic ceiling seemed to breathe with the wind, the air smelled of sawdust, and the tapping of hammers broke the rhythm of "Iron Man," a song the radio played at least once every day.

But when I looked outside, I noticed something new. In the moon garden, all around the chair where Dashay had sat, bloomed tiny white flowers. Her tears had been their seeds.

Chapter Two

*A*fter breakfast my mother led me outside, handed me a hammer, and introduced me to Leon, a member of the framing crew, who showed me where to put the nails.

We were nailing plywood to two-by-fours, don't ask me why. I'm sure Leon would have told me if I'd asked. My mind wasn't on what we were building. I wanted to be inside. Dashay would be getting up soon, and she and Mãe would be talking. I wanted to hear the details.

But no, I had to help rebuild the house. It felt like being outside a movie theater or a playhouse; all the drama was on the inside, and I was left to imagine the plot.

Leon offered me some of the lemonade in his thermos. He was a muscular man with a deep suntan, dark eyes, and multicolored tattoos of knives and roses along his arms and neck. The rest—I just *knew* he had more—were covered by his T-shirt and jeans.

"How old are you?" he asked me abruptly.

"Fourteen."

"Fourteen going on thirty."

My father had told me that. Some days (usually when I felt tired), I looked much older than others.

The lemonade tasted tart yet sweet. I watched blisters on my right palm raise and almost at once fade away, but I quickly closed my hand so that Leon wouldn't see. I figured he didn't know we were vampires, and Mãe had taught me not to flaunt the fact.

The radio played a song called "Love Bites." Leon said, "Ain't *that* the truth."

Quitting time was at five. I ran into the house and almost collided with Dashay. She wore a saffron-colored caftan and her long hair was wrapped in a green silk scarf. She looked aloof and regal. But she gave me a hug—not nearly as emphatic as her usual hugs—and a strained smile.

"I missed you," I said.

Tears appeared in her caramel-colored eyes.

"Enough crying." Mãe's voice was brisk. She wore a dark blue dress and a string of lemon-colored beads. "Hurry and change, Ariella. Put on a dress. We girls are going to town."

∞

Happy hour at Flo's Place wasn't happy that night.

The regulars sat at the bar and in the booths, glasses of red wine and Picardo in their hands. But not everyone drank the red stuff. Here and there you could spot a glass of beer or white wine, mostly in the hands of mortals.

No one at our table was talking. Mãe and Dashay looked like beautiful statues.

So it came as a relief when the door to Flo's was flung open and Mysty and Autumn strutted inside. They walked in short steps, leading with their bellies, prominent thanks to low-slung jeans and abbreviated, tight tops. I adjusted a strap of my cotton sundress and thought I must look about ten.

Autumn and Mysty had done something to enlarge their hair. Their sunglasses were pushed back on their heads, and their eyes were lined and lashed and shadowed. Autumn glanced at me, gave me a nod and a wave. But they didn't come over. They headed straight for the bar.

Mãe and Dashay didn't notice them at first, but I watched as the girls tried to order beer.

After some exchanges with the bartender, Autumn said, "Ain't our money good here?" in a high-pitched voice that cut through Johnny Cash singing "Ring of Fire." Everyone in the place stopped talking.

"This ID is fake. I can't serve you." The bartender, whose name was Logan, was tall and good looking, with dark red hair. He was one of us. "We'd lose our license," he said.

Autumn turned and looked directly at me. "Well, you served *her*."

A half-full glass of Picardo sat innocently before me on the table. "Who *are* they?" Dashay said.

Mãe said to me, "Those are the girls you met the other day?"

I nodded. Autumn kept staring at me, waiting for me to say something, to come to their defense. But what could I say?

Logan laughed, and some of the tension went out of the room. "She's drinking Picardo. There's no alcohol in that. You want to try some?"

He poured an inch of Picardo into a shot glass and handed the glass to Mysty. She looked at it dubiously, then raised the glass and shot the bright red liquid down her throat. Almost immediately she made a gagging sound and spat it onto the floor. "Gross!" she said.

"It's an acquired taste," I said. A few of the regulars smiled at me.

"You girls don't want to be hanging around a dump like this," Logan said. "You'd be more at home over at Murray's."

Without another word they left the bar, Autumn throwing me a look of contempt as they went.

Logan said something under his breath, and everyone close to the bar laughed.

"I always thought there was alcohol in Picardo," I said.

"There is." Dashay took a long sip from her glass. "Plenty."

∞

My mother took Logan to task for lying to Mysty and Autumn. "You could lose your license for giving them Picardo," she said, leaning her elbows on the bar.

Logan poured us another round. He grinned at Mãe. "I know. But the girl wanted a taste. Now she knows what bitter is."

I wondered why we could drink so much Picardo and never get drunk. Mãe and Logan both began to speak at once: "Because we're not—" They laughed. Mãe finished the sentence: "—susceptible to alcohol."

I helped her carry the glasses back to our booth.

"Watch out for those girls," Dashay said as we sat down. "They gave me a bad feeling." Abruptly she stretched her hands toward me. "Let me look at your eyes."

She pushed my forehead back and leaned in close to cup my chin. I stared into her eyes: caramel brown from a distance, but flecked with orange and green and black and yellow, I saw now. It felt odd to look into them so closely.

After several seconds, she pulled away. "No, you're all right."

"What was that about?" I asked her.

She didn't answer. She stared off into the distance.

"Her mind is elsewhere," Mãe said, her voice gentle. "Let her be."

And so we spent the rest of Unhappy Hour in silence, listening to the jukebox play a strange mix of songs that smelled of stale cigarette smoke and loneliness, each of them plaintive in its own way.

When we left the bar, I noticed a beige van parked down the road, near Murray's Restaurant. "That looks like the van I saw yesterday," I said.

It drove away before I could tell for sure.

Mãe and Dashay didn't even hear me. They were each thinking about Bennett.

∞

Later that night, when Dashay had retired to her room, I came back to the living room, sat on the sofa, and tried to tune in to her thoughts.

My rationale was simple: she was my friend; she was in trouble; and, clearly, she and my mother weren't ready to tell me what had happened in Jamaica. I couldn't stand being left out any longer.

Mãe glided into the room, wearing a white silk robe that shimmered as she moved. She took one look at me and knew exactly what I'd been doing. "You did hear what I said about eavesdropping?" She spoke in a fierce whisper. "It's a bad thing—"

I said quickly, "Father always said that there are few if any moral absolutes." I was suddenly reminded of how much he disliked people who interrupted others. *The art of conversation in America is utterly dead,* he'd said once. "Excuse me for interrupting," I added.

"And so how would you justify eavesdropping?" She sat in the armchair facing me.

"Well, the infringement of her privacy is outweighed by the possible benefit," I said, thinking as I spoke, hoping it sounded plausible. "I love Dashay. And I might be able to help her."

"I don't think you're being logical," my mother said slowly.

"You let me listen to your thoughts. What's so bad about eavesdropping?"

"I let you listen sometimes," she said, and proved it by blocking them; it's easy to do that, if you're one of us, though I often don't remember to make the effort. "I'm not an ethical *expert* like you and your father, but in my opinion it's not fair to eavesdrop or listen to the thoughts of someone who's upset. It's meddling, pure and simple, and meddling is wrong."

I folded my arms across my chest. "Even if you think you can help them?" It was the first time I'd talked back to my mother, and I found it exciting. I wondered if I'd have had the nerve if the room wasn't so dark.

Suddenly Dashay swept into the room. "Let it *go*, Ari," she said.

But I had what I thought was the last word: "Dashay, you must have been eavesdropping."

Sassy girl, Mãe thought. And Dashay thought, *Just like her mother*.

In spite of what I'd said, I knew that Mãe was right: listening to others' thoughts was an intrusion, warranted only in exceptional circumstances. The trouble was, so many circumstances felt exceptional, that year.

∞

In the end, I didn't have to eavesdrop to hear the story. Dashay told me herself, a few days later.

Bennett had never wanted to go to Jamaica, she said. Dashay hadn't been home for years—she left soon after her parents died in an accident—and the funeral of a grandmother didn't strike him as the right occasion to meet her family. But Dashay cajoled him into going. (Bennett was easy to cajole—he was the sort of man who danced through life, laughing easily, making women want to flirt.)

From the first night, things didn't go well. For starters, Dashay's family had no idea that they were entertaining vampires. Dashay had grown up an ordinary mortal, but when she left home she was "vamped" (her word) in Miami—a city popular with the more vicious sorts of vampires. (Bennett was an *other*, too—but how that happened is another story entirely.)

In any case, Dashay's family was a suspicious bunch, and her auntie was the worst. She wanted to know what was in the blood-colored flakes Dashay and Bennett sprinkled onto their food. She wanted to know why Dashay "didn't smell right"—of course, vampires have no smell.

Auntie had always blamed Dashay for leaving Jamaica when her parents died, for not waiting until their souls were truly at rest. When someone dies, it's thought that her spirit, or "duppy," wanders for several days. There are special rituals to make sure the duppy is laid to rest.

One night Auntie saw Dashay and her cousin Calvin under a cotton tree. Dashay held Calvin's chin in her hand, staring deep into his eyes. Auntie got it into her head that Dashay was a witch, putting a spell on her son. So Auntie went off into the hills above Montego Bay to see the obeah man—a sort of shaman who links the spirit world with this one. The obeah man listened to Auntie ranting about her niece, the witch, and he laughed at her.

Auntie came back home in a furious mood. She said to the assembled family members, "He tell me, what sort of woman are you, worrying about witches when you have vampires sleeping in your house?"

Dashay was speechless. And Bennett wasn't there to defend her. Later, she wondered if maybe he'd seen Dashay and Calvin together that night. Maybe he got the wrong idea.

"Duppy get the blame, but man feel the pain." Dashay repeated the phrase. "When things go wrong, Auntie always puts the blame on duppies, or on me."

Dashay ran out of the house to look for Bennett, but she couldn't find him. "The love of my life," she said, her voice low. "Just like that, he was gone." She blew across her palm, scattering imaginary dandelion fluff. Then she began to cry again.

∞

That August I spent several more days helping Leon; we moved onto the roof, nailing strips of shingles into place, then came back down to staple stripping around the openings for doors and windows.

Once I looked up from my work and found Dashay face to face with Leon, her eyes inches away from his. I stopped, not knowing what to do.

"She's making sure he's all right." My mother's voice came from behind me. "She thinks that she can tell someone's condition from their eyes."

Apparently Leon passed muster. Dashay said something to him, then abruptly walked away. He looked baffled.

"Your friend is one strange lady," he said to me later. "She said she was checking out my 'sasa.' What does that mean?"

I couldn't help him. He was hoping it meant "sex appeal."

That night at dinner I told Dashay what he'd said. But she didn't laugh. "He has a small one, right near his liver," she said, her voice low, close to a whisper. "Not big enough to worry about, just yet. I tell him if he won't drink so much, the thing should leave him."

"A small *what?*"

"A small sasa," she said. She pronounced it "*sah*sah."

"Like in Homo*sassa?*" My vowels sounded harsher than hers.

Dashay nodded. "Not spelled the same, but the same sound, and I think the same meaning. Though some folks will tell you this place was named for pepper plants!"

My mother sighed and left the table.

"Sasa is spiritual power," Dashay said. "People have it. Animals have it. If you kill a dog, say, that animal's sasa comes into you, puts a spell on you, takes its revenge."

"You can see this sasa?"

"I can tell when it's in someone, yes."

My mother carried a plate of risotto to the table. She sat down without saying anything.

"What does it look like?" I had to know.

"On the right edge of his right iris, it looked like light, like a spot of light, flickering." Dashay passed a bowl of salad to me. "That's the place tied to the liver."

Mãe was eating, but I sensed her skepticism. "Can everyone see them?" I asked.

"No. First you need to be a foy-eyed." Dashay coughed. "That's a Jamaican word. *Four-eyed* to you. It means you can see ghosts and spirits and such."

"I've seen a ghost." The words came out, and then I wished I could take them back. They conjured up the image of my best friend Kathleen, who had been murdered the year before.

We finished dinner without talking. Afterward Dashay came up to me while my mother put away the leftovers. "I can try to teach you, if you want," she said. "Teach you how to see a sasa."

"Maybe someday." Curious as I was, I didn't feel ready to see any more ghosts. The one I'd seen still haunted me.

∞

"Still snooping?"

From the living room doorway the next morning, Mary Ellis Root glared at me. She was my father's research assistant.

I dropped the letter I'd taken from a pile of my father's mail. Like the others, it was addressed to Arthur Gordon Pym, the name he'd assumed when he moved to Florida. Raphael Montero had "died" in Saratoga Springs.

"What are *you* doing here?"

Root looked different. Same oily dark hair pulled back into a bun, same beetlelike body stuffed into a greasy-looking black dress. But the three long hairs that had sprung from a mole on her chin like misplaced antennae—they weren't there anymore. I wondered, had she plucked them?

"He asked me to collect his mail." Her voice was raspy as ever. "And just in time, I see."

It was so like her to accuse me of snooping when *she* had walked unannounced into *our* house. But I didn't try to defend myself. After all, I'd been caught in the act of prying. And Root and I had a history of mutual hostility. I'd always wondered why she resented me so much; I suspected that she hated anything and anyone that interrupted my father's research.

Mãe walked in, carrying a coffee mug. "Mary Ellis," she said. "What a surprise."

Her voice suggested the surprise was a pleasant one, but I knew better. She didn't like Root any more than I did.

"I came for his mail." Root never used my father's name.

"Of course," Mãe said. "Would you care for some coffee? Or do you prefer pomegranate juice?"

We all were sitting at the kitchen table, sipping juice, pretending we liked each other, when Dashay walked in and said, "They're all either dying or dead."

Root didn't ask who "they" were. I wondered if she could hear thoughts. Although I suspected that she was "one of us," I didn't know for sure. I'd never been able to tune in to her thoughts, and her personal habits were a mystery to me.

"They act as if they've been drugged," Dashay said. "That is, the ones that haven't disappeared. The ones who stay, they walk around in circles like they're lost." Dashay talked with her hands as well as her voice. I felt relieved that she'd taken the trouble to check out the bees, sorry that it had taken a crisis to reanimate her.

"What's their disease?" Root's voice sounded clipped and professional.

"It's called Colony Collapse Disorder," I said. "I checked it out on the Internet. Nobody knows the cause, but there are plenty of theories."

"Most likely the cause is stress," Root said, "brought on by something humans created. Pesticides, possibly." For the first time, I had an inkling of what my father appreciated in her.

Mãe said, "I got a response from the Florida Department of Agriculture. They've had calls from all over the state. They haven't come up with a definitive answer yet. But normally, if bees leave a hive, other insects and animals move in to eat the honey. Nobody's touching this honey."

"No bees, no cross-pollination." Dashay's hands flew outward. "Imagine what could happen to the food supply. What will people eat?"

"Just deserts." Root's eyes gleamed as she said it.

I turned to my mother, sent her the thought: *Root has made a* pun?

Mãe didn't respond. Her eyes moved restlessly around the table.

Root began to pile my father's mail into a canvas bag she'd brought with her. She said she was staying with a friend near Sarasota. "Do *you* know when he's coming back?" she asked my mother.

"Not yet." Mãe shook her head, as if to clear it. "He's looking for a new home."

"I knew that much." Root pushed back her chair. "What I need is a time frame. Our research can't go on hold indefinitely."

My mother said, "Neither can our lives." The passion in her voice surprised us, perhaps herself most of all.

Chapter Three

I've never much cared for Sundays—dull brown days, according to my personal synesthesia. Synesthesia is common among vampires. For my mother, Sundays were gray. Dashay said her days of the week stopped having colors when she was thirteen, soon after she began seeing sasa.

I was staring at the survey chart that hung on the kitchen wall when Mãe came in and threw her arms around me.

"What's this about?" My voice was muffled by her shirt.

"You looked glum," she said.

"I think I'm homesick." The words came out in capital letters, deep and dusky blue. They brought with them memories of Saratoga Springs—of gray winter skies and green spring mornings—and of life with my father in an old Victorian house. He'd taught me in the library every day, the world outside shut out by thick velvet drapes. Now I felt those lessons had ended too soon.

Mãe released me. "I could teach you," she said. "Not the same things he did. I can teach you about cooking and plants and horses. About myths and legends, and other things that he doesn't know. And about kayaking."

If there's any antidote for Sunday, it's kayaking. Even on that hot Florida day, there was a breeze on the river and a sense that time had stopped—that nothing had changed since the Seminoles paddled the same waters.

Mãe's kayak was yellow and mine was red. She gave me a crash course in basic kayaking skills. Then our boats glided out into a green and golden world.

"I did something stupid this morning." Mãe's voice floated across the emerald-tinged water. "I phoned Bennett."

It didn't seem stupid to me. "What did he say?"

"No one answered."

A kingfisher cackled loudly from a branch overhead, and we stopped talking to admire his fierce little face and punk haircut. *Punk*—that's a word I learned from watching television at my friend Kathleen's house. Our house in Homosassa had no TV.

"Anyway, I wanted to hear Bennett's side of things," Mãe said. "Dashay's story doesn't all make sense to me."

"Then it *isn't* wrong to meddle, so long as your intentions are good?"

She grinned. "I guess I had that coming. Yes, it's still wrong. But it's not as wrong as doing nothing when your best friend's heart is broken."

I was about to point out the fallacies in her reasoning when I heard Dashay's voice in my head: *Let it go, Ari.*

So I let it go. Over our heads, the tips of the mangrove trees bent and nodded.

∞

I'd barely begun to explore the area, so when Mãe was ready to turn back, I went on alone, toward Ozello, a village I'd never seen.

Alongside the kayak, a large gray mass suddenly surfaced in the clouded water—a manatee, his rough, wrinkled skin gray and green, crusted with plankton. He came so close I could have touched him, but I didn't. Mãe had told me once that she didn't think much of humans interfering with manatees. "They prefer to be left alone," she said. "Just as we do."

Two deep scars ran along the manatee's back, probably made by boat propellers. The state park in Homosassa Springs ran a refuge for injured manatees, releasing them when they'd recovered. I wondered if he'd come from the refuge. He sank out of sight again, the muddy water closing over him. Separation was a means of self-preservation, I supposed. That's why vampires didn't intermingle more with mortals, why we had our own culture—our own values, our special tonics, even our own bars.

I moved on, not sure whether I was on the Salt River or St. Martin's. Homosassa is riddled with inlets. Seven spring-fed rivers run toward the coast, shaping the land like pieces of a jigsaw puzzle.

White smoke trailed along the horizon and now I saw its source: two hyperbolic cooling towers, part of a nuclear energy plant. Putting aside all the arguments for and against nuclear power, one thing is for certain: the towers don't become one with the landscape, by any means. They sat, squat and ugly, a testament to man's disregard (or contempt?) for landscape and natural beauty.

∞

I heard the powerboat before I saw it. The whine of its engine shattered the peace of the place and made a great blue heron perched on a mangrove take flight.

As the boat rounded the bend, it was moving so fast I had no time to maneuver. I saw a blur of a white hull aimed straight for me.

Then I was in the water.

Mãe had told me to pull the release strap on the kayak's skirt if I needed to get out fast, and I tried that, holding my breath underwater, vowing not to panic. The strap resisted at first, then came free.

Mãe's voice in my head said: "Kiss the boat. Push up."

Kissing the boat meant leaning forward, putting my hands on either side of my body so that I could straighten my legs and push up and out. I was nearly free when I felt someone grab me, twist my body, yank it hard.

Then I was breathing again, and when I opened my eyes, I saw unbearably bright shades of yellow and green. My right ankle hurt. I lifted my leg, let it float in the water.

"She's okay!" The voice behind me sounded elated.

Someone was supporting me, dragging me away from the kayak. He wasn't tall, but he was muscular, and he reeked of beer.

"Lay back in the water," he said to me. He wore aviator sunglasses that hid a good part of his face, but I thought he must be seventeen or eighteen. "I'll pull you to the boat."

He spoke with so much authority that I didn't correct his usage, although a stubborn voice in me was crying, *It's* lie *back*. The shock of being capsized made me somewhat compliant.

The boat was more than twenty feet long, with the name MY DOLL painted across its stern, beneath two outboard engines. A green canopy shaded the cockpit. I was hauled aboard as if I'd been a case of beer, passed from hand to hand. I shut my eyes, suddenly dizzy. When I opened them, I was lying on the deck under the canopy, in the company of my rescuer, another boy, and my "new friends" Mysty and Autumn.

The girls looked at me with barely concealed dislike. I sent them back one of their favorite words: *whatever*.

But I must have not only thought it but said it, because the boys laughed. All of them, it occurred to me, were very drunk.

I didn't know whether to feel angry or grateful. At least what had happened to the manatee hadn't happened to me.

∞

They insisted on taking me and the kayak home. I had misgivings, but I let them. My ankle pain was bearable, and I knew the sprain would heal rapidly; most injuries do, when you're a vampire. The intensity of the sun did worry me. My scalp had begun to prickle, meaning I'd been overexposed.

I lay beneath the canopy and—forgive me—tuned in to their thoughts. All was not shipshape aboard *My Doll*. The boat didn't belong to anyone aboard; the boys had "borrowed" it for the day from the marina where Jesse, my rescuer (and in his mind *hero*) worked. Jesse was Autumn's brother. The other boy was Chip, one of his friends who'd come along to "hang out" with Autumn. The encounter with my kayak cut short their outing, and Autumn and Mysty directed their resentment entirely at me.

Feeling stronger, I sat up. "You know, this is a manatee zone," I said. "You were speeding."

The boys couldn't hear me because of the engine.

Autumn said, "Give me a break. Really." She wore a black bathing suit that made her look exotic, too sophisticated to be on *My Doll*.

"Manatees migrate in the summer," Mysty said, thinking, *Or is it winter?* She'd been forced to watch a nature documentary in school.

"Some are still around. I saw one today." I wanted to shout at them, but I knew it wouldn't change anything. "Should they be driving?" I asked. "They're pretty drunk."

"You've got to be kidding." Autumn's voice was sharp-edged. "Big deal, they had a few beers. You're the one who drinks that Picardo stuff. We saw it in the liquor store. That stuff is eighty proof!"

"That bartender lied to us." Mysty looked at me as if *I'd* told the lie back at Flo's Place. "Why didn't you say something?"

"I was with my mother." I spoke without thinking.

The words mollified her. She assumed my mother didn't know I was drinking alcohol and that the bartender had lied to protect me. She was accustomed to complicated lies, particularly when dealing with parents.

"Your ankle still hurting?" Autumn tossed a pack of cigarettes to me. She'd stopped blaming me.

"I can't smoke now. Almost home." I was glad to see Mãe's dock looming ahead.

At the last possible minute, Jesse slowed the boat. I told him where to tie up, and they lifted me and the kayak ashore.

"I'm fine," I lied, and managed to walk a few steps. "Thanks."

"You sure?" Jesse wanted to be a hero as long as he could.

"Very."

"Come on!" Mysty wanted to get back to the beer party.

"We'll call you," Autumn said, her thoughts inscrutable as ever.

I knelt to tie the kayak to cleats on the dock, and I waited until they were gone before I hobbled up the path to the house. I hoped they wouldn't call.

∞

When I came in, Mãe was sitting on the sofa in the living room, her head bowed, weeping.

"What's wrong?" I forgot all about my ankle.

She straightened and wiped her eyes with her hand. "I'm sorry, Ariella." But after she spoke she began to cry again.

I sat next to her. Tentatively I stretched out my hand. She clasped it. Hers was damp.

"It's everything," she said. "Dashay. The bees. Your father."

On her lap was an envelope addressed to her in his handwriting. "What did he write?"

"Nothing." She wiped her eyes again. "He writes nothing about himself. It's all about househunting and research and the *colors of the Irish countryside*." She rubbed her hand on her T-shirt. "Today's our wedding anniversary! He's the man who says he remembers everything."

I tried to think of words to console her. "He doesn't like to talk about his feelings," I said.

"I know that," she said, "better than anyone."

"At least he writes to *you.*" I'd had only two postcards from my father, postcards that anyone might have read with cursory interest—nothing like the thick envelopes of thin blue paper that came for my mother.

"He wrote to you, too." Mãe gestured toward the envelopes on the side table. "It came yesterday, along with this one. I was so upset about the bees that I forgot to open the mail until today."

I reached for the envelope with my name on it, surprised at how happy I felt. But I didn't open it. I wanted to be alone for that.

Mãe nodded. Then she must have tuned in to my thoughts, because she said, "Oh no. Your ankle? I should have taught you how to roll a kayak."

∞

Alone in my room I tore open the envelope. It was mostly travelogue: the coast of County Kerry was stark, yet more beautiful than he'd imagined—gray outcroppings of rock against deep green fields, and ruins of castles a commonplace sight.

"History intrudes everywhere," he wrote. Had I heard about the Skellig monastery? Monks had lived in stone huts resembling beehives on a rocky island in the Atlantic, off the Kerry coast. They'd abandoned the monastery during the twelfth century, he said. They left because of divisiveness after some of the monks became Sanguinists.

He hoped I was keeping up with my reading. Then he quoted some lines from a poem by William Butler Yeats: "O may she live like some green laurel / Rooted in one dear perpetual place."

At the end, he wrote, "I miss you."

It was not enough.

∞

Mãe said I had to spend at least a day resting my ankle. Lying immobile made me grumpy. To cheer me up, she brought me magazines she'd bought at the drugstore in town.

These weren't my preferred magazines. They focused on current events: government, politics, crime, and war. I leafed through them, growing more and more queasy and depressed. My father had called such events "ephemera," saying that they recurred cyclically. He said that to pay attention to the current phases of the cycles would produce "delusions of control, and in the end, frustration."

I wondered if my father was correct. True, I couldn't do much to end war or stop crime. But some part of me felt grimly pleased that I knew a little more about them.

Until now, war had been a historic term to me; historians made wars sound reasonable, understandable, even noble, with analyses of all sides of the conflicts. I looked at the photos in the magazines and thought, *History is just another kind of story.*

Mãe came in carrying dinner for two on a tray. (Dashay was "out," Mãe said, her tone telling me not to ask where.)

When she'd set it down, she said, "You still look sad, Ariella."

"I've been reading about politics." I unfolded a napkin and spread it across my lap. "Father never paid any attention to them."

"All the more reason why you should." She handed me silverware. "If we ignore the world, we do so at our peril."

"I guess. But I miss the old days." The sentence sprawled across the table, a pink-tinged sentimental mess.

"So do I, at times."

"What do you miss?" I asked.

"I miss Saratoga Springs, sometimes. Did you think I was going to say I missed my privacy here, before you came?"

"Maybe." The thought had occurred to me more than once.

"I'm glad you're here. It means everything." She opened a covered dish and began spooning creamed oysters onto a bed of sautéed spinach and toast points.

"I miss my bicycle." That thought, too, came out of nowhere. With my father, I'd almost always thought before I spoke.

"Your bike must be in storage, along with the furniture from the old house." She handed me a plate, which I balanced on my lap.

The oysters smelled of lemon, cream, butter, and tarragon—they hinted of faraway places I'd yet to visit.

"Why don't we go and get your bike?" she said. "We'll need furnishings, once the house is rebuilt. Raphael said we should take what we need from the storage unit and give away the rest."

Mãe said she'd book us a flight to Albany early in September. We'd rent a truck, go to Saratoga Springs, and drive back with our possessions. I liked the idea of seeing my hometown again, in the company of my mother.

Over dinner, we talked about my father. "You're right—Raphael never had much of a sense of politics," Mãe said. "Maybe because he had no sense of family, or of being connected to a group. He never knew his father. His mother died when he was born, and he was raised by an aunt."

"Then you'd think he'd want to be around us even more," I said. I'd barely touched the food, and Mãe's creamed oysters were almost irresistible. "He could have stayed long enough to give us a chance." *A chance to be a family,* I thought, finding the words too sentimental to speak.

Mãe heard them anyway. "But if someone grows up without that closeness, they don't know how to experience it with others. They may be afraid of it."

"I grew up without it." I pushed away my plate. "Are you saying I'll never be close to anyone?"

The words hurt her, but she tried not to show it.

She moved the plate toward me again. "If you want your ankle to heal, you should eat."

I speared an oyster with my fork and took a bite.

"It's easy to assign blame," she said. "I blame myself for leaving you all those years ago, and for letting you go out alone in the kayak today. Those are legitimate blames. I know the part I played, and I know the circumstances. But to blame someone who can't help being himself—that's not fair."

I sensed that she was right. But I couldn't give up the story I'd written in my head of a family reunited, living in harmony. No, I wasn't ready to let that story go.

∞

It must have been close to midnight when I awoke. Often the tree frogs' noise or the night song of courting birds or the bright moonlight was intense enough to wake me, but tonight I sensed nothing—no frogs, no birds.

And no moon hung in the night sky. Yet when I looked out at the moon garden, I saw the orange glow of a lit cigarette.

I limped into my mother's room, then Dashay's room. Both beds were empty.

So I went out to the garden alone. I moved silently, keeping close to the house until I drew close enough to see who was there.

Jesse sat on a wrought-iron bench, wearing shorts and a T-shirt. Without the sunglasses, he looked handsome; his features were even, and he had large, dark eyes with long lashes. But something about the way his mouth and jaw moved suggested that he felt at odds with the world, and belligerence had become his preferred way of dealing with it. He didn't notice me until I stood right in front of him, and he didn't seem surprised to see me. "So this is where you live," he said, his words slurred. Clearly the beer party had been a long one.

His shoes were crushing some of the white flowers raised by Da-shay's tears. "What are you *doing* here?" I said. And I wondered, *Where are Mãe and Dashay?*

"Wanted to make sure." He belched. "You okay." He smiled and patted the bench next to him. "Have a seat."

"This is private property." I kept my voice low, but I felt furious. "You have no right to be here."

He laughed. "Come on. Ari. Ari, you need to lighten up. Mysty and my sister said so, too." He belched again. "Whoops. I need a drink. You got beer?"

"Go home." I'd come close enough to read his T-shirt: THE TRUTH IS OUT THERE.

"That's not right. Least you can give me—the dude who saved your life—is a couple beer or three." He smiled again, trying to charm me. Then his mouth and jaw twisted back into their habitual clench.

I moved as close to him as I dared. "Look at me." *Can a drunk person be hypnotized?* I wondered. That hadn't been mentioned in the articles I'd read online.

For the record, the answer is yes. It took longer than I care to remember now—long minutes of me urging him to stare back at me, to breathe deeply, to hear only my voice, to go deeper and deeper into relaxation, until I felt the little click of engagement, the moment when he couldn't look away, and I knew that I was in charge.

"You will go home." I paced my voice slowly, evenly. "You will drive slowly." I assumed that he'd come by boat, since our front gate had an alarm system. "You will not exceed the speed limit tonight. Or ever again."

Suddenly I began to enjoy myself. "You will never come back here. You will not be able to drink beer. The taste of it will nauseate you." I wondered how far I should go, and decided I'd gone far enough. "Go now. When you arrive home, you'll regain your conscious state."

And he rose obediently, turned, and headed for the dock.

I went inside, back to bed, congratulating myself on a job well done.

But not done well enough. Next morning at breakfast, Mãe and Dashay let me know that in emphatic terms.

At first they were contrite about not being home when it happened. They'd gone to Bennett's house—Dashay first, Mãe later, looking for Dashay. Bennett had not come home.

Then they interrogated me about what I'd said to Jesse. Mãe reminded me that she didn't approve of hypnosis in general, but given the circumstances, she could understand why I'd done it.

"The girl had to defend herself." Dashsay looked exhausted, but she spoke vigorously. "And telling him not to speed or drink, that can only help him. Maybe save a few manatees, maybe his own life."

I smiled. I craved their approval.

Then Mãe said, "What else did you say?"

"I told you everything."

"You didn't tell him that when he became conscious again, he wouldn't remember what you'd said?"

The looks on their faces told me I had more to learn about the art of hypnosis. "They didn't mention that in the articles I read online," I said. Most of them had been scripts to help someone quit smoking or lose weight—scripts designed to be remembered.

"Oh, Ariella." My mother's words had heavy gray bottoms like snow clouds.

I sat without moving, numbed by her worry.

After a while, Dashay said, "Maybe he won't say anything. Maybe the alcohol will make him forget."

But I was remembering something my father had said. "Remember that what you learn carries weight. With knowledge comes the obligation to use it justly."

Chapter Four

*H*ave you ever heard a good song that had the word *eternity* in its lyrics? I haven't.

Since I received a portable music player from Mãe for my birthday, I'd downloaded hundreds of songs and looked up their lyrics on the Internet. When I did a search for *eternity*, what came up were lines such as: "I know we'll be happy for eternity." "We will be together for eternity." "I'll wait for you for all eternity." All written by mortals, who didn't have an inkling of what they were talking about.

I was thinking about writing my own song when my cell phone rang. Mãe had bought me the phone to "stay in touch with friends." So far I'd used it only a few times. When it rang, I jumped.

"That Ari?" The voice was distorted, but I could tell it was Autumn's.

"Hi," I said.

"We're going to the mall. You want to come?"

The alternative was helping Leon sand window frames. "Sure," I said. I couldn't read any emotion in her voice, and I was curious to see what sort of reception I'd get. Even if it was hostile, I figured that at least I'd know what Jesse had told them about the night I'd hypnotized him.

They showed up at the front gate an hour later. Autumn had said half an hour, so I'd been waiting awhile when the dusty brown car appeared, moving slowly up the road.

Jesse was driving. He smiled at me and waved—not what I'd expected.

Autumn sat in the front, and I slid in back next to Mysty. Jesse's eyes met mine in the rearview mirror. "Morning, Ari. How are you doing?"

"I'm fine. Thanks."

Mysty looked from me to Jesse and back again. Autumn turned around in her seat. "Jesse says you two had quite a *talk* last week." She winked at me.

She and Mysty both wanted to know what had happened. That meant Jesse hadn't told them.

I decided to be as honest as I dared. "I gave Jesse some advice," I said. "Slow down and don't drink."

Mysty's blue eyes were skeptical, but Autumn said, "It worked. This whole week, he hasn't had even one beer for breakfast. Or any other time that I've been around."

"He's sure not driving the way he did," Mysty said. "It took us two years to get over here. What's up with that big fence around your house?"

"It's to keep out hunters," I said. Many vampires gate their houses for security reasons. It's not that we can't handle intruders; it's that we prefer not to.

Jesse kept glancing back at me, his eyes full of devotion. He thought I was pretty. He didn't have a clear memory of being hypnotized, only a sense of admiring me, trusting me, and thanking me for the opportunity to be a hero.

Autumn and Mysty noticed the way he looked at me. Autumn said, "We going to the mall, or what?" She stared out the window, her eyes invisible behind sunglasses that always made her look bored.

∞

The mall near Crystal River was my second shopping mall; the first had been outside Saratoga Springs, NY. Both had movie theaters and Sears and such—but the Crystal River mall suffered from a pervasive retail malaise. "Going Out of Business" signs were on half the stores.

Nonetheless, on a Saturday morning, this was where local teenagers came to parade. A long line waited at the Piercing Pagoda, and another snaked from the movie ticket counters. Autumn and Mysty headed for a clothing store. Jesse stopped walking, and I hesitated, not sure where to go.

"Do you ever look up at the sky at night and wonder who's looking back at you?" Jesse said. His eyes had a dreamy look. He tipped back his head and gazed at the mall ceiling, as if he were at a planetarium.

"Yes," I said. "Sometimes." My father had given me a telescope for my fourteenth birthday.

"Ever think about what it would be like to get out there in deep space?"

"Yes." I'd often imagined it.

He shook his head. "I'd like to travel at the speed of light, so that when I came back, I'd be the same, but the rest of the world would be different. All my friends would be old guys, and I'd still be in my prime."

"It's theoretically possible." But not likely to happen in Jesse's lifetime, I thought. And even if it did, not likely to happen to Jesse.

Then Autumn and Mysty were there. Autumn had her cell phone to her ear, and she was saying, "Okay, okay. Whatever." She hung up. "I got to go meet my parole officer."

From Mysty's eyes, I knew this date came as news to her.

"I can't miss another one," Autumn said. "We can leave you guys here and come back for you after."

Mysty said, "Great." She looked down at her shoes, pouting.

I wondered why Autumn couldn't drive herself. She was old enough. But then I considered the possible reasons she might need to see a parole officer.

"It's not far," Jesse said. "We'll be back soon."

"Sooner if you stop driving like an old man." Autumn punched his arm. Then she seemed confused, as if she'd expected him to hit her back.

∞

Mysty and I had lunch at a place called Friendly's. Before I'd taken two bites of my tuna sandwich, she'd devoured a cheeseburger and eaten half of her French fries. She noticed that I wasn't so fast, and she wondered if eating slowly kept me thin.

"You haven't lived here long?" I asked her.

"Four or five months." She dragged a French fry through a puddle of ketchup. "My stepdad, he moved us here. He got a transfer to work at the power plant."

"You like it?"

She popped the fry into her mouth and tried to chew slowly. "It is *so* boring. I thought I'd die of boredom, until I met Autumn. And Jesse." She blushed, and suddenly she looked much younger.

So she thinks she loves him, I thought. *And she thinks I'm competition.*

The server asked us if we wanted refills on our sodas. Without waiting for us to reply she dumped half a pitcher of cola and ice into our glasses, liberally splashing the table in the process.

"Jesse is a nice guy," I said. "But I'm not interested in him."

She looked cheerful, but only for a moment. "He likes *you*," she said. "When we were coming to pick you up, you were all he talked about. 'Ari said' this and 'Ari said' that. I mean, you got the guy to stop *drinking*." She spoke as if I'd performed a miracle.

"He's stopped for a few days," I said. But I had a feeling he wouldn't resume, unless I told him to. And for a moment, I admit, I basked in my power to make a man do as I commanded.

Her head tilted to the right, Mysty smiled. She knew what I was thinking. She really was a pretty girl, I thought, noticing her tanned skin and carefully curled hair. Everywhere we went, people stared at her. Even though we both wore jeans and T-shirts, hers fit better than mine.

"I want you to teach me," she said. "Teach me how to make Jesse like me. Teach me how to talk to him, the way you did that night."

I wasn't going to try to teach her hypnosis, but maybe I could help her some other way. "You could teach me something, too." I gestured toward two teenage boys in the next booth. Their eyes had been fixed on her since we walked in.

She got the point. She winked at me.

After lunch we strolled around the mall. From time to time Mysty pointed out clothes that would make me look "hot" and told me I should use my hips more when I walked; when I stood still, she said, I should keep most of my weight on one foot and bend the knee of my other leg, to emphasize the shapes of my calves. In between these lessons, she told me her life story and the stories of her parents and older sister. Her stepfather was inclined to drink when he wasn't at work, but he was "a sweetie," not "a creep" like her "real father." Her mother was "an old hippie" called Sunshine who'd named her daughter Mystic Rose; now Sunshine worked as a clerk at a local drugstore, where people called her Sunny. Mysty had two stepbrothers living in Tennessee.

Telling me her story was her way of letting me know that she trusted me. All I gave her back were generalities: a vague sense of my parents being separated, my mother breeding horses and bees, and some generic tips on how to handle Jesse.

"Look into his eyes when you talk to him," I said. "It's amazing how few people really look into each other's eyes. Look deep, and speak slowly. Tell him what you want."

Mysty treated this advice as if it were a revelation. As I spoke, she touched my arm with her small tanned hand to signify agreement and thanks. I moved farther away, so that she couldn't reach me. Then I felt it—the familiar tingle up and down my skin that comes when someone is watching me.

I looked around, but saw no one. A few boys were eyeing Mysty.

My instinctive urge was to run away.

"Tag," I said, knowing how stupid it sounded. "You're it." And I ran off, down the mall. Mysty raced after me. After a minute I ducked into a side passage that led to a cash machine. She came after me, slapped my arm. "You're it!"

I put the index finger of my other hand against my lips. We stood still for a few seconds, catching our breath.

Then Mysty said, "Ow!" She held out her arm. "Look, something pinched me, hard. I didn't see anything, did you?"

I hadn't seen a thing. But I'd felt the presence of something approach us, pause, then go on. I looked at the bright red mark on her arm. "Maybe it's an insect bite."

∞

By the time Autumn and Jesse returned, Mysty considered me her best friend. She sat next to me again in the back seat on the drive back to Sassa, chattering about clothes, scratching at the welt on her arm. "You think this is a spider bite?"

"Who knows?" I said.

The car's air conditioning didn't work. Even with the windows open the air was thick with cigarette smoke and the musky smell of Autumn's perfume.

Mysty reached over and touched my arm again. "Feel how cool you are!" she said.

Autumn turned around, sunglasses on, her face impassive.

"Feel her!" Mysty said.

Autumn stretched out a hand and let her fingers brush my arm. "Cold," she said.

"How do you do that? You're not even sweating, and it must be ninety degrees in here." Mysty's eyes were wide with wonder.

For a second I considered telling them the truth: vampires don't perspire, and our normal body temperature is lower than that of humans. Instead I said, "You know the old saying: 'Cold hands, warm heart.'"

"My uncle says that." Mysty was easily distracted. She went back to scratching her arm. Jesse simply smiled, oblivious. But there was something wary in Autumn's face, in the set of her mouth and jaw. She turned around again without saying anything. Once again, I found that I couldn't read her thoughts.

"Stop scratching," I said to Mysty. "You're making it bleed." The streak of blood across her arm made me nervous. I forced my eyes to look away.

∞

"You can let me out here," I said when the car reached our front gate. "Thanks."

Mysty said, "Ari?"

I'd already opened the car door.

"Can I call you?" she asked.

"Sure," I said. I stepped out of the car. "Autumn has the number."

They were watching me, and I didn't want them to see the code I used to unlock the gate. I sent Jesse the thought *Go now,* and a second later he drove away. The last thing I saw was Mysty's face in the back window, her mouth framing the words *Thank you.*

The house looked less like a ruin now. The workers weren't there—some sort of holiday was being observed. Labor Day, I think. Mãe and Dashay were finishing a late lunch in the kitchen, and I helped myself to salad.

I sat down. Both of them stared at me. "You're *smoking*?" Mãe asked.

No, I told them. My friends were the smokers. The smell of their cigarettes lingered in my clothes and hair.

Mãe said, "Friends? Those troublemakers we saw at Flo's?"

"Don't be a snob," Dashay said to her. "Who else is she going to be hanging out with?"

"Are there any *other* ones around?" I asked. "My age, I mean. I'm the only one my age at Flo's."

"I thought you knew the facts of life," Mãe said.

"I do," I said, feeling confused. "Dennis taught me."

"That explains a lot."

She and I had mixed memories of Dennis. He'd been my father's assistant and our close friend. He'd taught me how to swim and ride a bicycle, as well. But he was mortal, and sometimes he made mistakes. The last time I'd seen him, he'd asked me to make him a vampire—a request that shocked me.

"Dennis is no expert." My mother cleared a space on the table, carrying plates to the sink, and returned with a notebook, a ruler, and a pen. She ruled in the lines for a chart, then began to fill it in. I watched, fascinated.

"You never saw Sara do the chart thing before?" Dashay made a face. "She's always making little maps and such."

"I need my information to be organized," Mãe said, still writing.

By nature, her mind wasn't organized—it enjoyed flitting around too much.

"Next thing she'll be making PowerPoint presentations at breakfast," Dashay said. "And that will be the day I move out."

Mãe's chart looked like this:

SECT	ORIGIN	LOCATION TODAY	CHARACTERISTICS
Sanguinists	England, 12th c	worldwide	Environmentalists; ethicists; mostly celibate; proponents of equal rights for vamps & mortals; subsist on blood-based sera and artificial blood.
Colonists	Germany, 19th c.	Germany, Latin America, China, and U.S. (outposts in Arizona and Idaho?)	Use humans for food and sport; favor their extinction through cultivating & harvesting; subsist on human blood.
Nebulists	England, 20th c.	England (Oxon) & N. America (Toronto, Miami, and LA)	Proponents of vampire rights; mostly celibate; believe human extinction is inevitable, but prefer to take victims one at a time; subsist on human blood and artificial blood.

I didn't want to appear ungrateful, but I already knew most of the information. Well, I hadn't known when the sects had begun or in which parts of the world they were popular, but I'd heard about most of the general preferences.

Mãe heard that thought. "Okay, Ms. Know-it-all. What do most sects have in common?"

I reread the chart, but it didn't help.

"Come on, Ariella, this is basic stuff. What do most vampires have in common?"

"We have special diets?" I said.

"Yes. What else?"

"We need to be careful about sunlight and fire." I felt more confident now.

"True. And?"

Dashay was trying not to laugh.

I looked back at the chart. "Um, some of us are celibate. I think."

"Yes." Mãe was relieved that the conversation was finally going somewhere. "Sanguinists in particular favor celibacy. Why?"

"Because they think it's wrong to have sex with mortals?" It was a guess.

"Their tradition says sex is wrong, period," Dashay said, glancing at my mother to make sure it was all right to butt in.

Mãe said, "Trust you to come in right at this point," but her voice was amused.

"Remember, the first Sanguinists were priests," Dashay said. "Maybe that should be listed on this pretty pretty chart."

My mother ignored her. "Even after they left the church, they favored celibacy. Of course, there were exceptions."

"Yes, but the girl doesn't need to know about all of that." Dashay turned to me. "What you need to think about is this: What do all of these sects have in common besides what you said?"

I reached across the table for a bowl of mixed berries. I felt thoroughly confused.

"They don't want vampires to breed!" Dashay reached out and brushed Grace, the cat, off the table. "They each have their reasons. Sanguinists think the world is overpopulated, Nebulists think it's nasty to have sex, and the Colonists want the humans to breed because it means more food. But vampires having children? None of them think it's the right thing to do."

"Why not?" I felt insulted, somehow.

Mãe was watching me closely. "If a vampire and a mortal have a child, that child is likely to have health problems," she said.

Dashay said, "That's only a part of it. These sects, they think the vampire blood is pure, and the world belongs to those *pure folks.*"

A "half-breed" myself, I made an effort not to take any of this personally. "What about vampires breeding with vampires?"

Dashay shook her head. "Can't happen."

"Well, that's what the lore tells us." Mãe's jaw clenched, a sign that she felt worried or sad. "Who knows? There's been no research to speak of. All we have to go on are gossip, myths and folk tales, Internet chat rooms. Most vampires are like Victorians—they prefer not to talk about sex. Anyway, now you know why there aren't other teenagers like you in Homosassa. You're a rare breed, Ariella."

I felt—here's that word again—dizzy. The conversation hadn't convinced me of anything. "Let me see if I understand," I said. "I shouldn't ever have a child. Is that what you're telling me? Because if I fall for a vampire, having children *can't happen,* and if I fall for a mortal, the child might have *health problems.*"

I wanted to ask questions. How severe were the possible health problems? Was I likely to be sick? I looked down at the well-intentioned chart, and I wished I'd never changed the subject.

Then Dashay picked up a pencil. Mãe winced, but didn't stop her. Dashay added another sect at the bottom of the chart: US. In the ORIGIN column, she wrote WHO KNOWS, and under LOCATION, she wrote SASSA. And for CHARACTERISTICS, she put a large question mark.

"*We* are not part of any sect," she said. "And what we do, whatever characterizes us—that remains to be seen."

I reached over and nudged Grace off the table again, thinking hard. For my father, being a vampire seemed such a complicated business, bound up in duties and ethics and obligations of all sorts. For my mother and Dashay, it wasn't such a big deal. And for me?

Something else the sects have in common: they all keep their distance from humans. Even the Sanguinists, who believe in peaceful coexistence, don't mingle much with mortals.

"I have a question," I said. "Why don't we tell people what we are? Why do we go to Flo's and not to Murray's? Why aren't we out in the open?"

"Because exposure can be dangerous." My mother spoke slowly, patiently, but she was surprised by the naïveté of my question.

"Some vamps are out of the box," Dashay said. "Mostly in the entertainment business. You can be a rock star or an actor and say you're a vamp, and the mortals think, 'Yeah, right.' They don't feel threatened by that, for some reason."

"Because they think it's a pose. And they tell themselves that there's no such thing as vampirism." Mãe pushed her hair back from her forehead.

I remembered the line from *Dracula* (we call the 1931 version simply "The Movie"): "The strength of the vampire is that people will not believe in him."

"If they don't believe, then where's the harm in calling yourself a vampire?"

Dashay shook her head at me, as if I were being deliberately obtuse. "Because we have been known to bite."

"*We* try not to." My mother's voice tried to soothe me. "But the Nebulists have no qualms about biting. They seem to get away with it, by and large—if incidents come to light, mortals are usually blamed. The Colonists prefer to kill in batches—they say it's more efficient, even claim it's more *humane*."

"Has my father ever bitten anyone?" I'd wanted to know that for years.

"Not to my knowledge," Mãe said. "It would go against all his principles."

"Well, he had to bite the man who vamped him—otherwise Raphael wouldn't be a vamp." Dashay lifted Grace and set her outside the kitchen, shutting the door.

Mãe and I exchanged a look, and a name: *Malcolm,* the name of my father's old friend, who had turned on him, made him a vampire against his will. Malcolm had vamped my mother, too, after I was born.

"Do we need to keep on talking?" Dashay yawned. "I want to wash my hair."

"Have we answered all your questions?" Mãe asked.

I swallowed a mouthful of berries without tasting them. I said I supposed so.

"Wait," Dashay said. "The reason we don't go to Murray's? It's too bright in there. Those fluorescent lights make me batty. Plus, they don't serve Picardo, and they have a terrible cook."

∞

Later, when we were alone, Mãe told me she'd driven by Bennett's house that morning and seen a FOR SALE sign on its lawn.

"Oh, rats," I said. We were working in the herb garden, and I stopped weeding. "Have you told Dashay?"

"Not yet."

"You have to tell her. And it will break her heart all over again."

"Tell her what?" Dashay leaned out of her bedroom window, her hair wrapped in a towel. Then she heard what we were thinking. We didn't have to say a word.

My mother and Dashay made a date with Bennett's real estate agent to see the house later that night. They pretended that they wanted to buy it.

"Why not be honest?" I asked. "Tell her that you want to find Bennett."

Dashay refused, and Mãe agreed with her. "This is the best way," Mãe said. "Ariella, are you packed yet?"

We were leaving for Saratoga Springs the next day.

"I need my metamaterial suit," I said.

"No, you don't." She didn't like the suit, which my father had given me in order to let me turn fully invisible. "I don't know where it is, and in any case, we're going to be visible on this trip."

That meant I'd be packing jeans and T-shirts. "Whatever," I said.

They both looked shocked. "I'm sorry," I said. "I'll pack."

Mãe said, "Don't forget to bring a dress. We'll go out to dinner, you know." She liked to dress up and go to fancy restaurants.

Left on my own after dinner, I turned on my laptop and decided to try to answer some questions by myself.

It took a while, but after reading more than a hundred posts by strangers, I arrived at the definitive reason why vampires and mortals tend not to mix: lack of trust.

Vampires lie. They lie to mortals almost all the time, by hiding their identity. And they lie to each other for all sorts of reasons. When a vampire blocks her thoughts, she may be lying—or she may want you to think she's lying, which is a more sophisticated tactic.

Of course mortals lie as well. But because we can hear their thoughts (not to mention hypnotize, scare, and bite them), we have a decisive strategic advantage.

Could vampires and humans ever really coexist in the peaceful, productive way envisioned by the Sanguinists? I began to doubt it. Could vampires lead ethical lives if they couldn't be trusted? Weren't honesty and trustworthiness essential to ethics?

If my father had been there, we would have talked for hours

about those questions, considering an array of interpretations and implications, redefining terms, using language to link the objective, social, and subjective worlds. But he wasn't there, and the questions remained a muddle to me.

When my cell phone rang, I was happy to stop thinking. Mysty's voice, breathier and higher-pitched than mine, informed me that she had a date tonight with Jesse.

I knew she wanted my approval. "That's good," I said. "Really good. Great."

"We're going down to the dock to, um, *stargaze*."

"It's a good night for it," I said. "A full moon, and Mars will be rising in the east."

She giggled, as if *stargaze* meant something else. In terms of talking to a friend, I was out of practice.

"I'll be sure to ask Jesse about Mars," she said. "I hope the bugs aren't bad. Mosquitoes love me."

I thought about recommending herbs that repel mosquitoes. My mother grew some. Then I realized that she didn't want advice. She wanted sympathy.

Have you ever analyzed human conversation? Most of it lacks purpose in the sense of accomplishing a task or seeking information. Most of it attempts to establish a personal relationship based on mutual agreement. I knew this from conversations with my friend Kathleen, who, for a while, had called me almost every night.

"Mosquitoes," I said now. "Yuck." Mosquitoes don't bother vampires. I guess our blood isn't to their taste.

"I hate mosquitoes." Mysty's voice had a faint Southern drawl, softer than Autumn's Florida accent. "I hate birds, too."

"Why do you hate birds?"

"I'm afraid of them. They have such mean little faces." Mysty made a funny sound, a kind of guttural chirp, like the noise cats make when they're unsettled. "They look like they want to peck out your eyes."

I couldn't think of anything to say.

"What are *you* afraid of?" she asked me.

"Being left out." I said it without thinking.

"Oh, don't you worry about that." She sounded amused. "I'll make sure you're part of all our parties. And when we start school again, I'll introduce you around."

"I don't think I'm going to school," I said. It hadn't even been discussed.

But I don't think she heard me. "Do you think Jesse likes skirts better or tight jeans?" she said.

Our phone call meandered for another hour. My ear hurt. I said that I needed to go, and then came ten minutes more of Mysty saying, "Okay. Bye. Wait," and launching into new conversational threads that wove around, looped back, and veered off again. I pictured our conversation as an enormous spiderweb, knotted and hitched and so convoluted that it made my head ache.

When we finally did say good-bye, I stood up and walked around the house for a while to clear my brain. Then I took my new telescope out onto the lawn.

It was an eight-inch reflecting scope that weighed fifty-four pounds. My father had taught me to use it before he left for Ireland. "The purpose of a telescope is to gather light," he said. "Homosassa is a good place to see the sky, since it's relatively free of light pollution."

When I looked through the eyepiece for the first time, I'd felt disappointed. All I saw was a blur of darkness and light.

"Be patient, Ari," my father said. "You need to learn how to see. Remember when you first tried to find constellations? You couldn't find a bear or a lion."

I remembered. At first I could barely see the Big Dipper. Then, one night, I was suddenly able to see the same figures named by star-gazers thousands of years ago—with a few exceptions. Cygnus to this day doesn't look much like a swan to me, and Perseus doesn't look like a man, much less a hero.

My father said, "With practice, your eye will pick up details that are invisible to you now."

The humidity level was so high that I felt as if I were swimming as I set up the scope. It reminded me of the air before the hurricane hit—dense and hot and gusty. I wondered if another tropical depression was on its way.

Tonight was not optimal for stargazing after all. Clouds kept scudding across the sky. But intermittently I glimpsed craters and mountains on the moon, and the strange shadows the mountains cast on the plains. I repositioned the scope. I was looking for constellations when I saw a dull red glow, an enormous star, twinkling from Orion's right shoulder. Before I could study it, it was covered by cloud.

But I remembered its location, and later I identified it as Betelgeuse: a red supergiant star more than six hundred-fifty times as large as the sun. The Web site I found said that Betelgeuse is "nearing the end of its life."

Imagine the supernova explosion predicted for Betelgeuse. The dying star will shed its outer layers and form a cloud of glowing gas and plasma. The scientists don't agree on the explosion's effects on Earth. Some think we'll be bombarded with particles and gamma rays. And they don't agree on its timing; some think it might take place in the next thousand years or so. But they are unanimous about one thing: Betelgeuse will die. I wondered where I'd be when it happened.

Suddenly, from the outer corner of my left eye, I saw a small movement in the trees near the deck. At the same moment my skin began to tingle. I pulled away from the eyepiece, and then I fell backward, onto the deck's bench, the night world around me spinning. A sense of nausea rose from deep in me, and I felt something approaching out of the dark. I put my hands on either side of my head, trying to stop the spinning. But I couldn't make it stop, and I couldn't make what was out there go away. Then I passed out.

When I opened my eyes again, cold air swirled around me. I sat up. I felt no dizziness, no sensation of being watched. The telescope was still there. The stars hadn't changed position.

Have you ever been outside at night and sensed that you were not alone? Odds are, your sense was correct. The night is as full of things, seen and unseen, as the sky is full of stars.

Chapter Five

*W*hen Mãe and Dashay came home that night, Dashay walked through the living room right past me without saying anything. Her lips pressed tightly together, but nonetheless they trembled.

I lay on the sofa, wrapped in a blanket. Mãe shook her head, warning me to stay quiet. After Dashay shut her bedroom door, Mãe said, "Well, that was a mistake."

The real estate agent had been delighted to see them at first. "She said she'd put up the sign only this morning, and she knew the house would sell fast. She offered us sweet tea."

Ignoring the realtor, Dashay had headed straight for the bedroom, opened a closet door, and said, "His clothes are still here."

Not, my mother observed, the most subtle tactic. And in complete disregard of the strategy they'd planned on the drive over to Bennett's place.

"The agent said she'd never met Bennett," Mãe said. "She listed the house after he faxed her a letter. They've hired professional movers to come in tomorrow to pack up his things."

"So where is he?"

"Atlanta." Mãe sat on the sofa and kicked off her sandals. "She didn't tell us that straight out. She let it slip later, when I asked her about the advantages of living in the South."

"Atlanta's not so far." I'd seen it on a map. That was one thing my mother had taught me: how to read maps. Before I tried to find her, I'd never thought I needed them.

Mãe laid her head against the cushions. "We asked her why the owner was selling, and she said he'd made the decision all of a sudden. She said she thought he was going to be married in Atlanta."

I thought, *Poor Dashay.*

My mother tilted her head forward and opened her eyes. "At first, Dashay didn't move. She stood there, not even blinking. Then she picked up Bennett's globe—remember the crystal globe? She picked it up and threw it at the door."

I did remember the globe, sitting on a pedestal in Bennett's living room. Dashay had given it to him. It was an antique—a clear sphere with continents delicately etched across it and signs of the zodiac engraved on its base. To me, it epitomized fragility.

"Why did she have to *break* it?"

My mother flinched. She was recalling the graceful arc of the globe's trajectory. Instinctively, she'd bent forward, stretched out her hands, thinking she might catch it in time. The globe flew past her fingertips.

I watched my mother stretch out her hands, look at them critically. She wasn't accustomed to them failing her.

"Don't you ever have moments where you find yourself doing things you'd never intended to do?" she asked. "Moments when your feelings swell up and take over?"

Yes, I'd had such moments. And she knew I had.

My mother flexed her fingers. "Sometimes, we need to break things." Then she noticed me and the blanket. "Aren't you feeling well?"

I told her about the dizziness, the spinning, the passing out. "Darkness was all around," I said, unable to think of more precise words.

She said, "Sounds like vertigo. Vampires are prone to it."

"And I felt that someone was watching me."

Her jaw clenched tight, and her eyes darkened. "If you're not well, we'll postpone our trip."

"No," I said. "I'm fine now. And I'd really like to get away for a while."

∞

Next morning, Dashay insisted on driving us to the airport in Orlando.

Mãe was still ready to cancel the trip, but Dashay wouldn't hear of it.

"You are going to get up there and bring us back some furniture," she said. "This place needs furniture. Chairs and bookcases and all those little things, rugs and lamps and pictures. We need to make this place like a home again."

Mãe kept glancing at Dashay, trying to figure her out. Dashay smiled at my mother—a wide, artificial smile, a parody of a real one. Her eyes were solemn.

"Stop smiling that weird smile," Mãe said. "You win. We'll go. But stop smiling."

Dashay stopped smiling. We went. We drove across the rolling green terrain of Citrus County toward flat Orlando. I felt too nervous to talk. I'd never flown before.

The Orlando airport was bedlam. Hundreds of children wearing mouse hats and T-shirts, almost none of them happy, made a din unlike anything I'd heard before or since.

My mother looked lean and cool in a white suit. Most of the tourists wore T-shirts and shorts. She looked like a separate species, as indeed she was.

She leaned back in her chair, watching the chaos, her eyes serene.

"Every one of us has a story of our lives." Mãe stretched out her legs, about to kick off her shoes, then realized where she was and kept them on. "Some of us make them up as we go. Others buy into the stories told on TV or in the movies." She looked at an old man wearing mouse ears. "Stories help us get by. They don't have to make sense."

She went to check the arrival board and came back to say our plane was late. "What shall we do?" she said. "How about a dance?"

Speakers in the ceiling played classical music—an attempt to drown out the screaming children, I supposed. At the moment, a waltz was on.

"I don't know how to dance." I hated to confess ignorance to her, yet I seemed to do it at least once a day.

"Then I'll teach you."

So I had my first dance lesson at the Orlando airport, moving across the industrial carpeting in three-four time to the music of Strauss, accompanied by the shrieks of unhappy children.

∞

On the plane, Mãe was thinking ahead, to renting the van, checking into a hotel, finding a place for dinner. She often lived in the near future, I thought. Like my father, she liked to make plans and watch them come into being. If the plans failed, she'd think ahead to new ones.

I preferred to live in the present. Everything about the plane—the uncomfortable seats, the tiny screens that showed a safety video, the attendants' peculiar costumes—was fascinating, to me. And as the plane cruised up the Northeastern coastline, I looked down at the rivers and streams that ran into the ocean and saw them light up—first silver, then gold, then indigo—as the plane flew over them. A trick of the light? The sun was almost directly overhead. Whatever caused the phenomenon, it made the earth appear to be a living body, with rivers for veins.

"You're feeling better." Mãe looked over my shoulder, down at the beautiful earth. "The vertigo is gone."

"Yes." Yesterday's sense of foreboding already was far behind us.

I didn't let myself think ahead, about returning to the city where I'd been born. In the present moment, I felt alive.

∞

From the air, upstate New York seemed a hundred shades of green, a mosaic of fern and moss and pine. If I were able to name colors, I'd create a hue called mountain green—a mixture of pine and gray asparagus, it was the predominant color of the landscape that day.

On the ground upstate New York—Saratoga Springs, at least—seemed a place trying to live in its past, trying to become what it once was.

We chose an old hotel downtown, a place I'd often ridden past on my bicycle, wondering what its rooms might be like. The wallpaper, carpeting, and furniture had "seen better days," Mãe said, and I wondered if it was literally true, if inanimate objects retained any memory or connotation of past events. Was that armchair less happy now than in the late nineteenth century, when it had been built? *Yes,* I thought. *It must be.*

I had a similar sensation the next morning, when we drove past our old house. A stately Victorian with a cupola, it had been painted gray when last I saw it, and a wisteria vine had trailed along its left side.

The vine had been chopped down and the house painted lime green with violet trim. Since then I've heard a term for such houses: "painted ladies." The name described the house well. The house's windows, once reminding me of hooded eyes, had been stripped of curtains and shades. Now they were wide open, vacant. Stone cherubs stood on either side of its brick walkway. A large wooden sign on the lawn read BETTY'S HAVEN B&B.

My mother and I said, at the same time, "Oh."

The house emitted signals of distress—visible sparks, faintly yellow in the morning air. It didn't like what had been done to it any more than we did.

I tried to send the house a message: *Someday, you will be rescued.*

∞

Here was one thing Saratoga Springs had in common with Florida: storage units. The repositories of cast-off lives. Our unit smelled of dust and memories. It was lined with neatly stacked boxes and furniture shrouded in plastic covers.

Mãe said, "There's more here than I'd imagined."

In cartons marked simply "A," I found clothes, books, old notebooks in which my handwriting looked unbearably eager, and CDs that Kathleen had given me. I didn't want to read the notebooks or listen to the CDs, but I wasn't ready to give them away. I sealed two boxes and loaded them into the back of the truck we'd rented. When I came back, Mãe was sitting cross-legged, a pile of green fabric in her lap, crying.

"I'm sorry," she said. She held up the cloth, and it unfurled into a chiffon cocktail dress. "I bought this to wear when I met your father in London."

"He mentioned that dress once," I said. "He said it reminded him of lettuce."

She smiled, and cried. Except for three boxes of books, photographs, and artwork, and several pieces of furniture, she was giving most of her possessions away.

I found boxes of toys I'd outgrown years ago—stuffed animals and picture puzzles and books. I moved them to the give-away pile.

But when we finished loading the things to take home, I changed my mind. "These come, too," I said.

Mãe knew what I was thinking: that one day I might have a child who would play with those toys. She considered it a bad idea. But she didn't argue.

Late afternoon on the following day, we arrived at the thrift shop's donation center. After we'd taken out all of our giveaways, I thought of one last thing I had to have. I'd untaped four of the cartons marked KITCHEN before I found it: my mother's old cookbook. She'd written comments next to the recipes, long before I'd known her.

Mãe was tired and hungry and eager to get back to the hotel, but when she saw what I'd been looking for, her face brightened. "You can't know how much that means to me," she said. "It was a present from my mother."

For me, finding the cookbook justified the entire trip.

My cell phone rang. The ring tone was an excerpt from Tchaikovsky's *Swan Lake,* which happens to be the only music in The Movie—but that's not why I chose it. I thought the tune mournful and romantic.

It was Dashay, asking to speak to my mother without saying "Hello" or "How are you?" to me.

Mãe held the phone with the pads of her fingers, as if it were a dead fish. "Yes?" she said. Then she listened for a while.

"Yes." My mother's voice sounded strained. "Well, I'll tell her. We'll be on the road first thing tomorrow." She said good-bye and handed me the phone. "Bad news."

"I gathered that."

"You may be getting a call from the county sheriff's office. It's your friend," Mãe said. "That girl Mysty. She seems to have disappeared."

"Disappeared?" I thought of Mysty, small and doll-like. How could she be *gone?* Was she lost? Had she been hurt? "She called me the night before we left town. She said she and Jesse were going star-gazing. And after she hung up, I took the telescope outside and did my own stargazing. That's when I got dizzy, remember?"

"Jesse's the one you hypnotized?" Mãe's eyes were serious, almost cold.

"Yes."

She wondered if I might have made him hurt her, and I reassured her. We didn't put any of that into words. *He's an oaf, but an amiable oaf,* I thought. *He wouldn't hurt her.*

My mother said, "She's probably wandered off, the way girls do sometimes. She'll likely turn up in a day or so."

∞

Mãe said we should try to buy Picardo for the trip home, since so few places along the road stocked it. Whatever is in Picardo (its ingredients are a secret kept by the manufacturer) helps us get by without blood.

We walked a few blocks to a liquor store. The clerk dusted off the bottle Mãe handed him. "Not much call for this stuff," he said. "Tell you what—I'll give you a discount if you buy two."

"Thanks." Mãe set money on the counter.

He wiped off the second bottle. "This is your lucky day," he said.

"We're not lucky," I said. Words and worry spiraled through me. I might have said more, but Mãe said, "Why don't you wait outside?"

So I stood outside the liquor store while she made small talk with its owner. Three teenagers sat in a car in the parking lot, debating which of them would go inside and try to buy a bottle of vodka. I noticed them idly, the way one takes in surroundings that don't matter. One of them left the car, slamming the door behind him.

I was thinking about Mysty's voice on the phone that night, the soft drawl that lingered over words of more than one syllable and sped up when she was excited. Wouldn't she have told me, if she'd been planning to go away?

"Ari?"

One of the boys in the car said my name, twice.

I recognized the voice. "Michael."

He got out of the car. He was thinner than I'd recalled, but otherwise the same: long hair, dark eyes, dark clothes. I looked at his mouth and thought of our first kiss. It had happened the previous summer, at a fireworks display; I'd seen the reflection of a red chrysanthemum shower in his eyes as he kissed me.

"I can't believe it's you," he said.

"It's me," I said.

"How long have you been in town?"

Behind him, someone opened a car door and got out—a tall person with short hair. I couldn't be sure if it was a boy or a girl.

"Two days. We're leaving tomorrow," I said.

"You should have let me know." For a moment we didn't speak. Then I said, "You haven't changed."

"But I have," he said. "I'm a vampire now." The figure behind him moved into the light from the storefront. It was a girl, and she felt jealous.

Mãe came out of the liquor store carrying a large paper sack.

"This is my mother," I said, and told Mãe, "this is my friend Michael."

All the while I was thinking, he's *one of us*?

∞

You might wonder how one vampire recognizes another.

There are a few tests. Does he cast a shadow? Is he susceptible to sunburn? (UVB rays burn our skin more than a thousand times faster than they burn human skin.)

Neither of those tests works at night, of course. Others are more subjective. I mentioned earlier that vampires have cool skin, don't perspire, and have no smell; humans, particularly those who eat meat, have a pronounced sweet, salty odor that deodorants and antiperspirants can't mask or prevent. Because we monitor our diets, vampires tend to be thin; there are tales of Colonists who gorge themselves on red meat, but I think those are urban legends, all in all.

Many vampires, including my father, suffer from periodic sensory overload syndrome (SOS). Artificial light and sunlight, as well as complex visual patterns that overstimulate the optic nerve, may cause dizziness, anxiety, and nausea.

Since most vampires are aware of SOS, they tend to avoid patterned clothing, particularly paisley, herringbone, and polka dots, as a courtesy to others. And most of us have acute sensitivity to sound, smell, and texture. That's why we avoid op art, tend to play music low and wear ear protection when we go to rock concerts, don't wear perfume, and get nervous around shag carpeting and sandpaper.

My mother had told me that vampires are prone to vertigo induced not only by heights and loss of balance, but by enclosed spaces that appear to have spiral or labyrinth patterns.

Short of testing susceptibility to these stimuli, we rely on instinct and observation. Does he speak in carefully phrased sentences? Does he have a low, well-modulated voice? Does he demonstrate near-perfect memory? Since we associate these traits with fellow vampires, we become guilty of the same tendency humans have: to stereotype, or profile, one another.

When Mãe invited Michael to join us for a drink back at the hotel, I was relieved when he said he'd come. It would give me a chance to figure out who he was.

∞

The bartender was falling in love with my mother.

Michael and I sat in high-backed wicker chairs on the glassed-in porch of the hotel bar, a pretty place with tall ficus trees and votive candles glimmering on each table. Mãe stood at the bar trying to order. But the bartender wanted to flirt with her. And she wasn't stopping it.

Half of my attention was on her, the rest on Michael. As far as I could tell, he was not a vampire. His voice was low enough, and he did think before he spoke. But his thoughts didn't have the same texture as those of my mother, my father, and Dashay, the vampires I knew best. His were wispy, soft; theirs had more substance, even when they were emotional or perplexed.

"I've been meaning to call you." Michael was watching my mother, too, thinking how pretty she was.

Why isn't she wearing a wedding ring? I thought suddenly. *After all, she's still married.*

Michael looked at me. His brown eyes had an unfamiliar, docile expression.

"Are you taking drugs?" I asked. I felt glad that no one was sitting near us.

"Well, yeah." He smiled. "I told you, I'm a vampire now."

I noticed that he was perspiring slightly. *No, you're not,* I thought.

"You haven't tried V?" His voice trembled slightly.

"V as in . . . ?"

"Vallanium. The drug that makes you a vampire." Michael pushed back his long hair with both hands. "Ari, it's amazing. You take two a day, and you live forever."

"This stuff is a pill?"

He reached into his shirt pocket and pulled out a small black canister, like the ones film comes in. He snapped off its lid and shook two dark red capsules into the palm of his hand.

"Want to try it? It's a nice buzz, kind of like smoking weed, but if you take it with vodka you get these images . . ." He shook his head. "It's hard to explain."

"Is it expensive?" I looked down at the capsules. Each was inscribed with a tiny *V*.

"Yeah. But I have a job now. I'm not in school anymore, I'm working at the All-Mart warehouse."

The bartender was pouring the drinks, finally.

"Maybe I'll try it later," I said. "I'll pay you, if you like."

He shook his head. "No, that's cool. You should try it." He handed me two capsules, which I slipped into my jeans pocket. "I'm sure you can find a dealer down in Florida," he said. "Everybody I know is on V."

"Put them away before my mother comes back." She was paying for the drinks.

He slid the canister back into his shirt pocket.

Mãe carried a tray to the table: two glasses of Picardo and one of cola. Michael looked disappointed. "What are you drinking?" he asked.

"It's called Picardo. Want a taste?"

Mãe gave me an inquiring look. *I'll tell you later,* I thought.

The red glass glowed in the candlelight. Michael lifted it to his lips, took a sip, and began to cough.

Sorry, my friend, I thought. *You are so not one of us.*

∞

My mother said all the right things. She brought up the subject of Kathleen so delicately that Michael wasn't upset. Then again, maybe the V kept his emotions in check.

"It's been hardest on Mom," he said. "She's on antidepressants, and they make her kind of numb. At least she gets out of the house now. For months she stayed in bed."

"And they never found out who did it?" Mãe's voice was soothing.

"No, although for a while there they thought Ari or her father might be involved." He glanced at me. "You knew that."

"The FBI agent even showed up in Florida," I said.

"People still say it's funny that you left town after the murder." His mind filled with hazy suspicions.

"I could never do anything like that." I said. "Neither could he."

"I know," he said. "Hey, I was sorry to hear that he died."

Mãe briskly changed the subject. She asked Michael about his plans for college, and he explained at some length, in the vaguest possible terms, why he didn't have any.

After Michael left us that night, with promises to stay in touch that we all knew would not be kept, Mãe and I stayed at the table, talking about the things we couldn't say before.

"Doesn't he deserve to know the truth?" I asked.

"What's the truth?" Mãe finished her drink and waved her fingers at the empty glass.

The bartender had never taken his eyes off her, and he refilled the glass at once. He wanted to linger, but she cut him short with one glance, and he retreated. I realized that she'd put up with his flirting before to give Michael and me a chance to talk in private.

"All we know is what Malcolm said in Sarasota," she said. "He might have been lying. He's good at that."

But I'd heard him confess, and I remembered the details—he'd talked about the way he killed her. He'd done it because she was a nuisance, he said.

"Even if Malcolm did kill her, what good would it do to tell Michael?" Mãe's eyes were dark. "We don't know where Malcolm is. We have no proof. Trust me, Ariella, it's better not to say anything."

I trusted her. But I felt the weight of knowing, like a kind of sickness inside.

Chapter Six

We left Saratoga Springs the next morning with boxes and baggage shifting behind us in the truck.

On the drive out of town, I made my mother stop at the cemetery. Kathleen's name was engraved on a large stone, next to a smaller one headed with the names of her parents. All of their birth dates were on the stones, followed by dashes and spaces to fill in the years of their deaths. Kathleen was the only one with two dates. I left one of the CDs she'd given me near her stone. I'm not sure why.

"And so we bid farewell to Saratoga Springs." Mãe turned the truck onto the ramp for Interstate 87. She sighed and glanced at me. "I'm sorry."

"For what?"

"I'd thought coming back here would do you good. You know, give you some sense of closure—"

"I hate that word." Then I apologized for interrupting her.

"Catharsis, then." She pressed down on the gas pedal, but the truck kept its own pace, barely above the speed limit. "I hate automatic transmissions," she said.

"*Catharsis* means 'purification.'" I stared out at the rolling green hills. "I don't feel particularly pure."

"It's not your fault that Kathleen died." Mãe edged the truck into the right lane. "And it's not your fault that Mysty disappeared."

We'd barely crossed the New Jersey state line when my cell phone rang. The Citrus County Sheriff's Office had tracked me down.

The detective told me at the beginning that they were "following leads," but that Mysty hadn't been found. My sick feeling intensified.

He said. "Did she say anything to you about leaving town?"

"No." I went over the substance of my phone conversation with her, twice. But it all seemed so trivial. "She sounded happy, yes. She had a date with Jesse that night, she said. Jesse Springer. He's Autumn's brother. No, I don't know him well."

The detective asked where I'd been the night she disappeared, and I told him home. I knew better than to tell him about my vertigo that night, or about sensing the presence of something evil. I agreed to come in to the sheriff's office after we'd returned.

"Mãe?" I said. "When will we be home?"

The truck was merging onto the New Jersey Turnpike. "Tomorrow night, I guess. We still need to eat and sleep."

I told the detective that I'd come in on Tuesday morning, and hung up. "I wonder where she is." The cab was cold, and I wrapped my arms around myself.

"You don't think she ran away?" Mãe drove the way she danced—smoothly and rhythmically. She rarely used brakes.

"No." I couldn't picture Mysty having the gumption to run away. "She was bored, sort of, but she was in love. Or she thought she was."

"How about you?"

My mother's mind didn't work the way my father's did; it impulsively jumped from idea to idea, while his was methodical, even when it leapt to connect disparate concepts.

"Are you asking if I'm in love?"

She lifted her right eyebrow. (I couldn't lift only one. I'd tried.) It was her way of saying *You know very well what I mean.*

"No." I said it decisively. Whatever I'd felt when I saw Michael, it wasn't love. More like regret, for what might have been if Kathleen had lived.

One thing I'd learned: the death of a loved one changes everything for those who survive.

Later that day I noticed the capsules' bulge in my jeans pocket and took them out. Mãe asked what they were, and I told her.

"A pill to make people vampires," she said. "Not possible."

"I thought maybe we could have them analyzed." I wondered who was selling the stuff.

"Good idea." She flicked the truck's turn signal. "We're in Maryland now. I say we stop for lunch. We'll find a good seafood place."

I said okay, even though I didn't have much appetite.

∞

We stopped for the night at a hotel in South Carolina and got an early start the next morning. We drove into Homosassa Springs as the sun was setting. It sank between patches of trees, a fierce tangerine-colored orb.

As the truck idled at a traffic light, I saw, stapled to a power post, the first sign: MISSING, the headline read. A photo of Mysty (younger, wearing no makeup) smiled beneath the words. The sight of it chilled me, made her disappearance not an absence, but a scary presence.

The light changed and we drove on. The poster was on every third electric pole.

When we finally turned onto our road, and into our driveway, I felt weary relief. *This* was home, not Saratoga Springs. Lights within the house glowed yellow through the windows (real windows—the glass had been replaced). Forever after, yellow lights against a darkness have meant home for me, and home always signifies love and mystery.

Dashay didn't wait for Mãe to switch off the engine before she came outside, carrying Grace to greet us.

"So," she said. "Do you want the bad news first? Or do you want the *bad* news?"

∞

Inside, we heard the bad news: she'd got a report back from the Department of Agriculture researchers who had analyzed our dead bees. They'd found multiple pathogens in the bees, possibly caused by pesticides or a virus, along with evidence of mite infestation.

"You're going to love this part," Dashay said to me. She perched on the arm of a chair, adjusting her turban-like towel. She'd taken to washing her hair every night, something Mãe said was "typical of lovelorn women." "The mites are called varroa mites, little parasites that suck the life out of the bees. Their nickname is 'vampire mites.' Nice, huh?"

Mãe stretched her arms over her head and interlocked her hands to crack her knuckles. "Lovely," she said.

"Where do they come from?" I asked.

"From Asia, years ago. Some bee nut probably brought them over, in a suitcase. They already wiped out most of the feral bees. And medicines won't kill them."

"Mites and pesticides have been around for years." Mãe's eyes were focused on a spot far away. "Healthy hives like ours have been pretty much resistant. I suppose moving them during the hurricane might have made the bees vulnerable."

"We have to destroy the hives." Dashay looked at Mãe.

"I'll do it tomorrow." She sounded numb.

"I'll help." Dashay took a deep breath. "And now you want the *bad* news? The deputies were here today. They went through the house and all around the property."

Mãe unclasped her hands and dropped her arms. "Did they have a warrant?"

"No. They asked me if they could look around, and I said we have nothing to hide. They swooped through here and then they left. They didn't take a thing. I watched to make sure."

I dipped a shrimp into a bowl of red sauce and ate it. "Dashay, did you really think they'd steal our stuff?"

She and my mother looked at me with disbelief, then sympathy. "Not steal," Mãe said. "She meant take away evidence."

It took me a few seconds to come to terms with the idea: the sheriff's deputies thought I might be involved in Mysty's disappearance. Meantime, Grace jumped onto the sofa between my mother and me. I petted her.

"That other girl, the one who came into Flo's with her that night?" Dashay waved her hands, as if to conjure a name.

"Do you mean Autumn?"

"Autumn, yeah. She was here. She came last night, rang the buzzer on the gate. She wanted to talk to you."

"She has my phone number." Grace licked my arm and began to purr. Did she love me, or was she after the shrimp?

"Yeah, well. She said she needs to talk to you, and she said she'll be back."

But Autumn didn't return that night. We went to bed early, mindful that the next morning I would be talking to the police.

∞

The Citrus County Sheriff's Office was a brick building in downtown Inverness, and the interview took place in a pale green room with a large table, plastic chairs, and a huge United States flag mounted on a wall. Mãe was asked to be present. The detective, whose name was Pat Morley, was a balding man of medium height wearing dark trousers and a white shirt with short sleeves. He had a face and voice so ordinary that you'd never remember them. His gray eyes looked as if they'd been bleached. He sat opposite us, and he asked me questions in a low voice, taking notes on a pad.

He asked me the same questions he'd asked on the phone: how

I'd met Mysty, how long we'd been friends, how much time we'd spent together, where I'd been the night she disappeared; he looked at Mãe from time to time, inviting her to confirm what I'd said, and she always said, "That's correct."

He asked about our trip to the mall, and I told him about my lunch with Mysty. "I had a sense that someone was watching us," I said.

"What kind of sense? Did you see someone?"

"I felt it. I didn't see anyone."

He didn't bother to write it down.

He asked about Jesse in more detail: Did he and Mysty have a relationship? How close were they? And he knew about Jesse's visit to our place the week before she disappeared. What had we talked about?

Then it became awkward. Up to that point, I'd answered every question honestly, without cheating—in other words, without listening to his thoughts. But now I needed to know what was in his mind, so I tuned in. And what I heard shocked me, so much so that my face must have shown it, because Mãe sent me a thought, *Be careful.*

Detective Morley didn't really care what I said! He was going through the motions, asking questions, but his notes were mostly scribbles that would never be transcribed. He'd made up his mind: Jesse had killed Mysty. It was only a matter of time, he was sure, before her body was found.

"We talked about drinking and driving," I said, my voice clear and emphatic. "I told him he needed to stop drinking."

Morley said, "Yes, he told us that. He has a very high opinion of you."

But he was thinking, *Dumb kid. Lost control one night and ruined his life, and for what? A little tramp like that?*

I began to say, "Mysty is not a tramp," but I stopped myself.

"Mysty isn't a bad girl," I said. "She's bored with her life, maybe. And Jesse isn't a bad guy."

He thanked us for our time.

Mãe said, "Wait. What are you doing to find her?"

"The family put together a search team," he said.

Something was bothering me, something I couldn't quite remember. I went over all of his questions again in my mind, and then it came to me: the man in the van.

I told Detective Morley about seeing the van the day I'd met Mysty and Autumn, and again on the night they'd walked out of Flo's. He opened his eyes a little wider, and he took some notes—real ones, this time. "What kind of van was it?"

I tried to visualize it, to see it as it moved out of the parking lot. "It was beige. There was a name in silver on the back door," I said slowly. "Chevrolet."

"Did you notice its license plate?"

"No," I said, "but the driver—" I'd been going to say, "had no eyes," but I got a strong warning from my mother not to say it. "He was leering at the girls, the first time I saw him," I said.

The detective wasn't interested in that.

"He was heavyset," I said. "He was bald."

We left the station and got into Mãe's truck—her own, not the rental van, which Dashay was beginning to unload back at the house. She waited until we were out of the parking lot before she said, "Why didn't you tell me about seeing the blind man?"

"I tried," I said. "Twice. Both times, other things intervened."

We drove back to Homosassa Springs without talking.

As she pulled into the lot in front of Flo's Place, I said, "I've seen him before. In Sarasota."

She said, "Okay."

"Have you seen him, too?"

"No, but I've heard about him." She switched off the engine and turned toward me. "Didn't your father ever tell you about harbingers?"

∞

Harbingers, she explained over an early lunch at Flo's, are signs of things to come.

"Not everyone sees them," she said. "I don't. But your father has seen the blind man twice, and it sounds as if you've inherited him."

"The blind man in Glastonbury." I remembered my father talking about seeing the man in England, not long before my father was made a vampire. I'd seen the man in Sarasota; the next day, the hurricane hit and our condominium caught fire. Of course, he couldn't be blind. He drove a van.

"But who is he?" The mere thought of the blind man made me uneasy.

"Your father thinks harbingers are Jungian shadows." She took a bite of her grouper sandwich.

I'd read only a smattering of Jung and Freud. My father had treated their essays as fiction, by and large. "Do you mean they're not real?"

"They're very real to those who see them." She took another bite and chewed it slowly. "Jung thought shadows were visions of our own unconscious selves, which we repress."

"But I *saw* the man in the van." I knew he was more than a shadow. "So did Autumn and Mysty."

My mother believed me. "Yes, you saw a man in a van. But was he really blind? You saw what you most fear: someone full of malice, someone with an absence of vision. He's your shadow man."

I asked, "Do harbingers always mean bad news?" Flo's was unusually noisy that day, and I had to raise my voice to be heard.

"For your father, yes. But not for everyone. Dashay's harbinger is a black bird, a grackle, that swoops at her. It happens when change is coming, for better or worse."

The concept of a harbinger didn't make much sense to me.

Logan, the bartender, came over to our table—a rare occurrence, since he liked to stay behind the bar. "Heard you were visiting the sheriff this morning," he said to Mãe.

One aspect of living in Citrus County that I never liked: everyone knew everyone else's business. Someone had spotted Mãe's truck and lost no time spreading the word.

Mãe said, "Yes, and why were we there?"

He grinned and pointed at the TV set over the bar. The Tampa station was broadcasting a photo of Mysty, then shots of two distraught-looking people; the caption read PARENTS OF MISSING GIRL.

"Only one circus in town this week." Logan looked at me. "So you knew this Mysty?"

"I knew her," I said. "But not well."

"She and her friend looked like trouble waiting to happen. Still, it's shameful when a girl disappears." Logan turned to my mother again. "Remember the last one?"

She nodded, her eyes on me. "There was another one?" I asked.

"Over the years there have been a few," Logan said. "The worst one was the last one, two years ago. They found the little girl buried in her neighbor's yard—"

"You have customers." Mãe tilted her head toward the bar. She didn't want me to hear the details. She didn't want me to be further upset.

But in the days to come I heard all sorts of details, things that I'd never imagined. While I was growing up in Saratoga Springs, sheltered from TV and newspapers, learning about philosophy and mathematics, people were disappearing all over America—all over the world, really. Every year, tens of thousands of people vanish—most of them adult males. But the media attention tends to go to pretty girls and children—about three hundred children are abducted every year and never return. More than a million teenagers run away from their families every year. Most return home within a week, but roughly seven percent—seventy thousand teenagers—are never heard of again.

It was hard for me to believe such things happened at all, let alone with such frequency. I felt as if the world I lived in was only a façade—that beneath its skin, a darker world raged and rampaged. I'd glimpsed that world before, but I'd never known how vast and malignant it might be.

Afterward, whenever we drove in Mãe's truck, I noticed teenagers wearing music earbuds or talking on cell phones, paying no attention to either world—to the posters of Mysty, or to strangers who might be watching them. I wondered who would disappear next.

∞

When we returned home, Mãe and Dashay burned the trays of the beehives. I didn't help. I didn't want to see them burn. The acrid air came into the house and lingered for days.

For dinner that night I made a salad, but none of us ate much. Mãe excused herself and went off to have a bath. Dashay and I played Crazy Eights, but we both were thinking of other things and played poorly. The game dragged on.

When the front gate buzzed, Dashay said, "It's that girl again." And a second later, Autumn's voice came through the intercom.

When I went down to the gate, she was waiting for me. She wore sunglasses, tight black jeans, and a tank top with one word printed on it: NOT.

"I need to talk to you," she said.

"Why didn't you call me?" I unlocked the gate and beckoned her inside.

"Cell phones can be traced. Or bugged." She wheeled her bicycle up the driveway.

We sat in the moon garden. Even though the sky was growing dark, Autumn kept on her sunglasses. The air stayed hot and humid. It didn't bother me, but Autumn wiped her forehead with her hand from time to time. "I hate Florida," she said.

"Weren't you born here?"

"Yes," she said, "and I'm counting the minutes until I leave. So, what did you do to Mysty?"

I hadn't expected that question. When I tried to hear what she was thinking, all I heard was a static-like buzz. *Who are you?* I thought.

I heard, in response, a soft, high-pitched whining sound. It came from Autumn—not from her mouth, but from somewhere inside her.

Then Dashay was there, her back to me, bending toward Autumn.

"Somebody call me?" she said softly. She took off Autumn's sunglasses, and Autumn didn't move.

I craned my neck and had a brief glimpse of Autumn's eyes—wide open, with light moving across her left iris.

Dashay moved to block my view.

"Yes, my pretty pretty," she said. "You're the one calling me. I hear you now. I can't hear you! I hear you loud and clear. You're not there! I don't hear anything."

She went on, crooning nonsense ("I see you, I can't see a thing. I can feel you, you're no place at all"). I wondered if Dashay was mad—if Bennett's disappearance had disconnected her sanity. Discomfort, hot and prickling, climbed up my spine.

But I didn't leave. I closed my eyes, and my eyelids turned colors, twists of violet. After a minute or so, I heard the whining sound again, and then a sudden popping noise.

I opened my eyes. Dashay turned away from Autumn, her face triumphant.

"Want to see?" she said to me, She held out her right hand, clenched tight.

Part of me did, but I shook my head. "It's Autumn's demon, isn't it."

"She had a sasa in her, yes. I heard it. Sometimes they sing at night. Sure you don't want to see? 'Cause I need to drown it quick."

I took a quick glance. Something small, dark, and slimy looking quivered in her palm. Then she closed her hand and walked off toward the river.

Autumn hadn't moved while we'd talked. She sat, her eyes open, breathing normally, her palms flat against her knees. She blinked and stirred. "So what do you think happened to Mysty?" Her voice was matter-of-fact, as if nothing had happened.

I told her I didn't know. She nodded, but she was thinking, *She knows more than she's saying.* I could hear her thoughts, now that the sasa was gone.

I wondered what she'd done to acquire a sasa.

"Jesse took a lie detector test yesterday." She said it so casually. "Today they told him he failed and he has to take two more."

"Poor Jesse." I hoped that being hypnotized hadn't affected his performance.

"My brother is no liar," she said. "He says she stood him up that night." But she was wondering, *Did he kill her?*

"I don't think he did it," I said. "He doesn't have that kind of temper. Besides, why do you think she's dead?"

"It's been four days." Autumn hunched her narrow shoulders. "They're usually dead by now."

"You don't seem very upset," I said.

"Well, it's not like she meant that much to me." Autumn stood up to leave. "It's not like I even knew her very well."

But she was lying. Mysty was the only friend she'd ever had.

I walked her down to the gate. "Aren't you scared to be out alone at night?"

She draped one leg over her bike and mounted it. "I'd like to see somebody try to come after me," she said.

Chapter Seven

Once upon a time, my mother thought that place names with the letter *S* in them were lucky. That's the entire reason she'd chosen to live in Saratoga Springs, and later, *S* attracted her to Homosassa Springs.

Conversely, she decided that places that began with the letter *D* were unlucky. She thought they attracted negative energy. For her, that explained why so many murders and other crimes occurred in places like Deltona and DeLand, Florida.

But Mãe outgrew those superstitions. Luck, she decided, was more about a person's attitude than about anything else. Good and bad things happened randomly, everywhere.

Attitudes aside, when bad things happen it's natural to try to find reasons, to look for patterns. "Bad things happen in threes" was a saying I heard often in Homosassa Springs, after Mysty disappeared. It's always quoted after two bad things have happened, and people go out of their way to find number three. If I'm sure of anything, it's this: number three will find *you*.

∞

I never did learn who started the rumor that I killed Mysty. Before Autumn lost her demon, she might have done it; after her encounter with Dashay, she lacked sufficient malice. Most likely it was one or more of Jesse's friends, trying to shift attention away from him.

Dashay was the one to tell me. The lunch crowd at Flo's Place thought that Mysty was dead ("like that other poor girl two years ago") and that I was somehow responsible, since I was apparently the last person who'd talked to her.

I'd been deep in conversation with Mary Ellis Root when Dashay burst in, wearing a striped shirt, white jeans, and red sneakers—it had been her summer uniform that year. She looked particularly jaunty next to Root, who wore a lumpy dress and oversized men's sunglasses. I didn't appreciate being told in front of Root that the town thought me a killer, but Root enjoyed the spectacle; I could tell from the way she clasped her hands. I'd never been able to hear her thoughts; I decided that she must block them all, all the time. *She must be a vampire,* I thought. Yet I hated to think she was one of us.

Root had come by to collect my father's latest mail, and I'd asked her about Vallanium. I'd shown her one of the little red capsules that Michael had given me.

Yes, Root said, she'd heard of it. She'd heard the drug was popular in Tampa, near where she was staying. Apparently it was sold in the high schools.

"What's in it?" I asked her.

"Who knows?" She rubbed her hands, looking uneasy at not having an answer.

"Could you analyze this for me?"

Then Dashay sauntered in with her rumor story.

One thing about vampires: we generally disregard rumors. When you don't have a presence in society, it doesn't matter much what people say about you, unless things go to extremes. Then you simply disappear and move on.

But for some reason this one did matter to me. "It's not fair," I said. "I had nothing to do with Mysty that night. And why does everyone assume that she's dead?"

From their faces alone, I saw that Dashay and Root assumed the same thing.

"Here, give me the capsule." Root stretched out her hand, which reminded me of a paw; thick hair grew like fur across its back. "I'll find out what's in it, and I'll let you know."

Then she gathered up the mail and left without saying good-bye, as if she'd had more than enough of our company.

"So that Root is a friend of yours now?" Dashay's voice dripped skepticism.

"At least she doesn't spread rumors." I felt miffed, but I couldn't stay mad at Dashay. "I have a question," I said.

"You always do."

It wasn't easy to phrase this one. "It's okay to kill a demon?" My father was an advocate of nonviolence, and I'd grown up thinking that all killing was wrong.

Dashay listened to me without moving, without even blinking. "It's like removing a cancer," she said. "Once you know it's there, it would be wrong not to get rid of it."

I took a deep breath. "So what does it look like?"

"Every sasa is different." Dashay walked over to the bowl of nuts on the coffee table. She lifted out a walnut. "It was about the size and shape of this nut, but dark, and without a hard shell. It's softer, you know. Like a tumor."

I'd never seen or felt a tumor, and I hoped I never would. "So it doesn't have eyes?"

Dashay laughed. "You looked at it, remember? No, it does not have eyes or ears or a nose." Then she laughed again. "Don't look so disappointed. It does have a little mouth—that's how it attaches itself. And it vibrates and sometimes it sends out a high-pitched sound that only foy-eyes hear."

I didn't tell her that I'd heard it, too.

∞

Later that day we received a visit from the FBI.

At the sound of the buzzer, my mother went down to the front gate. She returned a moment later, followed by Agent Cecil Burton.

I'd seen him only a month ago. He'd turned up at the place in Kissimmee where we stayed after the hurricane. He was still trying to find out who killed Kathleen.

Now that I was a "person of interest" in Mysty's disappearance as well, he wanted to ask me some questions.

I was lying on the living room sofa, reading *The Count of Monte Cristo* and thinking about the nature of honor, when he came in. From our first exchange of glances I knew this interview wasn't going to be anything like the last one.

Agent Burton's eyes had always been world-weary, but this time they had a look of cold determination. His fingernails, buffed and trimmed the last time I'd seen him, were ragged now, as if he'd bitten them.

He said, "How are you, Miss Ariella?"

I sat up. "I'm fine."

He sat in a chair across from me. Mãe offered him a drink and he said that water would be very nice. As usual, he wore a suit and tie, in spite of the heat. He looked fit, but his eyes were bloodshot, as if he hadn't slept well in a long time. I had a sense that personal problems were keeping him awake.

"Lovely place you have here." He took a small tape recorder out of his pocket and set it on the table between us.

Mãe came back with two glasses of water, which she set on either side of the tape recorder.

Agent Burton said he had some questions for me that were important in finding out what happened to Kathleen and to Mysty. He asked if I wanted to help.

"Of course." I sent Mãe a quick question: *Am I allowed to listen to his thoughts?*

Mãe sent back, *Of course.* She sat on the sofa next to me.

The next hour went quickly, but I felt exhausted by the time it ended. Listening to Burton's questions and his thoughts required concentration. Answering the questions was the easy part.

By and large, I told him the truth. We'd been over the details of Kathleen's murder before, so I found myself repeating things I'd already said. Of course I didn't talk about Malcolm, or his admission that he'd murdered Kathleen.

From time to time my mother let me know that I was doing a good job.

When we got to Mysty, Burton's thoughts became fresher and more complicated. Now I had to think before I spoke. Yes, I said, I'd heard rumors that I was involved in her disappearance.

His thoughts told me he didn't take the rumors seriously. He was mostly intrigued by the coincidence: two girls I'd known had come to "bad ends." That was his phrase for it. Like most people, he assumed that Mysty was dead.

"Tell me about Jesse Springer."

I told Burton all I knew: the kayak accident, the trip to the mall, Jesse's interest in the stars and deep space, Jesse's decision to stop drinking.

I even mentioned Jesse's visit to our house the night I'd hypnotized him. All I left out was the hypnosis itself.

It was hard for me to talk at times, because Burton was thinking such contrary thoughts: that Jesse had deliberately capsized the kayak to get attention, that he'd only pretended to stop drinking, and that he'd killed Mysty without a qualm.

The polygraph tests indicated that Jesse was lying in response to some questions. He'd said that he'd agreed to meet Mysty that night at one of the river docks, but that she never turned up.

Apparently Jesse fit the FBI profile for Mysty's abductor/murderer: a white male between twenty and thirty who tended to be a loner and substance abuser who'd had previous problems with the law. Mysty's stepbrothers in Tennessee also had been interviewed, but were ruled out as suspects since both had solid alibis.

Burton asked me about the man I'd seen driving the beige Chevrolet van, but he was thinking that the man-in-van was a long shot. Jesse was the one.

I was so intent on listening to his thoughts that I stopped in mid-sentence, having no idea of what I'd been saying. "I'm sorry," I said.

"It's natural for you to be upset," Burton said, but he was thinking, *All in all, she's a pretty cool customer.*

Mãe said, "She's only fourteen."

Finally the tape recorder was shut off. Burton looked at me, his eyes still cold and detached. "If you think of anything else," he said, and handed me his card.

I already had this card, but I took a new one.

That's when Dashay came in. She'd been swimming in the river, and she strode into the living room, wrapped in a red towel, beads of water flying from her shoulders. Her skin gleamed, and her hair was hidden by a vintage bathing cap festooned with white rubber zinnias. Anyone else would have looked ridiculous in this getup. Dashay looked stunning.

Agent Burton dropped the tape recorder as he stood up.

Mãe and Dashay tried not to laugh.

"How do you do?" Dashay extended her hand as my mother introduced them and smiled her dazzling fake smile. She stood close to Burton and looked into his eyes.

A spot near the kidneys, she thought. *Nothing sizable yet. Probably a result of consorting with criminal types—or with the ex-wife.*

∞

A week later, I stopped riding my bicycle.

I'd developed the habit of riding into town three or four times a week, going to the library or the drugstore, drinking a soda, and stopping for a swim on the way home. The city streets were quiet those days. Most of the locals had volunteered for the Mysty search parties.

I saw one group, fanned out in the forest between the town and the river, walking slowly, looking from side to side. I knew they were hoping to find a body, and the thought made me shiver.

At the library and the drugstore, people stared at me with suspicion. I heard them thinking: *That's her. She's the one. Poor Mysty.* And sometimes I had the sense that I was being followed, although no one was visible. Finally the unpleasantness outweighed my need for exercise. I stayed home.

We were visited again by the sheriff's detectives, who asked the same questions as before. I felt like a parrot, repeating syllables that carried no meaning for me.

Our house was finished now, stronger and larger than it had been before the hurricane. Mãe had added three new rooms and a deck for my telescope. But I didn't feel like stargazing, or helping her arrange the furniture and artwork we'd brought from Saratoga Springs.

The days were quiet with the work crew gone. Mãe mourned her honeybees and Dashay brooded about Bennett; both tried to hide their feelings. We were living in a house of heartbreak.

Mãe tried to interest me in Florida folk tales. Dashay renewed her offer to teach me about sasa. I wasn't interested. And I didn't want to go to Flo's to eat oysters. I had no appetite.

My mother told me that many vampires are prone to bouts of depression. "Some of it is justified," she said. "When you look at the state of the world, it makes you more than sad."

My father, I thought, had given me a classical education but had kept me from knowledge of current events and crime. He'd wanted to keep me optimistic for as long as he could.

The strangest thing about that time: words failed me. I couldn't find the right phrases or terms. More and more, I resorted to nodding and shaking my head, and then to avoiding opportunities for conversation altogether.

At night I lay awake for hours, thinking about Mysty and Kathleen: people who'd been presences in my life only briefly, and now were voids. I remembered my father talking about presence and absence, tension and release, as the basis of all art and all science. I wanted to think about the implications of that, but my head was too foggy to get anywhere.

One morning, after a nearly sleepless night, I came out to the kitchen and found Mãe sitting at the table, doing the *New York Times* crossword puzzle. She downloaded it on her computer every morning.

"What is the football term for 'shoving away'?" she asked me.

I shrugged and traced a spiral pattern with my finger on the tablecloth.

"I hate sports clues." Mãe set down her pen. "How about some oatmeal?"

I made a face. The idea of thick, congealed food lacked appeal.

Neither did the bowl of fresh fruit and yogurt she set in front of me. "Ariella," she said. "You are beginning to worry me."

I thought, *I'm worrying me, too.*

"I understand how you feel," my mother said, her voice full of concern. "It's hard when people are talking about you, thinking you're part of whatever happened to Mysty."

And Kathleen, I thought.

"Why aren't *you* talking?" she asked.

Speaking requires too much effort, I thought. *Words have lost their meaning.*

"Sounds like teenage angst." Mãe went back to the crossword, trying to hide her worry.

Part of me, I have to admit, enjoyed the experience of teenage angst. I spent days lying around the house or going down to Dashay's mourning garden. It had been wrecked by the hurricane and patiently restored by her; she'd replanted the flowers and foliage, all in shades of black, and replaced the obelisk fountain with a new one: a statue of a woman that wept black tears. I sat on a black iron bench and contemplated death, because that's what one is supposed to do in a garden of gloom.

My mood lasted for nearly two weeks. Then, one afternoon in late September, when the humidity dropped and a sweet breeze blew in from the Gulf, I found a letter from my father to my mother lying unfolded on the kitchen table. I saw my name written in his handwriting. I didn't even have to touch it to begin reading it.

My father wrote: "I'm sorry to hear that Ariella is feeling depressed, but not surprised, given all she's had to endure this year. The disappearance of the local girl is regrettable, not only for her family but for ours."

I liked the "ours."

"Since the FBI is involved in the investigation, I won't return as I'd planned," he wrote. "But Ari's lessons should not be suspended indefinitely. Her current mood no doubt reflects a degree of boredom as well as the shock of recent events. My suggestion is that we begin at once to look into options for continuing her education. She's more than ready for college, and a change of place will do her good."

At that point I stopped reading. I wasn't at all sure I was ready for college. But I let myself imagine what it might be like to begin a new life in a new place. It might be exciting. It might even be fun.

That's when I decided I'd had enough angst. It had succeeded only in worrying my parents and in boring me.

∞

Mãe was in one of the new upstairs rooms, painting its walls a pale shade of turquoise that had a hint of silver in it. She said that yes, Raphael had planned to return the following month, and that she'd warned him about the FBI interest in me.

She handed me a paintbrush. "You can do the corners."

"I like this color," I said. "What's it called?"

"Indian Ocean," she said. "A glorified name for a simple blue."

"But it's appropriate," I said. I dipped the brush into the can, then tapped off the excess paint. "It looks like the color of an ocean far away."

She smiled. "It's good to hear your voice again."

"I read my father's letter to you," I said, fanning the brush up the inner corner of a wall.

"I know you did." She poured more paint into her roller pan.

She'd left it there for me to read, I thought. Mothers can be devious creatures.

For a while we painted. The windows were open, and the salty breeze mixed with the smell of fresh paint seemed to signal new beginnings.

"Do you think I'm ready for college?" My voice sounded as uncertain as I felt.

"I'm not sure." She'd finished two walls, and now began a third. "I think it might be worth a try."

∞

The next time Agent Burton called on us, Dashay was waiting for him. She met him at the gate, wearing a close-fitting dark red dress, her hair loose and wavy.

From the kitchen window, Mãe and I watched her talk to Burton as they came slowly toward the house. "She's *flirting* with him," I said.

"She wants him to help her find Bennett." Mãe's voice carried disapproval and understanding, both. "She says she has a plan. And when Dashay has a plan, things happen."

"Good things?"

Mãe said, "Things happen fast. And some things get broken."

We looked out at Dashay and Burton, and I had a sudden wild fantasy: Dashay would make Burton one of us, and then all our troubles would go away. But I knew better.

Root sent me an e-mail later that day. Normally I received nothing personal, only newsletters about music and books. When I saw her name on my laptop's screen, I felt repulsed, as if she herself had appeared in my room, and for the first time I questioned my reaction. Why did she bother me so? Was she part of my Jungian shadow?

Root's e-mail style was terse and to the point: "Vallanium capsule is a sugar pill."

She signed the e-mail: "ROOT."

I typed a thank-you, and added a question: "No eternal life?"

She wrote back within an hour: "Not a chance."

∞

My father hated e-mail and telephones. He preferred letters and face-to-face conversations, modes of expression that allowed verbal sophistication and style.

I respected the reasons for his feelings. Nonetheless, sometimes I wished he would pick up the telephone or dash off an e-mail. He was another void in my life.

For many vampires, telepathy doesn't work for long-distance communication—but like all traits, this one varies considerably. My mother had managed to send me messages that turned up in my dreams in Saratoga Springs. I don't think this was possible because she had unusual telepathic powers, but because she was my mother, and the psychic relations between parents and children are known to be atypical.

After lunch that day Mãe asked if I'd take my bike into town and buy more masking tape. The cooler weather made the prospect of a long bike ride enticing.

I saw no one that I knew, until I was outside the pharmacy, unlocking my bike from the rack, and a woman's voice said my name. I turned. A small woman, probably in her forties, with blond hair straggling past her shoulders, stood under a live oak tree, watching me. Mysty's mother. I recognized her from the TV news we'd seen at Flo's.

"Will you come here for a minute?" Her voice was soft, with a Southern accent more pronounced than Mysty's. "I'd like to talk with you."

I wheeled my bike over to her. She wore a faded denim shirtdress and sandals.

"I'm so sorry," I said, but she interrupted.

"Tell me what you know. You're that Ari girl, aren't you?"

I nodded.

"I heard the things people are saying about you," she said. "Tell me what you know." Her eyes were the color of spring grass.

"I didn't see her the night she disappeared," I said.

"Some say you killed her." Her hand flew out and clutched my arm. She had sharp fingernails. The red polish was chipped.

I tried to pull my arm free. She was surprisingly strong. When I wrenched it away, her nails gouged my skin. I stared at the slashes, at my dark red blood.

"Tell me what you know." Her voice reminded me of Mysty's.

When she tried to grab my arm again, I swerved away. "I've told you," I said. "I had nothing to do with it."

I climbed onto my bike and rode away, but I felt her eyes following me. She'd been spending most days since Mysty disappeared walking around town, watching and waiting.

For a moment I thought about turning back, about telling her I'd been thinking hard, trying to hear Mysty's thoughts—sending out what we call "locators," thoughts that sometimes tell us where others are. I'd sent them to my father, too. But, like him, Mysty wasn't sending anything back. She wasn't anywhere within my range.

The sight of blood clotted along my arm kept me pedaling. I rode fast, out of town, past another group of searchers gathered around a sheriff's car, into the country again. I was thinking unpleasant thoughts. *What if I did have something to do with it? What if whoever followed us at the mall that day was really after me?*

By the time I reached home, the gashes on my arm still hadn't healed.

Later that night, someone spray-painted the word KILLER across our front gate.

Chapter Eight

All my life, I've had the tendency to do things at the wrong time. The results have been mixed, but never boring.

Going to college at the age of fourteen would strike many people as a misguided idea. The contemporary general wisdom holds that the proper age for higher education is the late teens, after one has reached a degree of physical and mental maturity. Educational experts (mostly self-proclaimed) don't agree on whether the "proper age" might be different for students labeled "gifted."

Plato, whom I'd studied with my father, believed that higher education should begin in one's twenties, with advanced study of mathematics, then philosophy. Only students capable of understanding reality and making rational judgments about it were suited for such study, he said, for later they would become the guardians of the state.

At fourteen, I didn't know what I wanted to become, much less what was worth guarding. But I'd begun to wonder how I could contribute to society unless I actually lived in it.

My mother, Dashay, and I sat up late one night with our laptop computers, reviewing college sites. Since the spray-painting incident, they felt a certain urgency about moving me out of Sassa and into another part of the world.

"The timing is miserable," Dashay said, looking at academic calendars online. "If she applies by mid-January, she can't start till next August."

"*She* is sitting right here," I said, "and she appreciates your concern. But why the big rush?"

They looked at me. They were on either end of the sofa, Grace sleeping on a cushion between them. I sat in one of the velvet chairs we'd brought out of storage.

"Somebody got hold of a can of spray paint," I said. "So what?"

But I knew what they were thinking: that the spray paint might be only the beginning.

"This isn't the peaceful place it was," Mãe said. "We hope that it will be again, when the rumors and speculation die down."

It would die down faster with me somewhere else. I knew that. But I was too stubborn to admit it. "So the bullies win," I said. "They make me run away."

"Not running," Dashay said. "You are going to school. Retreating, maybe. Nothing wrong with that." She passed me a bowl of red popcorn, liberally sprinkled with Sangfroid.

I took the bowl. "What about the University of Virginia?" It was my father's alma mater.

My mother said, "It's too far away."

Dashay said, "Sara, you are a fool." But she said it with affection in her voice.

"Where did you go to college?" I asked my mother.

"I went to Hillhouse. It's a liberal arts school in Georgia."

"Were you happy there?"

She smiled. "Yes, I was. It's only five hundred students or so. But it's an alternative school. They don't assign grades—they give written assessments instead. I don't know if it's rigorous enough for someone like you."

"Do you mean I'm smarter than you?" The words came out before I'd considered saying them.

My mother laughed. Dashay said, "Ari, you watch out. That's your mother you're talking to."

I began to apologize, but Mãe said, "It's okay. It's a legitimate question. Yes, I think you are much smarter than I was at your age."

"Thank you," I said, trying to keep my voice modest.

She added, "And nearly half as smart as I am now."

∞

While my mother and Dashay surveyed university web pages, I decided to do something else: take an aptitude test online.

I scored high in the areas of science, art, and writing, and low in sales, clerical, and administration. My ratings for investigative and artistic thinking were much stronger than those for being attentive or conventional.

"You should major in liberal arts," Dashay said. She said she'd done that at the University of the West Indies.

"I think that Raphael wants Ari to go into medicine one day, but liberal arts is a good foundation for anything," Mãe said.

My father had never told me he wanted me to "go into" anything. "Ari is sitting right here," I said. "Why do you keep talking about me in the third person?"

"This is a big moment," Dashay said.

"Not *that* big." Mãe knew I was apprehensive and didn't want to make things worse. "You can choose one school now, have a trial year, then transfer later on. You have all the time in the world to figure things out."

All the time in the world. Even for vampires, it's hard to think in those terms.

"Ari's big problem is, she hasn't learned how to tell time," Dashay said.

∞

That night didn't want to end. Later I sat on a bench on our new deck, trying out the new mount for my telescope. I loved the idea that I was looking up at stars seen by Plato and Aristotle. Time seemed to dissolve when I stargazed.

Orion's belt jumped out at me: three white-blue stars, each more than twenty times the size of our sun, formed more than ten million years ago. And along the sword that hangs from the belt was the reddish swirl called the Orion nebula, a cloud of dust, gas, and plasma. Nebulae are where stars are born.

I sensed someone behind me and my body tensed, then relaxed when I smelled rosemary. Dashay used rosemary oil as a hair conditioner.

"You having fun out here in the dark?" she said. She wore an embroidered caftan, and her head was wrapped in a towel.

I pulled away from the eyepiece. "Want to have a look?'

She shook her head. "What's up there doesn't interest me much. What's going on down here is more than enough for me to think about."

"But it's so beautiful." Even without the telescope, the night sky pulled my eyes to it. The patterns of stars, planets, and haze were embedded stories. "Do you know the story of Orion?"

"I've heard the Greek story." Dashay tilted her head and stared up. "The hunter killed by his lover."

"By accident," I said. "Artemis was tricked by her brother into shooting Orion with an arrow."

"Yes, yes." Dashay looked at me. "What's the point of that story, Ari?"

"The point?" I didn't know the answer.

"What's the moral of the story?"

I didn't think constellation stories had morals.

"The point is: love is misery," Dashay said, and folded her arms.

∞

My tour of colleges was short and to the point. Mãe and I decided to visit four: two large state universities and two smaller private ones, all within three hundred miles of home.

Hillhouse was one of the private schools. I'm not going to name the other places we went; I don't want to influence anyone else's opinions of them.

It's enough to say that the large state schools did not appeal to me. Their campuses were overbuilt and ugly, despite elaborate landscaping that seemed entirely out of keeping with the utilitarian designs of the buildings. We'd been promised meetings with faculty members, but none was available. At each school we took a tour of the facilities, which included stops at dormitories that made me think of dog kennels. Our tour guides at both places were young women—pretty, blond, unflappable women whose cheerfulness knew no bounds.

"Here's the quiet dorm," Jessica said, leading us into a brick building at State U-A, down a corridor, and into the middle of a living room where seven people were smoking marijuana. "Oops," Jessica said, and, still smiling, led us out again.

"This is a state-of-the-art classroom," Tiffany announced at State U-B, opening the door of a room with beige cement-block walls and fluorescent lighting that hurt my eyes. *A prison cell might have more personality,* I thought. *Why would anyone design such antiseptic, uninspiring spaces as classrooms?*

Mãe didn't like either state U any more than I did. "We could try one more," she said, her voice doubtful.

"If we do, I won't get out of the truck." I was having second thoughts about going to college at all.

The first private school we visited was a marked improvement—an older, well-designed campus, all red brick with doors and window frames painted white, shaded by sycamore trees. The classrooms had posters and framed art on their walls. The dormitory lacked the zoolike qualities of the others we'd seen; students huddled over laptops at their desks or talked in small groups. I could almost imagine myself living there. Almost.

"Everyone is white," I whispered to Mãe.

When we talked with the admissions director, he said the school tried to recruit "a diverse population." I guess that population didn't want to come to a school where everyone else was white. The director seemed excited by my last name and appearance; I heard him think, *Our first Latina.*

One aspect of being home-schooled, I realized, was that I'd never been labeled, by others or by myself.

"I don't want to go to a school where I'm called the first Latina," I said to Mãe.

We were back in the truck, headed south. "Okay," she said. "It seemed a little prissy, anyway."

∞

We drove onto the Hillhouse campus on a sunny afternoon in October. Mãe had told me what to expect: the rural campus was built around a working farm, and all of the students had jobs either on the farm or elsewhere, helping to operate and maintain the campus.

The first thing we saw: a lawn with oak, sycamore, and maple trees, and students raking leaves. I hadn't seen a rake since leaving Saratoga Springs. And the students were a diverse assortment, ethnically and otherwise. They had hair of all colors, dyed vivid green and blue and orange and red, and many dressed in clothes that looked like stage costumes: jesters, gypsies, pirates, and rock stars. While some worked, others were jumping and rolling in the piles of leaves. They reminded me of a pack of raccoon babies I'd seen back in Sassa, tumbling down a slope for the sheer pleasure of it.

As I watched, a boy sprang out of a mound of leaves as if he'd been launched; the leaves scattered everywhere, and some of the others picked up handfuls and tossed them at him. "Thanks a lot, Walker," one said.

He had wavy hair the color of sand, blue eyes, flushed cheeks, full lips, white teeth. He smiled and took a running leap into another leaf pile. I wondered why I was noticing so much about him. I wondered why I hoped he'd notice me.

We parked the truck and made our way to the administration building. The buildings were made of dark-painted wood, with long narrow windows that looked out onto the lawns and fields. Most had porches, and every porch had a row of rocking chairs.

While Mãe and I waited for the admissions officer, I read a pamphlet entitled *A Brief History of Hillhouse*. The school's philosophy was modeled on that of Summerhill, a progressive school in Britain. Hillhouse was run as a cooperative community, to which everyone contributed at least fifteen hours of work a week. Everyone was expected to attend weekly governance meetings. Class attendance was voluntary; students designed their own curricula, and they received written reports on their progress rather than grades. The coursework was designed around a series of projects planned jointly by the students and professors.

The policies sounded sensible to me. I didn't realize how unusual they were until later, when I read the catalogs we'd collected at the other schools. The catalogs emphasized credit hours, exams, grade point averages: a system premised on penalties and rewards, with the underlying assumption that students were children who had to be pressured in order to learn.

Hillhouse didn't require applicants to take entrance exams or submit grade transcripts. Application decisions were made on the basis of the interview and on three essays submitted with the application.

The admissions officer, Cecelia Martinez, was a young woman with wide eyes and an open face. Like everyone we'd met at the other schools, she seemed relentlessly cheerful.

"So," she said, after we were introduced, "I understand that you're a legacy."

I'd never been called that before.

"Yes," Mãe said. "I graduated from Hillhouse twenty years ago."

Cecelia Martinez wondered what sort of plastic surgery my mother had had. "You two look like sisters," she said.

My mother didn't look more than thirty, I realized. And Cecelia Martinez wasn't one of us. I wondered if anyone at Hillhouse was a vampire.

Mãe left the room when the "formal" interview began. (Nothing was truly formal at Hillhouse.) First, Ms. Martinez asked me about my education. She asked me to describe my favorite teacher.

"I was home-schooled," I told her. "My father was my teacher." *What should I say about him?* I described his biomedical research, his work into the development of artificial blood. I talked of our lessons in mathematics, science, philosophy, and literature. I didn't say, *And he's a vampire. He can read thoughts and turn invisible, but he prefers not to.*

"That's great," Ms. Martinez was saying. "So you're an only child. Do you have lots of friends?"

I said I'd had a few close friends. I didn't say, *Both of them disappeared.*

Then she asked about my hobbies and interests, and I told her about my telescope, about horseback riding and kayaking, about learning to cook and surfing the Internet.

"Terrific," she said. "And what do you think you'd like to major in, if you come to Hillhouse?"

"I'm not sure yet," I said. "I think I'd like to work on interdisciplinary projects. I'm interested in the ways different cultures communicate within themselves and with each other. Maybe I'll become a kind of cultural translator." *Or a shaman,* I thought.

She loved that answer. "You should talk to Professor Hoffman," she said. "He leads the interdisciplinary studies department here."

When I came out of the office, Mãe looked at me and beamed. Her relief was almost too obvious. I thought, *Did she think I was going to talk about demons and harbingers?*

My mother looked even happier at the mention of Professor Hoffman. "He was one of my teachers," she said. "Does he still play the theremin?"

"He does." Ms. Martinez picked up the phone and called Professor Hoffman.

"What's a theremin?" I asked.

"An electronic instrument." Mãe's hands traced the shape of a rectangle. "It sounds like music from another world."

When Ms. Martinez put down the receiver, Mãe said, "And is he still writing letters to the editor?"

"I'm sure he does." She grinned. "But the local paper stopped printing them a while back. He was sending in two or three a week."

On the way to meet Professor Hoffman, Ms. Martinez pointed out the barn, the theater, the library, and the student union, whose basement, she said, was occupied by a cafeteria. "All the food we serve is organic, and most of it is grown locally," she said.

Around us, students meandered to and from classes, talking. I heard fragments: "spend the summer in Costa Rica," and "they said no, they already went broke paying tuition." Others continued to frolic (there's really no other word for it) in the leaves. Someone sat on a stone wall, playing a wooden flute.

The interdisciplinary studies offices were next to the chemistry department in another building, also made of wood and glass. The corridor we walked down was lined with crude portraits, all featuring the same dark-haired young man, painted on black velvet canvases.

"The chemists love the King," Ms. Martinez said.

I wanted to ask who he was, but Mãe sent me a quick warning: *Don't. I'll explain later.*

∞

Professor Hoffman's office door was open. "Well hello, Sara," he said, ushering us in. He looked at my mother as if he'd seen her only the day before: a quick glance, a nod. Then his eyes fell on me.

He was a thin man with graying hair, wearing rimless glasses, jeans, cowboy boots, and a shirt the color of mustard. "What do you think of this?" he asked, pointing at the corner of his desk.

Cecelia Martinez, I noticed, had left us. There wasn't enough space for another person in the room.

The desk, like the office itself, was covered with assorted objects: papers and books, of course, but also toys made out of tin, rocks, wooden blocks, bars of soap, cans of soup. I looked down at the corner and saw what appeared to be a dead snake.

"Is that a coral snake?" Its skin had bright bands of red, yellow, and black.

"Well yes, it is. We have several of them in the woods around here. Lately an unusually large number of them has been turning up dead." He turned to Mãe. "Are you still keeping bees?"

I wondered how he knew. "I wrote a paper on honeybees while I was a student," Mãe told me. "He remembers everything."

"Yes," she said to Professor Hoffman. "And an unusually large number of them has been turning up dead."

"It's happening with birds as well." He sifted through a pile of papers on the desk, and I half expected him to pull out a dead bird. Instead, he picked up a journal and leafed through its pages.

We stood, watching him. There was no place for us to sit. Every chair in the office was occupied by objects.

"Here it is. The Audubon Society says that common bird populations have been declining dramatically, in some cases down as much as eighty percent, over the past forty years."

"What's causing the decline?" Mãe asked.

He flipped shut the journal. "The most immediate causes are man-made. Overdevelopment means a loss of natural habitat. And the habitats that remain are often polluted. Not a pretty picture."

He tossed the journal onto his desk and turned toward me. "Well well, who the hell are you?"

∞

As we drove home that night, I told Mãe what she already knew: I wanted to apply for admission to Hillhouse.

The dormitories we'd toured weren't any cleaner or larger than the ones we'd seen elsewhere. Students everywhere seemed intent on packing as much as possible into the cell-like rooms. Ventilation was poor, and the scent of patchouli oil (Mãe told me its name) overpowered several other odors.

But these rooms seemed more inviting to me because they were older, and most had the same long, narrow windows that we'd seen in the other buildings. Every window was a framed picture of trees. And the students collectively had impressive energy; everywhere we looked we saw them running, skateboarding, dancing. Nearly everyone we'd seen on the other campuses moved slowly, hunched forward, carrying heavy backpacks; most held cell phones to their ears.

Yes, I told my mother, I could see myself at Hillhouse. "A legacy," I said.

"If you have to leave me, I'd rather you were there than anywhere else." Her profile turned away from me, but I saw her jaw clench and the right corner of her mouth turn downward.

"I'm not really leaving you," I said. "Am I?"

"You're beginning to take your place in the world." She tried to brighten up. "It will be good for you, Ariella. And it's not that far from home."

We drove for a while, not talking. Finally I said, "Mãe? Who's the King?"

She told me about Elvis Presley, the rockabilly singer who became an international pop idol. She told me that people still claimed he never died, claimed they saw him walking through malls and airports. Some thought he might be a vampire. Then she sang to me, a song called "Heartbreak Hotel." It might have been Dashay's theme song, I thought.

Now I knew about the King. Why he so appealed to the Hillhouse chemistry faculty forever remained a mystery.

∞

We came home to an empty house. But the half-full cup of tea on the kitchen table was still warm, and next to it lay a copy of the local newspaper, opened to a page with a photo of Jesse on it.

I skimmed the article. He'd told the police a new version of the night he'd arranged to meet Mysty—in this one, he couldn't remember whether she'd turned up or not. He claimed to have lost his memory of the night in question. He was now considered the only person of interest in the case. The police still didn't have enough evidence to name him a suspect.

"The night in question." "Person of interest." What a strange language people speak when they talk about crime.

When Mãe and I heard the sound—a low-pitched nicker—we stood up at the same moment. The horses had come home.

We ran down to the stable. A long white horse van was parked next to it. Dashay must have driven it from Kissimmee, where the horses had been boarded while the stable was repaired.

A stone statue of a woman riding a horse stood at the stable entrance. She was Epona, the goddess of horses, and she'd moved with us to Kissimmee when the hurricane struck. Dashay must have brought her back.

Inside, amid the sweet smells of new lumber and hay, they were waiting for us in their stalls: Osceola, Abiaka, Billie, and my favorite, Johnny Cypress. They were named after leaders of the Seminole tribe. Johnny shook his black mane at the sight of us.

Dashay was there, too, brushing Abiaka. "We got back this afternoon," she said. "I came down to tell them good night. They're happy to be home."

Some people claim that animals don't experience the emotions people ascribe to them—that they care only about food and water and shelter. Those people haven't spent much time around horses.

Or cats. Grace came into the stable and headed straight for Billie, her own favorite. Billie was a cream-colored mare with patient manners. She lowered her head and sighed through her nostrils as Grace rubbed against her foreleg.

Our family wasn't complete, but the horses helped. We spent the next day riding, going down back trails that meandered toward the gulf. Snails' trails, Mãe called them, because they twisted and turned arbitrarily. Billie stayed behind with Grace for company. In the old days, Bennett had ridden Billie.

At noon we stopped on a beach near Ozello for lunch at a little restaurant called Peck's. We ate oysters and shrimp at picnic benches outside. From where we sat we couldn't see the nuclear power plant, and I tried to forget it existed.

A cool breeze swept in over the water. The sight of my mother and Dashay, and the horses grazing nearby, made me feel at peace. I didn't let myself think about the future, about the prospect of leaving them.

After lunch Dashay went over to Abiaka and talked to her for several minutes. Dashay's mouth was close to Abiaka's ear, and her voice was too low for us to hear.

Mãe shook her head, telling me not to try to listen in, but somehow I knew that Dashay was talking about her heartbreak.

She reminded me of a short story by Anton Chekhov called "Misery." The story's epigraph is "To whom shall I tell my sorrow?" An old man tries to tell the story of his son's death to the customers who ride in his carriage. No one will listen, and in the end he confides in his horse.

Later that week, when I sat down to work on the application for Hillhouse, my personal experience essay was inspired by Chekhov, Dashay, and the animals who suffer our confessions so patiently.

Chapter Nine

Naming an emotion is the first step in coming to terms with it. Researchers have found that the amygdala, the part of the brain that triggers negative feelings, is calmed when we give our feelings names. That's why we feel better after we confess to animals.

The amygdala is considered a part of the reptile brain, devoted to our physical survival. Some scientists claim that meditation, or the Buddhist practice of "mindfulness," keeps the amygdala under control.

My father had taught me the practice of daily meditation, but I'd discontinued it when I left Saratoga Springs. Now, as I prepared to leave my home in Florida, I began to meditate again. It helped me cope with the anxiety I felt at the thought of leaving home.

Hillhouse had what were called "rolling deadlines" for applications, but I wanted to send mine in as soon as possible. The second essay was supposed to focus on art imitating life, or vice versa. I chose to analyze a poem by Gerard Manley Hopkins, which begins:

> As kingfishers catch fire, dragonflies dráw fláme;
> As tumbled over rim in roundy wells
> Stones ring; like each tucked string tells, each hung bell's
> Bow swung finds tongue to fling out broad its name;
> Each mortal thing does one thing and the same:
> Deals out that being indoors each one dwells;
> Selves—goes itself; myself it speaks and spells,
> Crying Whát I do is me: for that I came.

The images and the language mesmerized me. I'd seen kingfishers and dragonflies in the air, and I felt the truth of the lines, but I had to read them several times before I began to understand them. I wrote about watching kingfishers and dragonflies, about the congruence between what they are and what they do, and about how this truth applies to humans: their actions define them. I wondered, did that apply to vampires as well? But I couldn't write about vampires. Once again, I censored myself.

The final essay was to express how the applicant envisioned herself as a part of Hillhouse. This one stumped me. I went to find my mother.

Mãe was in her study, writing a letter on the thin blue paper that she used for transatlantic mail.

"How might I 'envision' myself 'as a part of Hillhouse'?" I asked.

She frowned. "Do you want me to be one of those parents who tells you the answers?"

"Of course not." I'd read online that some college applicants actually hired others to write their admission essays, and I wondered: Didn't they realize how such actions defined them? "But I don't know how much of an outsider I'll need to be. It's not as if I can tell everyone I'm a vampire."

She set down her pen. "Why don't you look at the student jobs listed in the catalog? One of them might inspire you."

I took her advice, and I ended up writing an essay about joining the stables crew, since I knew how to listen to horses as well as talk to them.

With the application sent off, I found myself daydreaming about the future. My father sent me a letter in which he discussed college in the most general terms. He made no mention of me becoming a doctor or a scientist. He quoted W. B. Yeats: "Education is not the filling of a pail, but the lighting of a fire."

The quotation struck me as a peculiar choice, considering that earlier that summer we'd nearly burned to death.

Then he wrote: "Speaking of fire, you and your mother had better burn my letters. With so many police around, it's better that I stay dead."

I wrote back a long description of Hillhouse and a summary of my essays. I told him I'd asked to live in one of the "quiet" dorms, where loud noise was prohibited after 10 P.M. Finally, I wrote, "We miss you."

But after I sealed the letter, I thought twice. If I sent it, he'd feel reassured that all was well in Sassa. And it wasn't.

I destroyed the first letter and wrote a new one. It began: "Dear Father, I have been learning how to smoke cigarettes." It went on to talk about my persistent sense that someone was watching me, about my vertigo, and about my dreams of the fire. I mentioned hypnotizing a local boy being questioned in the disappearance of a friend. I thought of adding that Mãe was flirting with bartenders, but that seemed cruel, so I simply said, "Mãe and Dashay are prone to crying lately." I ended with: "Yes, we will burn your letters. It's really a blessing that you're not here."

Then I went to Mãe's office to find a stamp.

∞

November faded into December—for many, the holiday season. When I was growing up, we celebrated Christmas in a most restrained, secular way: useful gifts for me from my father and his assistants, Root and Dennis. Dennis had made us observe the holiday.

My mother and Dashay told me they celebrated the winter solstice with a Yule feast.

"No presents?" I asked.

Plenty of presents, they told me. They knew I hadn't received many when I was growing up. And we'd even have our own Yule tree—something I'd only glimpsed through other people's windows, back in Saratoga Springs.

One mid-December day I decided to use my allowance to buy presents for them. December weather was much cooler (high temperatures in the seventies), and the ride into town went quickly. The streets were busier, now that the search for Mysty had been called off. According to the newspaper, the police said they had no leads.

Sassa didn't offer many shopping opportunities. I decided that the pharmacy was my best bet.

For Dashay, I found copper-colored eye shadow with glitter in it, two red candles, and a lemon-colored T-shirt captioned SASSY in silver. Mãe was more complicated. I finally settled on crystal-studded hair ornaments: two shaped like dragonflies, two like stars, one like a crescent moon, and one like a honeybee. Having decided the honeybee might depress her, I was sliding it back onto the display pin when someone said my name.

Autumn leaned against a cosmetics display as if she'd been there awhile, watching me. "I need to talk to you," she said.

I paid for my presents, and she followed me into the parking lot.

"I wanted to come to your house, but I think the cops might be trailing me." She beckoned me toward a bench under a live oak tree. "If we talk here, it's like we ran into each other, no big deal."

She looked thinner than she'd been the last time I'd seen her. Her jeans weren't so tight now, and her sweater sagged around her waist and hips. Her eyes had shadows under them, but no demon light gleamed from her irises. I checked.

"Listen, you got to help Jesse." She nodded, as if agreeing with herself. "He's in a bad way. He's using something, I don't know what."

"Drugs?" I said.

"Yeah, but not like X or crack." She bent her head, then looked up at me. "You know about that stuff?"

I'd read about it online. I nodded.

"So he's doing some drug that makes him really stupid. He can't remember anything. And I figured, since you got him off alcohol, maybe you could help him kick this stuff." Autumn rubbed her face hard, beneath her eyes, leaving reddish crescents along her cheekbones. "Ari, he screwed up the lie detector tests. And they found some of Mysty's blood and hair in his car. He respects you. Won't you help?" Her voice cracked, and that's when I knew that I would try.

∞

Autumn and Jesse lived in a trailer park. The sign called it HARMONY HOMES MANOR, but it was a trailer park: row after row of mobile homes, some well maintained, with fake shutters on the windows and small gardens near the entrances, others looking as if they'd been abandoned—or should be. As we walked our bikes into the place (the road was too pitted with holes to ride), Autumn told me about the case against Jesse. "All they have is a tiny spot of blood and a few hairs, but they definitely belong to her."

"She rode in the car quite a bit, didn't she?"

"That's what I told them."

"And that day we came back from the mall, she picked at her arm until it bled." I had a vivid image of the blood welling on her arm.

Autumn stopped walking. "I'd forgotten all about that. That's where the bloodstain on the seat must have come from."

I wasn't as convinced as she was. For all I knew, Jesse might be guilty.

But when I saw him, I was sure he wasn't. He was sitting at the kitchen table inside the trailer, his head supported by his hands, elbows braced against the oilcloth table cover patterned with small pink pigs. Pig-shaped salt and pepper shakers stood next to a large bottle of ketchup on the table, and the place smelled like years of fried food.

Jesse looked up when we came in. "Hey," he said. "Hey . . ."

I realized he was trying to think of my name. His eyes were bloodshot, and he'd grown a beard. "I'm Ari," I said.

"Ari." He smiled.

"I like the beard," I said. I sat at the table opposite him. "Autumn, leave us alone to talk, would you?"

When she went outside, I bent forward and looked into Jesse's eyes. The irises were dark brown with hazel flecks. No sign of inner demons, as far as I could see.

He didn't mind my scrutiny—in fact, he liked it. He batted his long eyelashes and tried to decide if I wanted him to kiss me.

Yes, I was listening to his thoughts. I felt the situation warranted it. But they were jumbled; as soon as one formed, it fell apart and became half of something else.

I said, "Tell me what happened the night Mysty disappeared."

He stopped smiling and slid his chin into the cup of his palm again. "I don't remember." He said it without expression. But he did remember; he was thinking of a car's headlights approaching out of darkness, while he watched, and Mysty was sitting next to him—no, she went back to his car for cigarettes—no, she stayed where she was. Maybe there weren't any car headlights.

"Jesse, look at me." He looked up, his eyes full of confusion. "I want to help you. Do you trust me?"

He nodded. "Ari," he said.

"Then I want you to look at me, look into my eyes, and I want you to relax . . ."

Before I'd figured out what to say next, he was in a deep trance.

∞

The night Mysty disappeared, she showed up at the river dock carrying an old plaid wool blanket. "I said, 'Why'd you bring a blanket? It ain't cold.'" Jesse's voice was soft and slow. "And she said, 'Who wants to sit on the cold hard ground?'

"I knew what she was thinking." His eyes were shut, but his eyelids twitched. "She wanted to make out. Whatever. But I like this other girl. Her name's Ari. She's got class."

I should not be hearing this, I thought.

"So you and Mysty sat on the blanket?" I said.

"Yeah, until she went back to my car. Autumn keeps a pack of cigarettes in the glove compartment. I was parked on the shoulder of the road—you know Maythorn Street? That's where we were, at the end of Maythorn. I sat there and watched her go. She was in my car when I saw the headlights—another car coming down the street. It stopped next to mine. I heard voices, but I couldn't hear the words, you know? I figured it was somebody she knew. So I was laying back, half asleep for I don't know how long. Maybe ten minutes? I don't wear a watch. I try to tell the cops, why wear a watch? It only gets in the way."

"So ten minutes went by," I said.

"I guess." His hands lay limp on his knees. The only things moving were the muscles in his eyelids. He didn't speak.

"And—?"

"And that's all I know." His breathing was smooth and regular. "She must have got into that car. Or maybe she went back home. She always liked to change her mind."

"You didn't see her again?"

"No, I didn't. People keep asking me that. I don't know why they don't believe me."

"What kind of car was it? The one that came down the street."

"It was too dark to tell. All I saw was headlights, set kind of high off the ground. Maybe it was a truck or an SUV."

Somewhere in the trailer, a telephone rang. I told him to ignore the sound. After six rings, it stopped.

"Jesse," I said, my voice reminding me of my mother's when she tried to calm me. "What kind of drugs are you taking?"

He smiled. "You want some?"

"Show me."

He lifted his right hand, moved it to the pocket of his flannel shirt. He managed to unbutton it, his eyes still shut, and pulled out a prescription bottle. He handed it to me.

The prescription label was in the name of his sister, for amoxicillin, which I knew was a common antibiotic. I opened the bottle and shook out a few pills into my hand. They were dark red capsules, each bearing a small black *V.*

"Where'd you get these, Jesse?"

"My buddy bought them in Crystal River. They're sweet. A good mellow high."

I thought of Root's e-mail: *Sugar pill.* I put the cap on the bottle and slid it into my backpack.

"You don't need to take these. You don't want to take them. Are you hearing me?"

He nodded, docile as ever.

"You want your mind clear. You will remember that night clearly, next time you talk to the police."

With his eyes shut he looked younger, despite the beard. I repeated my spiel, telling him not to take any more of these pills, telling him he didn't need them. But I wondered why he *did* need them. I'd got him free of alcohol. Why do humans think they need drugs? Are they in perpetual pain?

This time I remembered to tell him to forget that he'd been hypnotized, and while I was at it I told him to forget that I'd even been there. I could have gone further, told him to stop having a crush on a girl named Ari. But I didn't. I don't like to think why.

As I was finishing with Jesse, I looked outside the kitchen window and saw Autumn's shoulder. She was pressed against the lower window, listening.

"Stay here," I told him. "Breathe deeply. When I clap my hands, you will awaken."

I didn't clap yet. I went to the trailer door, threw it open. Autumn looked up at me, embarrassment in her face overshadowed by desperation. "Help *me*," she said.

∞

When I pedaled away from Harmony Homes Manor, I felt proud of myself—a feeling that lasted all of a minute or so. The hypnoses would prove successful, I was sure. Jesse would stop taking V, and Autumn would never smoke again. And neither one would remember being hypnotized.

Autumn had begged me to help her quit. I knew the health risks of smoking, and I figured I was doing something good. She was harder to put under than her brother, but once she went, she went deep.

Why, then, did I feel so guilty, after that first minute passed?

In my head I heard my mother's voice—*Meddling is wrong*—and father's words: *With knowledge comes the obligation to use it justly.*

And I answered them: *I didn't meddle. What I did was just.*

So why did the guilt persist?

I rode through town, a sudden wind rising to whip my hair out behind me and to spin the artificial wreaths and candles hanging from overhead wires strung across the street. The sky had turned the color of wet ashes. Two young men in the post office parking lot shouted something after me, but I couldn't tell if it was "Bitch!" or "Witch!"

Once I turned the corner onto our road, the wind seemed to propel me toward home, faster than I wanted to get there.

∞

I left the paved street and pedaled up the road leading to our gate. I found myself listening, listening hard. But the world was silent. No sounds of birds, or insects, or overhead planes. As suddenly as it rose, the wind had died off, and the trees were still. My bicycle tires rubbed softly against the dirt. I pushed my hair back from my forehead and tried to think of a song to push me the last mile home. All that came to mind was "Ring of Fire."

I rounded the last bend, reminding myself of all I had to look forward to. The Yule feast was only a few days off, and Mãe and Dashay were already baking gingerbread, and Dashay had made a Christmas cake using dried fruit and dark brown sugar. The house would be fragrant with ginger and vanilla and Sangfroid and pine from the Yule tree they'd planned to get today. *My first real holiday,* I thought.

Then I saw the beige van. It was parked facing our gate (on which I could see the faint outline of the word KILLER, even though Dashay had painted over it).

I braked the bike so hard that I nearly fell. Then I regained balance, jerked the handlebars, and took off in the opposite direction. My heart pounded, and I can't tell you all I felt. The sense of revulsion was almost familiar now, spreading through me like some dark viscous fluid, rising into my throat, making it hard to breathe.

When I heard the van begin to move behind me, I panicked. I swerved the bike down a side street and into the yard of the first house I saw: small, painted green, set back from the road. I jumped off the bike, let it fall, ran up the steps, and pounded on the front door.

A woman wearing a white apron stained with red blotches opened the door, and before she could say a word I pushed past her, into the house, and slammed the door shut. My hand shook as I set the dead bolt.

The woman was saying something, but I turned toward the front window, and through its lace curtain and gray window screen I saw the van roll up. It stopped. The driver lowered his tinted window. He smiled, showing rows of blackened teeth. I felt his eyes—the white eyeballs with no irises or pupils—pinpoint me, and for a second they seemed to blaze, to cut through the space and screen and curtain like a laser.

I slumped backward, and the woman managed to catch me. "Ariella Montero," she said. "You're Sara's girl. My goodness. Who's that in the van?"

"Is he gone?" I tried to stand, but my legs wouldn't cooperate.

"You're shaking." She wrapped her arms beneath mine and half dragged me to an upholstered chair. Then she looked outside. "Yes, he's gone."

My arms were streaked with something red where she'd grabbed me.

"Don't worry. It's not what it looks like." She had a dish towel draped over one shoulder, and she used it to wipe away the streaks. "I just made a red velvet cake. I use cherry juice, and plenty of Sangfroid."

I took a deep breath and lay back in the chair. "Thank you for letting me in."

She grinned. "I didn't have much choice, did I? You tore in here like the hounds of hell were after you." I recognized her voice, and she began to look like someone I knew. I'd seen her at Flo's Place, or at the supermarket. Probably both places.

"I'm sorry to interrupt your baking," I said. "I'll be okay in a minute, and then I'll go."

"You're not going out there alone." She was a small woman with curly, dark hair and a heart-shaped face, but her voice carried authority. "He might be waiting. He might come back."

Her name was Nancy Cousins, and to this day I'm grateful for her kindness. She insisted that I drink a glass of Picardo and tonic, that I eat a slice of red velvet cake, still warm from the oven, and then that I call home.

"Ariella, where are you?" Mãe's voice had an unusual silky quality to it. She sounded happy, without a care in the world.

Once I'd told where I was and why, she said only, "I'll be right there," in her more familiar tone: deliberate calm masking worry.

I hadn't even finished my Picardo when she showed up. *Why is she wearing a dress?* I wondered. The dress was boatnecked, made of dark green velvet, and against it her auburn hair shone. *Is she wearing mascara?*

She was thanking Nancy for taking me in. "So you saw it, too?"

Nancy said, "A Chevy van. Tan colored."

"And the driver?"

"Some weird-looking bald guy," Nancy said. "Spooky eyes. You'd better call the police."

Mãe rested her hands on my shoulders, as if to steady them.

He may not be alive, I thought, *but he's real.*

We saw no more of the bald man that day. Mãe loaded my bike into the truck, having declined a slice of cake. "We have company waiting at home," she said. "Thank you for being so kind."

I wanted to know who it was, but she opened the passenger door and beckoned me in. "Do some deep breathing exercises, Ariella. Calm down."

I focused on my breathing until we were through the gate. My T-shirt had red stains on it, I noticed. They smelled like cherry juice. "Is Dashay all dressed up, too?"

Mãe parked the truck and switched off the ignition. "She's fetching the tree. Don't worry about your clothes. You can change before dinner, if you want to."

As we walked inside, I felt a sense of déjà vu: the smells of ginger, nutmeg, and cinnamon warmed the air. Mãe had placed a large red bowl filled with holly and ivy on the table near the sofa, and that's where my eyes went first. But the air in the room had a strange shimmering quality that I'd almost forgotten.

He was sitting in one of the armchairs we'd brought from Saratoga Springs, wearing a charcoal-colored suit and a forest-green shirt. Without thinking I ran to him, threw my arms around him, pressed my face against his jacket.

I'd never embraced my father before, and I think it shocked him. But after a few seconds, I felt his arms lightly go around me. *"Meu pequeno,"* I heard him say. *"Como eu o faltei."*

Portuguese isn't one of my languages, but later my mother told me what he'd said: *My little one. How I've missed you.*

∞

Mae and I couldn't take our eyes off him. His dark green eyes, the thick black hair springing back from his forehead, the pale skin, the cupid's-bow mouth. And the mellifluous sound of his voice. Mellifluous: from the Latin *mellis* ("honey") and *fluere* ("to flow"). It described his voice perfectly.

He was talking about Ireland, but I didn't pay much attention to his words. I listened dreamily, as I might listen to music. But the sound of my name awakened me.

"Ari's letter brought me here," he was saying, "against my better judgment. I'd thought it important for the two of you to have some time together without me, since you'd been apart for so many years."

He took a sip from a glass of Picardo and set it back on the side table. "But Ari's experiments with drugs and hypnosis suggested to me that my presence here might be a good idea."

My mother said, "Drugs and hypnosis?"

"Cigarettes," I said. "Only cigarettes." The mention of hypnosis made me feel a new wave of guilt.

"Ari, no." Mãe had been listening, and she knew what I'd done. "She's been hypnotizing her friends out of their bad habits," she said to my father.

"What's wrong with that?" My guilt made me defensive. "If I can help someone quit smoking or using drugs, why shouldn't I?"

My father put up his hand, palm facing me—his old signal to stop. "It's commendable for you to want to help others. But hypnosis is an imposition of your will on theirs. Surely you see the impropriety of that."

"But if they're better off as a result, then it's not an impropriety, is it?"

"By turning them into puppets, you rob them of the freedom to take action on their own." His voice was crisp. "And you separate them from the moral consequences of their actions. Remember your Sartre, Ari."

I didn't want to remember my Sartre. I didn't want to lose the argument.

So I changed the subject. "Father, I saw the blind man today."

My father went along with the change of topic. "Where did you see him?"

"Parked outside our gate." I didn't want to talk about the man, didn't want his presence in our living room. But I made myself talk. "I ran away, and he came after me. And I saw him in Sassa a few months ago, before Mysty disappeared."

"You were right to run away," he said. "I don't know what he is, but he means us no good."

"Mãe said you've seen him more than once."

He rubbed his forehead, and I noticed the jade cufflinks fastening his sleeves.

"Yes. I first saw him in Glastonbury, and later, in Saratoga—" Then a wave of exasperation crossed his face and, as I watched, he disappeared—his body dissolved into air.

At the same moment, the front door opened, and Dashay backed into the room, both arms holding a burlap-wrapped tree trunk, followed by the tree itself, supported by FBI agent Cecil Burton.

Mãe reached over and picked up my father's half-full glass of Picardo. She hesitated a moment, then handed it to me. She already had one of her own.

By the time they'd set the tree down, there was no evidence that my father had been in the room. Once again, Burton had forced him to turn invisible.

"That's quite a tree," Mãe said.

The tree stood nearly ten feet high. It didn't resemble the ones I'd glimpsed through windows. Its branches were feathery, not pointed or sharp, and they grew in a spiral shape, winding up the trunk like a staircase.

Dashay leaned back, her hands on her hips, and gazed up at the tree. "I found it at the nursery in Crystal River. It's called a cryptomeria. Isn't it special?"

"It doesn't smell piney." I didn't know what to make of the tree.

"No, it doesn't. But later we can plant it outside, and it will grow maybe forty feet tall."

The tree didn't excite me. I wanted my father back.

Dashay seemed momentarily puzzled, but she kept talking. "Then I ran into Cecil in town, and I invited him back to help trim the tree. He's all alone for the holidays."

So she called him *Cecil*. My mother and I were furious, but we knew better than to show it.

"Would you care for a drink?" Mãe asked Burton.

"Sure," he said. He was wearing jeans and a T-shirt, which didn't fit him as well as his usual suit. "I'll have what you're having."

Mãe smiled, but didn't say anything. I followed her out to the kitchen. She took a bottle of pomegranate juice out of the refrigerator and diluted it until it was the color of Picardo.

"Why don't you hypnotize him?" I said. "I want to talk to my father."

"*We* don't do things like that." She gave me a chiding look, and I knew that later I'd be hearing more about the ethics of hypnosis. "Besides, your father left."

"He's gone?"

"Didn't you notice?" She garnished the drink with a sprig of mint. "When he leaves a room, the air changes."

We went back to the living room, and I saw that she was right: the air had lost its shimmer.

∞

Agent Burton—Cecil—stayed for only two hours, but for Mãe and me those hours dragged. We strung popcorn and cranberries and hung them on the tree. Burton and Dashay talked about music and dancing, and even demonstrated a few steps.

Mãe and I didn't try hard to hide how glum we felt, and finally Dashay said, "What's up with you two?"

My mother said, "Ariella had a bad experience today." She turned to me. "Tell them about the man in the van."

Burton listened to my story with real interest, this time. "Why didn't you call me?" he said.

"We'd barely arrived when you came in with the tree." Mãe's eyes were cold.

He asked me to describe the van again and again, and he jotted some notes on a pad. Then he said to Dashay, "Sorry to be talking shop."

"Are you kidding?" she said. "Go out there and find that creep."

When Burton finally left, Dashay said, "Isn't he cute? I think he's cute."

Mãe picked up his empty glass and carried it into the kitchen without a word.

"What is wrong with you?" Dashay trailed after her.

"Don't you remember the house rules?" Mãe set the glass on the counter with unusual force, and that's when I realized how angry she was. "We never bring anyone here without first checking with each other."

"I know, but he was all alone, and it's the holiday season." Dashay folded her arms. "Where's your Yule spirit?"

"Raphael was here." Mãe looked as if she wanted to break something. "When you two came waltzing in, he disappeared."

"He was *here*?" Dashay flung out her arms. "How was I supposed to know?"

I left them quarreling in the kitchen and walked out of the house, down to the dock. The indigo air was sweet and cool against my skin, and a mockingbird in a mangrove tree sang a bittersweet melody—a song that only bachelor birds sing at night. I sat on the dock and looked up at the stars, trying to find Orion, but the stars weren't visible. Venus hung low in the sky, beautiful and remote.

I remembered Jesse's words: "Do you ever look up at the sky at night and wonder who's looking back at you?" Tonight I felt too insignificant for anyone to bother watching. *What if we're puppets?* I thought. *What if we're only figments of some warped imagination?*

I sat there until it was dark, waiting, but the stars never appeared, and my father did not come back.

TWO

In Loco Parentis

Chapter Ten

Two weeks later I sat in my mother's truck, en route to college. Hillhouse had called in December, letting me know that I'd been accepted and that I could begin in January, if I liked.

Did I like?

My mother and Dashay had taken me to Orlando—first, to see a doctor (one of us), who tested my ears and hearing. He found no sign of accompanying hearing loss. He said my vertigo might have been caused by labyrinthitis: an inflammation of the inner ear canal, which usually goes away on its own. Then we went to a mall to shop for school clothes—jeans and T-shirts, now neatly packed into a trunk that rode behind us—and on to lunch, where they'd tried to get me excited about my "new beginning."

Now Mãe went so far as to quote something she'd read about leaving home being like giving birth to yourself.

"That sounds *disgusting*," I said.

As she drove, she told me about her experience of leaving home. "I always knew I wanted to go to Hillhouse," she said. "It's where the coolest kids from high school went."

I've been told I have a vivid imagination, but it wasn't easy to visualize my mother as a high school student caring about the "coolest kids." "Did your parents want you to go there?"

"My parents died when I was fourteen." She said it without emotion. "My sister and I went to live with cousins."

Losing one's parents at fourteen was impossible for me to imagine. I'd been brooding for weeks about my father disappearing, but to imagine him dead, never coming back—that was impossible.

"My mother died of cancer." Mãe turned the truck onto Interstate 75. "And my father had a heart attack soon after that."

"Were they old?" I asked.

"In their thirties," my mother said. "Not old. That's one reason I wanted to become a vampire—to never suffer as they did."

The landscape rushed past us. I sat back in the seat, thinking.

"Don't worry, Ari." My mother patted my arm. "Your father will come back."

"But where is he? Why haven't we heard from him?"

She said, "I don't know for certain. But I have a hunch: he's gone after your shadow man."

∞

We stopped for lunch—shrimp and grits in a small-town café in Georgia's Low Country, where silver and pale green marsh grass swayed along the roadside and the air smelled sweet, like dried hay. Back in the truck, my mother handed me a small laminated card. On it was a photo of me, my name, and the day and month of my birth. But the birth year listed made me seven years older.

"I had it made on the black market in Miami," she said.

I stared down at the photo of me, allegedly aged twenty-one. "I never heard of any black market."

"Don't look so shocked. How do you suppose we get driver's licenses and passports?" She rolled down the cab window. "Didn't your father ever mention Vunderworld? Vampire Underworld. It's an important part of our support network."

"Why do I need a fake ID?"

She put the key into the ignition, but didn't start the engine. "You'll find that most of your friends have it, in order to get into bars and clubs. There's no reason for them to know that you're only fourteen. The college administrators know your real age. They think you're a prodigy."

My college education would be premised on lies, I thought.

"Without a few lies, you'd never be able to fit in." Mãe kept her eyes on the dashboard. "You're only fourteen, Ari. Do you want them to treat you like a baby?"

I hadn't thought about it. Could I ever *fit in*? "What happens when I get older?" I said. "When I don't age, but everyone around me does?"

She started the car. "Some vampires have plastic surgery to mimic the effects of aging. That way, they can live in a community of mortals for many years without anyone knowing."

"They have surgery to look older?" It struck me as comical. Each time we'd driven through Florida, I'd noticed roadside billboards advertising procedures to make people look young. One read, NOT EVEN YOUR HAIRDRESSER WILL KNOW FOR SURE.

"The best surgeons, the ones in Miami, make the changes subtle," Mãe said. "They can even mimic the way a human looks if she's had minor plastic surgery or facial injections." We were driving down a rural road, the afternoon sun turning the marsh grass faintly golden. "Of course, it only works for a time—the span of a human life. Then we have to relocate, take on a new identity, and start again, the way your father did.

"There's one more thing we should talk about." Mãe slid her eyes from the road to me. "Sex."

"I know all about it," I said quickly.

My mother adjusted the truck's rearview mirror. "You know the facts of life. But do you know how they work for vampires?"

By the time the truck turned onto the Hillhouse campus, I knew all about vampire sex—at least in theory—and, for the first time in my life, I thought my mother was a prude.

Because our senses are so acute, vampires tend to experience the world with much greater intensity than humans. My mother said the same principle held true for sex.

"That's one reason the Sanguinists and the Nebulists advocate celibacy," she said. "Sex between two humans can be passionate, but sex between two vampires might be so powerful as to be all-consuming, even violent."

"Might be?" In spite of my reluctance to discuss sex with my mother, I did want to know more. "But isn't always?"

"I wouldn't know." Her voice sounded guarded. "Since I became a vampire, I've been celibate."

My mother has been celibate for fourteen years? "Not even a fling?" I asked.

"Nothing."

The thought shocked me. Then I realized that my father probably had abstained from sex for just as long—but for some reason, that didn't bother me so much.

"Mãe, this is an awkward subject," I said. "But I don't plan on *never* having sex, if that's what you're trying to get at."

"I want you to be careful." She looked away, and I wondered what she was feeling. "To weigh the possible consequences. If you decide to do anything, you'll need to take precautions."

"I know about birth control," I said.

"More than that." She turned toward me again. "Dashay has told me a little about how it was for her and Bennett—how her hormones seemed to surge out of her control, at times. You may have to handle feelings you've never felt before. And Ari, don't do anything until you know you're ready."

How will I know? I wondered. But I didn't ask my mother that. Much to my surprise, I felt sorry for her.

∞

The door of room 114 in Seward Hall had pottery shards and small rocks glued to it, spelling out the words INNER SANCTUM. The door was locked, and no one responded to my knocking, so I used the key we'd picked up at the admissions office. The door creaked as it swung open.

The room had two windows covered by black drapes, and it was lit by a bare bulb in a ceiling fixture. Twin beds stood along facing walls, with battered wooden desks at their feet. Four suitcases were piled next to one of the desks. A girl with long, dark hair sat cross-legged on the floor, sewing tiny pleats into a shirt. She looked as surprised to see us as we felt to see her.

"You must be"—I pulled a form out of my backpack pocket—"Bernadette."

She stared at us without speaking. She had enormous dark eyes and ears that reminded me of seashells, which she used to hold back her hair.

"I'm Ariella. Your new roommate. And this is my mother."

Her eyes went from me to my mother and back to me.

"Um, you can call me Ari," I said.

Slowly she uncrossed her legs and stood up. "I thought I was finally going to have a single," she said. Her voice was low and musical, lacking the resentment that the words implied. I noticed a poster of Edgar Allan Poe over one of the twin beds, and for a moment I wondered, *Can she be one of us?*

"You can call me Bernadette," she said. "Only my enemies call me Bernie."

I don't like to think about saying good-bye to my mother that day. After we'd carried my trunk, four boxes of stuff (including

Sangfroid and Picardo in bottles with prescription labels, thanks to the helpful doctor in Orlando), I followed her back to the truck.

"It's probably safer if you don't come home for a while." Mãe turned her face away from me, and I knew she was trying not to cry. "But write me. Call me. If you get homesick, I'll come and visit."

I nodded.

"It's only two and a half months until spring break." She tried to make her voice cheerful. "I'll come and pick you up then, okay?"

I tried to say "Okay," but my voice cracked. We hugged each other quickly, and I felt her press something into my right hand. Then I turned and headed back to the dorm. I didn't want to watch her drive away.

Inside the dormitory's lounge I opened my hand and unwrapped a square of red tissue paper. At its center lay a small greenish-gold cat strung on a black silk cord, and beneath it was a slip of paper reading: "This amulet was made in Egypt around 1170 BC. Wear it, and be safe."

Mãe's handwriting slanted to the right, as always. *Ever the optimist*, I thought. I slipped the silk cord over my head, and the cat nestled below my collarbone, as if it belonged there.

∞

Back in the room, Bernadette was holding a bottle of Sangfroid, reading its label. "Are you a sicko?" she said.

"I have lupus," I said—the same lie my father had told the world in order to pass as mortal. Mãe and I had decided it was the easiest way for me to get by.

"Some of them may make fun of you," she'd warned. "But most of them have been taught to be tolerant of people with chronic physical ailments."

Bernadette was more than tolerant; her face lit up at the word "lupus," and she pulled a medical dictionary from the bookshelf next to her desk. "'Lupus erythematosus,'" she read. "'A chronic inflammatory disease that can target joints, skin, kidneys, blood cells, heart, and lungs. Lupus develops when the immune system attacks the body's own tissues and organs.'" She looked up from the dictionary. "Wow."

"It's not contagious," I said.

"That wasn't a negative 'wow.'" She was reading further. "'Signs and symptoms include a butterfly-shaped rash, arthritis, kidney problems, and photosensitivity.' Not to mention those issues with the brain, heart, and lungs." She shut the book. "I have asthma, and I'm hypoglycemic. Nothing as interesting as your condition. Will you show me your rash?"

"I don't have one." I reached for the bottle of Sangfroid, and she handed it over. "You think illnesses are interesting?"

"More than that. They're marks of distinction." She gestured toward one of the curtained windows. "The world out there makes us sick. Big surprise. We're the sensitive ones—we've evolved beyond the so-called healthy people. They're the ones who scare me. Like my last roommate, Jackie. She was so healthy I couldn't stand it—she ate sugar and fast food and red meat, and they didn't even bother her. She hasn't developed the sensitivities we have, and if she ever does, they'll probably kill her.

"You and me—we're the lucky ones." When she smiled, Bernadette had an elfin charm. Then I noticed her shadow, cast by the overhead bulb onto the carpet. I tried not to show how disappointed I felt.

"What happened to Jackie?" I looked at the bare mattress about to become mine.

"She went back home, to Hilton Head." This time, Bernadette's smile was condescending. "She missed her mommy too much."

Bernadette insisted on helping me unpack. She put a CD on the stereo and told me the band was called Inner Sanctum. As she lifted sweaters and jeans out of the trunk and placed them in bureau drawers, she danced to the music, which was mournful. In her black jeans and ruffled white shirt, she looked like a Spanish dancer.

"I'm doing a minor in dance," she said. "Majoring in lit. What about you?"

I told her I was considering a major in interdisciplinary studies.

"That means you make it up as you go along." She deposited three shirts in a drawer, did a twirl, and ended up back at the trunk. "Hillhouse is a haven for kids like us. The ones who don't last are the more traditional types—you know, business majors and pre-laws and premeds. The ones who want every question to have only one answer. We get a few of them from time to time, but they tend to transfer or drop out."

"Drop out completely?"

"Some of them do, yeah. They're demoralized by this place. Some people can't handle freedom, you know?" She picked up a jacket and danced it to the closet. "Your clothes are cute, but they look very, very new. We can soon fix that."

I arranged books on a shelf near my desk. Bernadette's bookshelf held feathers, rocks, small pieces of glass, and a spectrum of spools of thread.

She was rubbing an emery board against the knees of my new corduroy jeans. When I asked why, she said she was "distressing" the jeans to make them look "lived-in."

"Why did you decide to come for the spring term instead of waiting for fall?"

Mãe and I had discussed how to handle such questions. "A girl disappeared in my hometown," I said. "My parents decided it was a good time for me to leave."

(Later, when I told her my best friend up north had been murdered, she seemed impressed. "Your life is so *dramatic*," she said.)

Now she said, "Your mom's beautiful." Back at the trunk, she pulled out my metamaterial trouser suit. Mãe had relented and let me have it after I made a strong argument that I might need to turn invisible in my new environment. "This looks like something you'd wear to a job interview."

"It's for special occasions." I watched her carry it to the closet and hang it up. I didn't want that suit distressed.

"What does your dad do?" she asked.

"He's a researcher." I put socks and underwear into a bureau drawer. "He's not around much. He sort of comes and goes."

"I know all about that. My parents divorced three years ago."

I took a large parcel from a box brought from the storage unit in Saratoga Springs, cut away sheets of bubble wrap, and lifted out my lithophane lamp. Its porcelain shade appeared unornamented, but when I plugged the lamp in and turned its switch, brightly colored birds emerged on the panels of the shade.

Bernadette said, "Ooh."

"My mother bought it. It's been by my bed since I was a baby," I said, setting the lamp carefully on the table next to my cot. "If I woke up at night, I'd turn it on and talk to the birds. I had names for them."

"What were their names?" Bernadette came over and ran her hand over the shade.

"Not telling." I didn't want her to make fun of me. The names had come from fairy tales; the dove was Cinderella, and the cardinal was Rose Red.

"At least you trusted me enough to tell me that you named them." Her voice was wistful. I gathered that not many others trusted her that well.

When we went to dinner that night, Bernadette stood on top of the cafeteria table and said, "Announcement!" in a voice so loud the whole room went quiet.

"We've got a new one," she shouted. "Stand up," she said to me.

Close to a hundred students were sitting in the basement cafeteria, which smelled of cabbage and stir-fried vegetables. I didn't want to stand up.

I stood up.

"This is Ari Montero," Bernadette said. "My new roomie from Florida."

Some people clapped, others made comments that blended into an indecipherable noise. Two or three whistled and howled, which I took as a compliment.

A boy with short blond hair said, "How long will this one last, Bernie?"

"Shut up, Richard." Bernadette sat down next to me. "He's president of the Social Ecologists Club," she said. "Membership one and a half: Richard and his girlfriend."

I didn't ask which one was the half.

∞

The next morning I took part in a brief orientation session. There were only three of us new enrollees, and our "facilitator," a young man called Jack, said, "If this was fall term, I'd tell you to look to your left, and look to your right, and ask yourself which two of you won't be here in four years. But with only three of you here, that felt kind of cruel."

One of the other newbies asked, "Is the dropout rate that high?"

I didn't hear Jack's response. I was looking at my fellow newcomers, wondering which two of us would disappear.

Jack went over our class and work schedules. I'd already decided to register for courses in literature, philosophy, and physics, and the night before Bernadette had talked me into signing up for American Politics, a class she was taking. "The American Politics prof can be a bore, but we get to go on field trips," she said. "You should sign up for Environmental Studies, too—that class goes on an overnight trip to the Okefenokee Swamp."

"Maybe next term," I'd said.

Jack told me my work assignment was with the recycling team. "The stables crew is full," he said. "Everybody loves horses, nobody loves trash."

I looked over the list of students signed up for the recycling team, lingering over the name *Walker Pearson*. I thought of the boy who jumped out of the pile of leaves. How many boys named Walker could there be at Hillhouse?

"I don't mind working with trash," I said.

∞

My first week at Hillhouse went so fast I had no time to feel homesick. The literature and philosophy classes were my favorites from the first day, because the professors were bright and clearly loved teaching. My American Politics professor seemed bright, but she spoke tentatively and had a hunted look in her eyes that made me wonder about her personal life. My physics professor, on the other hand, acted utterly confident, but I soon found out that he wasn't as smart as he thought.

During the second meeting of the physics class, I'd made the mistake of asking Professor Evans (Hillhouse didn't call professors who held PhDs "doctors"; the faculty members and administration thought that academic tradition elitist) a question after his lecture. From the other students' stares and from the professor's body language, I inferred that asking questions was considered inappropriate in this class. Professor Evans launched into a lengthy discourse on the Higgs boson, a particle my father had explained to me in lucid, elegant detail.

"All particles acquire their mass through interactions with an all-pervading field, called the Higgs field, carried by the Higgs boson," my father had said. "The existence of the Higgs boson has been predicted, but not yet detected. Its existence is necessary to the sixteen particles that make up all matter. In other words, observations of the known suggest the presence of an unknown." *Presence and absence, again,* I'd thought.

My father had extensive knowledge of the theoretical framework of particle physics, and he was able to discuss it in precise English—two traits not shared by Professor Evans. As the professor droned on, he began making factual errors as well as syntactical ones, confusing the names of particle accelerators and researchers. At that point I tuned in to his thoughts, and I was astonished to hear how bitter they were. He thought my question was designed to embarrass him, expose his ignorance. And so he talked on, making more and more mistakes.

Most of the other students had stopped listening to him.

I didn't know what to do. If I pointed out his errors, he'd be even more upset. So I kept quiet, and when the class ended, I was the first to leave the room.

"Hey, Ari?"

I turned around. Jack, our orientation facilitator, was standing by the door. I'd noticed him earlier, sitting in the back of the room.

"I know you're new and all," he said. "But the best thing you can do in that class is sleep with your eyes open."

"I can't do that." I folded my arms across my chest.

"Then I'd advise you to drop the course."

And that's how I ended up taking Environmental Studies after all.

∞

I joined the recycling team that afternoon. Their operations were based in a low cement-block building near the barn. I much preferred the smell of the barn.

Some crews gathered trash from campus buildings and brought the bags there, where another crew spread the assorted materials over the sorting tables, separating usable items from recyclables from future compost. My first assignment was to be a sorter.

The first time I walked into the room where the sorting took place, two students were scanning trash spread across a table, and near them the boy called Walker was juggling oranges. Everyone wore gloves.

I saw Walker first. When he saw me, he dropped an orange.

Since then I've read theories about what attracts people to each other—speculation that they're drawn by physical and psychological traits that remind them of their parents. I'm not sure how much any of that applies to vampires.

I prefer a simpler explanation: my eyes were drawn to Walker first because he was the most visually appealing person I'd ever seen, and second because he was volatile and enigmatic. His sun-streaked hair; his lean, tan body; his loose-fitting, raggedy clothes—none of the parts of him explained the appeal of the whole.

"Who are you?" His voice had a soft Southern accent.

I let my eyes linger on the table a second before I looked up at him. "My name's Ari."

His eyes were a lighter shade of blue than mine. They reminded me of the color of my mother's new guest room: Indian Ocean blue.

"You going to do any work today, Walker?" One of the other students pushed back the sleeves of his flannel shirt with his gloved hands.

He took a step to the side, then moved away from me, stumbling over nothing that I could see. It was one of the few awkward moves I ever saw him make.

I put on my gloves. Students threw away all kinds of things: photos, books, CDs, clothing, and even old TV sets, as well as genuine garbage. We took out the usable items and put them in a cart. Later they'd be cleaned and placed in the campus Free Store. We sorted out glass, paper, and cans for recycling, and we put food items in a wheelbarrow that would go to the compost pile.

The next time I reported for work, Walker stood at the sorting table next to me. We didn't talk much as we worked, but we were aware of the proximity of our hands on the table. He smelled fresh, like the woods around campus, in sharp contrast to the trash we were sorting.

He asked me what I was majoring in, and when I asked him the same question, he said, "I'm majoring in magic. My plan is to become a notable eccentric."

Later that afternoon we both reached for an apple at the same time. The shock of contact felt electric, even through our gloves.

The next day, I went to American Politics for the first time. Walker was there, sitting in the back row. I took the seat next to him. As the lecture grew monotonous, he did surreptitious magic tricks, pulling coins out of his ear and feathers out of his hair.

∞

"Inner sanctum" hardly described the room I shared with Bernadette. People came and went at all hours of the day and late into the night. They came to borrow books and CDs, to bring offerings of food or books or CDs or clothes. (Most of my new clothes had been "distressed" by Bernadette to make them cooler, and now they were much in demand.) Most of our visitors were Hillhouse students, but some were students from other schools or vagabonds who roamed from city to city, campus to campus, all across America. For a self-styled outcast, Bernadette was very popular.

She had a boyfriend, she said, back home in Louisiana. He never called or came to visit, but she showed me his picture: a skinny boy with a shaved head and eyebrow piercings, holding one hand outstretched toward the camera, as if he were asking for something.

From time to time, Walker showed up, and usually he'd ask me if I wanted to study with him. That meant he and I would walk across campus and find a quiet spot in the library. On the way, we talked about where we'd lived before (he was a North Carolina boy, and his accent struck me as sexy), and we talked about where we'd like to travel (both of us wanted to tour Europe; Walker particularly wanted to go to Prague, where his grandfather had been born).

One night Walker played his guitar for me. It was a battered acoustic, but he played well, I thought. That was the first time he told me I was beautiful. The word glimmered silver as it crossed the air between us, and when it reached me, I felt myself begin to glow with the compliment.

Did we study? Not often. We went to classes and completed assignments without thinking much about them. The class work, for me, was far less difficult than the lessons my father had set.

Contra dancing and drum circles were regular events at Hillhouse. So were poetry readings and bonfires. Smoking pot and drinking were popular recreational activities, but Bernadette said they were much more prevalent at the state schools. She didn't indulge in either. "It's all too banal," she said.

From time to time Bernadette tired of the constant activity, slammed the door, and locked it. Then she'd pull out a deck of tarot cards or volunteer to braid my hair.

In her tarot readings, Bernadette always represented me with the Knight of Cups card, because she said its profile resembled mine. In the last reading she gave me, the Knight was covered by the Ten of Swords, which she said signified misfortune, pain, perhaps the death of a loved one. The influence directly ahead of me was the Four of Swords, which she said meant solitude, convalescence, or exile. "It's not a card of death, even though that's what it looks like," she said.

On the card, a knight lay upon a tomb, his hands clasped as if in prayer. "Great," I said.

I was tempted to dismiss her readings entirely, but I didn't. I recalled my father talking about Jung's concept of synchronicity—the opposite of causality. Synchronicity finds patterns and meanings in seeming coincidences, and in the case of the tarot one could argue that the subject's state of mind or psychic condition is reflected by the choice of cards and their interpretation.

Was I concerned with misfortune, solitude, illness, exile? Of course. These are fears that most vampires and many humans live with every day.

As for the braiding: the light touch of her hands on my hair made me think of my mother, so I tried politely to say no. (I'd called Mãe twice, and each time the conversations had been strained, only reminding us of how much we missed each other. It felt better not to call.)

Some nights Bernadette read aloud her poetry, which was usually about death. Her villanelle about seeing her father in his coffin troubled me, even more because I knew he was alive and apparently healthy.

She was reading aloud a new sonnet. It began "Roses black as onyx crown my grave / And dew like pewter teardrops cannot save / Their youth, or mine—"

At which point my cell phone rang. I bolted from the room to answer it and stood in the corridor to talk.

"Hey, Ari." It was Autumn's voice. "Want to go to the mall?"

"Hi," I said. "I'm not there anymore."

I told her I was at college, and she said she hadn't realized I was old enough. She had never heard of Hillhouse.

"It's a small college in Georgia," I said. "It's pretty here."

"Maybe I'll come and visit," she said. "I got my license back, and it looks like I'll be getting Jesse's car."

"He's giving it up?"

"He's going into the marines," she said. "Didn't you know that?"

"I'm not *there* anymore," I said again.

"I thought he'd have called you." Autumn sounded confused. "I gave him your number."

"Why is he joining the marines?" I couldn't picture Jesse wearing a uniform.

Autumn said, "He's always liked to fight. And it's a good time for him to get out of town."

She said the police and the FBI were leaving him alone, but Mysty's mother had taken to following him around, asking questions. That was something I could picture easily.

"Any news about Mysty?" I asked.

"Nothing. It's like she dropped off the face of the earth." Autumn coughed, and I wondered if she might still be smoking. "You got a bed for me if I come visit?"

I hesitated to reply. Hillhouse was still new to me, and I didn't know if Autumn would like it—no, to be honest, I wondered if she'd fit in. Then I felt guilty. With Mysty gone, I was probably the closest thing to a friend she had.

"Better bring a sleeping bag," I said. "That's what most people do."

Chapter Eleven

*T*he night before our field trip left for the Okefenokee Swamp, Walker put on a magic show.

Like most of the Hillhouse community events, the show was staged in the old theater building next to the gym. The theater smelled of cedar and woodsmoke, scents that made the rigid metal chairs more tolerable. Bernadette and I had seats in the second row; we'd arrived early, but the first row was fully occupied.

The boy sitting in front of me turned around—he was Richard, the president of the Social Ecologists Club. (Aside from occasionally circulating pamphlets denouncing liberal politics, the Social Ecologists Club was largely inactive.) He also sat in front of me in American Politics. I'd grown very familiar with the back of his head; his short blond hair lay in tufts that curled tightly against his scalp and threatened to explode if allowed to grow longer.

"Hey, Bernadette," Richard said. "Why aren't vampires invited to parties?"

My heart jumped. Did he know about me?

"Shut up, Richard," Bernadette said, her voice disdainful.

"You should know. Because they're pains in the neck!" His voice was jubilant, and that's when I realized he was telling a joke, aiming it at Bernadette. With her hair dyed black and her pale skin, she looked more like a stereotypical vampire than I did.

"What's a vampire's—excuse me, what's *your* favorite mode of transportation?"

"Shut up, Richard."

"A blood vessel!"

Bernadette and I didn't laugh once, but the girl sitting next to Richard giggled incessantly.

"Where do vampires keep their savings? In blood banks!"

"Shut up, Richard."

I was delighted when a boy from my literature class came onto the stage and began pounding on a large African drum. Richard turned around, pleased that he'd managed to annoy us. He wanted attention, any way he could get it. Bernadette shot me a look of disdain and shook her head.

Walker took the stage, accompanied by a drum roll. He wore jeans and a flannel shirt—no cape or sequined suit. His hair and skin glowed in the stage lights. "Welcome," he said, "to the art of misdirection."

The first few tricks involved eggs and impressed me more than some of the later, more elaborate ones, because their magic was, in a sense, real. On a table in the center of the stage, a Bunsen burner was lit, and Walker, using tongs, passed an egg through its flame until the egg was black. Then he dropped the egg in a bowl of water, and it turned iridescent, almost silver.

I knew some kind of chemical reaction must be responsible for the color change. But what made the trick magical was the story Walker told while he did it.

"For thousands of years, magicians have studied the practice of scrying," he said. "It's another word for crystal-gazing—for seeing the future in a reflective surface. Crystals link our mundane world with the one lying beyond it. In the moment that we gaze into the crystal, time dissolves. Our inner self grows calm. Our spirit connects with the light of the universe, making us clear and pure.

"Poor magicians like me can't afford to buy a crystal ball, so we make our own with eggs."

After the transformation was complete, he invited a member of the audience to come onstage to look into the bowl of water. Richard volunteered.

"Anybody else?" Walker asked.

"I'll do it." Bernadette was on her feet in a second.

"That's not fair," Richard said, and she said, "Shut up," as she passed him.

"Relax and breathe deeply," Walker told Bernadette. "Look deep into the silver ball, and tell me what you see."

"I see the reflection of the candle flame."

The theater was so quiet that I heard the sounds of people breathing on either side of me.

"Try to unfocus your eyes," Walker said. His voice was soft, with a twinge of North Carolina in its inflections. "Try to see the mist forming in the crystal."

"It's an egg," Richard said, but people shushed him.

"I see it," Bernadette said. "It's like smoke on the surface."

"Let the smoke grow until it's all you can see." Walker signaled the drummer, who began to play a slow, rhythmic beat.

"It's all I can see." In her black shirt and jeans, her long hair hanging on either side of the bowl as she bent over it, Bernadette looked like a creature from another time, another world.

"Now let your eyes focus." Walker's face, intent and serious, was almost too handsome to watch. "As the smoke clears, tell us what you see."

"I see . . ." Bernadette paused. "It looks like—it's a skull."

"Of course it is," Richard said. "She's a vampire. All she sees is death."

But no one was listening to him, except me.

∞

"I really saw it," Bernadette whispered. She'd resumed her seat, and the magic show went on.

Walker did several tricks using scarves and coins that multiplied, thanks to the sleeves of his shirt, talking all the while about ancient India and Tibet and the tradition of magic. He used thin black threads (was I the only one to see them?) to move earthenware bowls across the table; he called them Babylonian demon bowls, explaining that they were placed in the corners of ancient houses to catch demons. I later learned that his story was true, and that the bowls were also used to gather demons to visit upon one's enemy.

I wondered what Walker would say if I told him I'd seen an actual demon. As if he heard my thought, he looked up from a trick and winked at me. Then he turned a lump of coal into a diamond. I stopped watching for the strings and sleights of hand and let myself be charmed. For a moment I fantasized about being the magician's assistant, dressed in my metamaterial suit, turning invisible when the trick required it, letting the magician take the credit. But how would Walker react to knowing what I was capable of—no, knowing what I was? He'd probably be terrified.

His final trick required an oversized trunk and the assistance of Jacey, a student notable for being the shortest person on campus. Under five feet tall, she sprang nimbly into the trunk, her thick blond braids trailing her.

Walker tucked in her braids, then closed and locked the lid. "Jacey volunteered to be disappeared," he said. "She's fully aware of the potentially devastating physical risks." He began to chant words that made no sense, and he tapped the trunk lid three times with a tree branch that he called a Druid wand.

Of course the trunk was empty when he opened it. I figured it had a false bottom, and that once it was closed and tapped again, Jacey would be inside.

But when Walker opened the lid, the trunk was empty. "Let's try this again," he said, sounding worried. Was he acting?

He closed the lid, muttered the nonsensical words, tapped the wand. He opened the trunk and it was empty.

"You screwed up, Walker." Jacey's voice came from the back of the room, and we all turned to watch her. Now it was clear to me that she and Walker were acting.

"So the stage has a trapdoor?" Bernadette whispered.

But I didn't answer. Someone was standing in the aisle behind Jacey. Autumn had arrived.

∞

"Since I quit smoking, I got fat." Autumn sat on the floor of our dorm room, ripping plastic from a cupcake. She'd stopped at a gas station and bought a variety of junk food, which she'd spread on the floor like a picnic.

I didn't like sugary stuff, but Bernadette took a brownie and a thing called a Twinkie. "You're not fat," she said.

Autumn was at most ten pounds heavier than the last time I'd seen her. Her face was fuller and her hips a little rounder. I felt a twinge of guilt, as if I were responsible for her weight. But wasn't quitting smoking worth gaining a few pounds?

To be sociable, I reached for a bag of potato chips.

We'd left Walker surrounded by a crowd of admirers, and I wondered which of them he might be talking to at that moment.

"Dreamy eyes," Bernadette said, looking at me. "Somebody has a crush."

Was it that obvious? I said, "How can you tell?" There was no point in denying anything—Bernadette was too observant for that.

"Every time you look at Walker, your eyes go gooey." Bernadette bit into the Twinkie and waved its creamy center at me. "Like that," she said.

"Walker is the magician, right?" Autumn wiped frosting onto the knees of her jeans. "That means you don't like my brother anymore?"

I didn't care for this conversation at all. "How's Chip?" I asked.

"We broke up." Autumn reached for a plastic-wrapped brownie. "He was cheating on me." Her voice was matter-of-fact. "I can see why you'd like that boy Walker. He's cute." She made *cute* have two syllables.

Then she and Bernadette began laughing, and I had no idea why until Bernadette stopped long enough to say, "Ari, you should have seen your face when she said that!"

"I think she's still a virgin, "Autumn said to Bernadette, who said, "No way." Then Bernadette turned to me. "Are you really?"

I took a handful of chips. "None of your business." But knowing that they weren't made me feel young and naïve, once more excluded from their world.

∽

Autumn and Bernadette chatted late into the night. I mostly listened, surprised at how quickly they found things to talk about. The room was dark except for the light from my lithophane lamp, which illumined the little birds on the shade but kept our faces in the shadows.

Bernadette talked about the field trip we'd be taking. "Too bad you can't come with us," she said to Autumn, who was sleeping on the floor. "We only have room in the canoes for ten. You can stay in the room while we're gone."

"Maybe I'll take me a tour of the campus," Autumn said. "I wouldn't want to go to a swamp anyway."

"But it's going to be really cool." Bernadette summarized a few of our Environmental Studies lectures, doing a better job than Professor Riley had.

"It's the largest swamp in North America," she said. "Once it was part of the ocean floor, but now it's covered by peat deposits and rainwater. During the early nineteen-hundreds people lived in the swamp, and loggers took out thousands of trees. Then it was turned into a wildlife refuge."

Autumn said, "Uh-huh."

"The Indians named it. In their language *Okefenokee* means 'land of the trembling earth,' because the peat is so unstable, you can make the trees shake if you stomp on the ground." Bernadette was clearly looking forward to making trees shake.

Autumn yawned.

"The biodiversity is amazing," I said, trying to support Bernadette. "More than four hundred species of birds, and alligators, and five kinds of venomous snakes."

"Snakes, huh?" Autumn sounded sleepy.

"There are no roads in the swamp, only trails and boardwalks," Bernadette said. "We're canoeing in, and we'll spend one night in a cabin and one on a platform."

"You ain't afraid? With all the gators and snakes?"

I wasn't afraid, but I didn't want to answer for Bernadette.

"I'm more afraid of the other stuff," she said. "We read some folk tales about strange lights and swamp things—"

"Swamp things?" For the first time Autumn sounded alert.

"Ape men, and giants, and ghosts." Bernadette's voice was worthy of a vampire, I thought. She knew how to make sentences into stories. "Creatures of the dark, who move silently from tree to tree. The cabin where we're spending the night is supposed to be haunted."

"It is?" I said.

"Jacey did an oral report on that the first week of class," Bernadette said. "You missed it. She claims a woman was murdered there, and her ghost walks at night. Professor Riley said it was all legend, but I believe it. Then there are reports of UFO sightings and abductions by aliens."

"I know all about those," Autumn said. "The government wants us to think they don't exist, but they got talk shows about UFOs on AM radio nearly every night. Sometimes I think that's what might have happened to Mysty."

"Mysty's the girl who disappeared from our town," I said, and Bernadette nodded.

"She went out there to look up at the stars," Autumn said. "Maybe something came down to get her. Who knows? Anyway, is that why you all are going out there—to see a UFO?"

"No, we're going to study nature." Bernadette yawned. "It's one thing to read about it, something else to see it up close."

"I don't think I'll ever go to college." Autumn's voice was suddenly decisive.

"So what will you do after high school?" I reached to switch off the lamp.

"I used to think I'd move in with Chip." Her voice sounded resigned. "Now I don't know. Some days, I feel like I'm going no place fast."

I wanted to say something to comfort her, but all I could think of were clichés: *You're still young. You'll get over it.*

Bernadette said, "Yeah. Some days I feel like that, too."

∞

Autumn was still asleep when we left the next morning. Bernadette wrote her a note, telling her to stay as long as she liked. "Don't be sad about your ex," she wrote. "You haven't met the right one yet."

She set the note near Autumn's sleeping bag. Autumn slept on her stomach, and all we saw was her out-flung arm and a mass of dark hair.

"Thanks for being nice to my friend," I said to Bernadette, once we were outside.

She shrugged. "I feel sorry for her. She seems a little lost."

We carried our backpacks to the parking lot and found two seats at the very rear of the Hillhouse van. The March morning felt crisp, the sky streaked orange by the rising sun. Other students took their time finding seats; some carried cups of coffee or hot chocolate, whose aromas perfumed the van. All I'd had for breakfast was a gulp of tonic, straight from the bottle; often that was enough for my breakfast, but today I felt hungry, and groggy from lack of sleep.

Professor Riley and Professor Hoffman were the last two to board. They looked sleepy. "No singing," Hoffman said to us.

When the van finally left campus, I turned to watch Hillhouse disappear—and that's when I saw a beige van pass, headed in the opposite direction. I couldn't see the driver or the make of the vehicle. Despite the heater in our van, I felt a faint chill.

Most of the students dozed on the brief ride to Okefenokee. I stayed awake. As the sun grew higher in the sky, my mood began to lift. There must be thousands of beige vans in Georgia, I told myself.

∞

By the time we arrived at the swamp's entrance near Waycross, picked up our camping permits, and packed our canoes, it was nearly ten A.M. The temperature was 65 degrees, warm enough to shed our down jackets and vests. We put our sleeping bags and supplies in trash bags, set them in the center of the canoes, and tied them down with bungee cords.

As I was tying my trash bags to the canoe, Bernadette said, "The poor thing—look!"

An alligator lay on the bank about a hundred feet away from us. It looked as if its skin had shrunk to cling to its skeleton—emaciated, but still alive. We could see life in its small, dark eyes.

"What's wrong with him?" I asked.

Professor Hoffman said, "Could be old age, or maybe he was hurt in a fight."

"Can't we do something to help?" Bernadette's voice carried across the water, and one of the park guides came over. "That's Old Joe," he said. "He's getting ready to die. We don't interfere with nature."

Bernadette didn't say anything, but her shoulders hunched, and I knew she disagreed. Later she said to me, "Something is dying. And no one is paying attention." She shook her head.

Each canoe held two, and Bernadette and I were partners. For the initial part of the trip, we both paddled; later, we took turns. I wore a thick coat of sunblock on my skin, and she had sprayed both of us with insect repellent. I told her that bugs never bit me, but she wasn't convinced.

The waterway we rode was called a canal. At first it was the color of slate—gray, with indigo veins and variations—and the canoes rode it calmly, our oars making barely a splash. There was no wind, and the only sound was the low groaning of frogs. Along the banks alligators lay, singly or in couples, some watching us, some ignoring us. Mating season was two months away, and they weren't yet inclined to be territorial.

For several minutes, none of us talked. The air smelled fresh and aromatic, reminding me a little of the smell of witch hazel. My mother kept a bottle of it in the bathroom at home. I didn't want to think of home, so I tried to categorize the scent more precisely: it was both acidic and sweet, with perhaps a hint of turpentine. Nothing like witch hazel, really.

After we rounded the canal's last bend, we entered a prairie—a wide expanse of flowering swamp. Here the water became deep brown, the color of steeped tea. A breeze began, and conical yellow flowers bobbed close to the canoe. As we went further, those flowers seemed to multiply, emerging from fleshy green foliage strewn across the prairie as far as we could see.

Professor Riley said the flowers were called golden club. Their other name was "neverwet," because their succulent-like leaves repel moisture. They resist the elements that do not favor them, he said. They are likely to endure.

∞

By the time we pulled our canoes ashore on the island late that afternoon, our eyes were as tired as our arms. We'd seen green and blue herons, sandhill cranes, ibises, kingfishers, and more gators than we could count. As I flipped our canoe over, a thick blue-black snake more than six feet long emerged from a sandy mound close by.

I didn't like snakes then any more than I do now, but they had more right to be on the island than I had. I stood still. As the snake slithered into the brush, I felt the presence of someone behind me.

Professor Hoffman didn't speak until the snake had disappeared. "Well, well," he said. "Recognize it?"

"An indigo snake?"

"Very good. They're an endangered species, you know. Their natural habitat has been turned into shopping malls and housing developments. Now, unfortunately, they've developed the habit of napping on roads."

After dinner that night (potatoes and vegetables and herb-seasoned tofu, wrapped in foil and roasted in the fire), Hoffman talked about the species that we hadn't seen that day.

"The Carolina parakeet—the only parrot species indigenous to the United States—was wiped out in the usual ways. Its habitat was destroyed by foresters. Some birds were captured and kept as pets; their feathers were used to decorate hats, but the tame birds weren't bred because they were considered so common, and eventually they died off. Most of the wild ones were hunted by farmers, who thought they were pests.

"The Carolina parakeets were highly social creatures. When birds were shot, the rest of the flock would return to the site and gather around the dead bodies. Of course, hunters were waiting for them. We don't know what caused the birds' ultimate extinction, but it's suspected that the remaining few succumbed to poultry disease."

Bernadette set down her plate. "This is so depressing." Her voice was low, but I'm sure it carried.

Nonetheless, Professor Hoffman kept talking. "Similarly, the ivory-billed woodpecker was wiped out by heavy logging and by hunters. By the 1920s it was considered extinct. One pair—the birds mate for life—turned up in Florida, but they immediately were shot by specimen collectors."

"Idiots!" Bernadette said. The other students ignored her.

"A few years ago, research teams found evidence of ivory bills in Florida and Arkansas. If their findings are confirmed, the bird would be called a lazarus species. Anybody know what that means?"

The girl called Jacey said, "In the Bible, Lazarus was raised from the dead by Jesus. It was considered a miracle."

"Well, in scientific terms, it's no miracle. It's simply a sign that the original survey claiming the species extinct was flawed. When a creature presumed dead forever reappears, the scientific community is always glad to be proven wrong."

Bernadette nudged me. "I have to pee. Come with."

The cabin had no bathroom, but an outhouse wasn't far away. So far only the girls in the group had used it, the boys preferring to go behind trees. Bernadette went into the wooden hut, complaining about men using the world as their toilet.

I waited outside, watching the lighted windows of the cabin and listening to the night. The air was filled with the sounds of frogs, occasional moans from owls, and rustles from the woods near us. And then, the sound of Bernadette screaming.

The outhouse door swung wide and slammed against the wall. Bernadette leapt onto the grass, clutching the waist of her jeans.

The cabin door opened. Professor Riley said, "You okay?"

Bernadette ran inside the cabin, and I followed.

"Something in there bit me!" she said. "Do you think it was a snake?" She held out her ankle, turned it to show a red welt.

"That's not a snakebite," Riley said. "More like a blackfly."

A fly bite was so much more acceptable than a snakebite. I confess, my first thought had been of the huge indigo snake, slithering through the long grass into the outhouse to wait for one of us. (Later I learned that the indigo isn't poisonous. It swallows its small prey alive.)

The food and exercise made all of us sleepy. But Jacey refused to spend the night in the cabin. "This place creeps me out," she said.

We'd brought along two tents, and Jacey proposed setting one up. She said she wouldn't sleep outside alone.

No one else wanted to join her, so I volunteered.

Bernadette said, "You're crazy."

"The bugs don't bother me," I said. "And the air in here is a little stale." It smelled musty, like dead fires and old clothes.

So, Jacey, whom I knew only as the smallest girl with the longest braids in school, and I spent the night in the tent. We didn't sleep much. The rustlings I'd heard before seemed louder as the night passed, and we heard nearly constant movements on the ground near the tent.

"Raccoons," I said, but Jacey said, "Too big for raccoons."

We dozed off and awoke to more sounds: something seemed to be walking around the perimeter of the tent. It made a rattling sound as it moved.

Jacey sat up in her sleeping bag. She whispered, "Ari, Ari. I'm scared. I think it's the fetcher."

"Who?"

She breathed loudly. "The devil's fetcher. Coming for our souls."

Like most vampires, I'm not easily frightened. I remember watching horror movies at my friend Kathleen's house; I was more intrigued by the faces of her family responding to the movies than by the monsters on-screen. But that night, on an island in a swamp so remote that our cell phones didn't work, I let myself succumb to the sensation of fear. It was curiously pleasurable.

"What does he look like?"

"He can change his appearance." Jacey whispered in bursts and breathed deeply in between. "Sometimes he's an animal—a dog or a wolf or a calf. Other times, he's a person—an old man, or a woman with bloody hands. Sometimes they cut out your heart and eat it."

"How do you know about them?"

"I've always known." She took another deep breath. "I've dreamed about them, too."

Outside, the footfalls slowed, then sped up again. They sounded too loud to be an animal's, too fast to be a human's. Around and around the tent they went, accompanied by the strange rattle.

"I'm scared," I whispered, and I heard the surprise in my voice. Fear tingled and spread through my blood with each heartbeat.

"We could call for help," Jacey said.

"Wake everyone up?" I wasn't *that* scared. "Jacey, they'd make fun of us all over campus. We'd never live it down."

Then the thing outside stopped moving. It began making sounds, softly at first, then louder. I can't describe what they sounded like—imagine a puppy yelping, then pitching its voice higher, and finally so high that it threatened to shatter your eardrum.

Jacey made a strange sound too, a low gurgle in her throat.

Fear wasn't fun anymore. She grabbed my shoulder, and I held her hand. I don't know how long we stayed that way, wrapped in our sleeping bags, clutching each other, listening to the keening that came out of the dark. Sometimes I thought I heard words in the howling. Once I thought I heard it speak my name.

I heard Jacey thinking, *And tomorrow they'll find our dead bodies in the tent.* I wondered what she'd think if she knew she was holding the hand of a vampire.

We didn't sleep again that night. The thing outside eventually went away, but we knew it could come back anytime it chose.

Once daylight was strong, I unzipped the tent flap and saw only grass and trees and sky. I chided myself for being a coward. Why hadn't I simply gone outside to see what made the noise?

The scariest things are the ones that visit us in darkness, the ones we never see. And the fear that kept us paralyzed in the tent that night left a funny residue, a bitter taste in my throat, a reminder that, after all, in some ways I was vulnerable as any mortal.

Chapter Twelve

*H*umans see things differently than animals do. Humans are much better at detecting unmoving objects. Animals' nervous systems have evolved to detect movement, since motion may indicate the approach of a predator or prey. But a frog can't even see a stationary object because of neural adaptation; its visual neurons don't respond to unmoving things, in order to save energy.

Theoretically, humans do better at seeing stationary objects because their eyes are always moving, counteracting neural adaptation. But sometimes they fail to see objects in their field of vision because their attention is directed elsewhere. Skilled magicians know how to induce and manipulate states of inattentional blindness. That's why tricks work.

Not much research has been devoted to examining vampires' vision, but based on the little I've read on the Internet and on my own observations, it tends to be more acute than humans'. A vampire's retina has more rod and cone cells than a human's, making it more responsive to light and color. Yet even with that enhanced vision, the vampire eye may be susceptible to inattentional blindness. Like humans, and like frogs and dragonflies, we sometimes fail to see what is right in front of us.

∞

Jacey and I avoided each other for the rest of our time in the swamp. Each of us reminded the other of the sour experience of fear that began as fun and progressed to something malignant.

Bernadette—who said she'd slept like a baby—did the paddling that morning. I slumped in the rear of the canoe, half-asleep, ignoring the alligators slumped along the banks, half-asleep.

Professor Hoffman, wide awake, gave us an impromptu lecture that drifted back to me in partial sentences. He was talking about alligators' vision—how their eyes have layers of reflecting tissue behind the retinas that act like mirrors. "We call the tissue *tapetum lucidum*," he said. "Anybody know what that means?"

It means "bright carpet," but I felt too sleepy to volunteer. Hoffman said the tissue acts like a mirror to concentrate available light, helping the gators to hunt in the dark. And it's also responsible for the way alligators' eyes look at night if you shine a flashlight on them—they glow red, like burning coals.

Bernadette said, "Creepy."

The whole trip had been a little too creepy for me. And I wasn't looking forward to spending the night on a wooden platform, surrounded by who knew what. Vampires need sleep even more than humans do, to keep our immune systems healthy.

Hoffman was talking about something called succession—the natural process of change that occurs in a habitat. If the peat in the swamp built up, the swamp would become a shrub, and later a hardwood, habitat. "What keeps the swamp a swamp is the natural occurrence of wildfires," he said. "As fires burn away peat, open lakes are left. Without the fires, this place would be a forest."

One moment, I was half-asleep, half listening to the lecture, feeling mildly annoyed at the prospect of what I thought lay ahead. The next, we were all fully awake, thanks to Jacey's screaming.

She saw it first: close to the shore, amid the golden club plants, something dark was floating.

Jacey said, "What? What?" She screamed again, and then someone else screamed.

I sat up, but the other canoes blocked my sight. But as we drifted, I had an open view of the shape in the water—dark clothes billowing out and a head of dark hair. The shape looked terribly out of place. It looked *wrong*.

The professors took out their cell phones. Neither had a signal. Then they pulled out maps, trying to identify our location and find the best route to a place where the phones would work.

"Jacey, you okay?" Professor Riley said.

She'd hunched forward, panting. Later she told me she was trying not to vomit.

Hoffman told the other girl in Jacey's canoe to do the rowing. "The rest of you—everybody paddle."

We turned the canoes around and Hoffman led us back toward the landing where we'd launched them. The pace of our paddling was twice as fast as it had been on the trip out.

From time to time I glanced over at Jacey to see if she was okay, but all I saw was the back of her jacket. She still bent forward, head inclined so that she couldn't see anything beyond the canoe's interior.

Bernadette kept looking at Jacey, too, and I heard her say something indistinct. "What did you say?" I said.

She turned her head sideways. "Jacey looks like the Six of Swords."

I remembered the image of that tarot card: a cloaked woman leaning forward in a punt, a ferryman behind her, using a long pole to propel them to shore, and six swords before her, holding her in place. Bernadette had said the card signified escape.

∞

We felt exhausted by the time we reached the landing. Professor Hoffman called 911, and Professor Riley arranged for the van to pick us up. We'd had enough wilderness to last us a long time.

The other students were uncharacteristically quiet. No one wanted to talk about what we'd seen until we knew what we'd actually seen, yet no one could think of anything else. Once the van came and we were headed back to campus, Riley insisted on stopping at a fast food place, but no one ate much.

The campus and our dormitory building looked and smelled reassuringly familiar. Bernadette and I carried our trash bags of supplies and sleeping bags into the room, and I dropped mine in order to turn the light on. But I couldn't find my lamp.

"Turn on the overhead," I told Bernadette.

When she switched on the bare bulb, the room's details jumped out at us—our unmade beds, Autumn's sleeping bag on the floor, and across and around it, the remains of my lithophane lamp. It must have fallen hard, because fine shards of glass and porcelain glittered in a wide arc across the floor. Autumn wasn't there.

I felt too shocked and tired to say what I was thinking: *Why did Autumn have to break my lamp?*

"Let's clean it up later," I said.

Bernadette looked from the broken glass to me. "But where will Autumn sleep?"

"We'll leave her a note," I said. "We can crash in Jacey's room, and Autumn can have the sofa in the lounge." I didn't care where she slept. I wanted my lamp back.

Bernadette picked up her trash bag again, and I followed her down the hall to Jacey's room.

Bernadette knocked. When Jacey opened the door—her face white, eyes red—Bernadette said, "You've got company."

When it was time to go to dinner, we stopped back at the room. Autumn still wasn't there.

"Where do you suppose your friend is?" Bernadette asked.

I thought of Autumn and her tendency to get into trouble in the past. "She's an independent kind of girl," I said. I hoped she hadn't broken anything else.

∞

Very early the next morning, my cell phone rang. Dashay's voice sounded odd, lacking emotion and inflection. She said, "I'm calling to tell you to expect some visitors."

The way she spoke made me think someone else might be listening to our call, so I made my voice neutral, too. "Who's coming?"

"Your mother," she said. "And Cecil. Agent Burton."

"May I talk to Mãe?"

"She's not here," Dashay said. "She's in Georgia, visiting family."

The only family my mother had was a sister in Savannah, and she never visited her.

"Is everything okay?" I asked.

"She'll explain when she gets there. She's already on her way."

"How are you?" I asked, feeling as if I were in a play.

"I am all right." Her voice bordered on singsong. "I took a trip to Atlanta last week, to look up an old friend."

She must mean Bennett, I thought. "How is he?"

"He and his fiancée are very well."

Dashay's artificial calm began to worry me. Soon after that, we said good-bye.

I went back to our room and stepped around the glass shards to get my towels and shampoo. After a shower and a change of clothes, I realized how hungry I was. Bernadette was still asleep, so I went to the lounge to see if Autumn wanted breakfast. But the old couch in the lounge was vacant.

I went to breakfast alone.

Back in the room again, I was sweeping up the remains of my

lamp when Mãe came in. I dropped the broom to hug her. When we pulled apart, the sight of her face alarmed me—she looked drained, as if she hadn't slept in days.

"What's wrong?" I asked.

That's when Agent Burton walked in. He apologized for disturbing us, but his voice didn't sound sorry.

At his suggestion we went to the library, to a closed-off nook called a carrel. Burton took out his tape recorder and coughed a few times to test it. He looked more somber than I'd ever seen him.

Then he told me that the thing in the swamp was a body, and the body was Autumn's.

∞

Later—after a week of being interviewed by Burton and the Georgia State Police, of being given a series of polygraph tests, of walking around in a state of shock—I listened to my mother apologize. She said she'd wanted to call, warn me about what was coming, but she and Dashay decided it was better for the police to witness my first reactions to the news.

By the end of that week, Burton felt fairly certain that I hadn't caused Autumn's death (she'd been strangled, he said, but they weren't sure where it had happened), but he was troubled by what he considered the "unbelievable coincidence" of three girls who knew me disappearing and two (at least) ending up dead. (To a lesser degree, he was troubled by the polygraph's measurement of my abnormally low skin temperature, which Mãe persuaded him was a side effect of treatment for "a rare form of lupus—the same kind that killed her father").

Then came word that one of the dorm's resident advisors told police she'd seen a stranger carrying an oversized trash bag out of the dorm the morning we'd left for the swamp.

"I figured he was part of the canoe trip," she said. She hadn't been close enough to get more than a general impression of the man. Medium height, she said. Bald. Wearing sunglasses and dark clothes.

I told Burton about the beige van I'd seen approaching campus as we left for Okefenokee.

"We put out an alert last time you mentioned a van," he said. "Nothing turned up."

"Well, you'd better put out another one," my mother said. "Someone killed that girl, and he's still out there."

He thought I'd imagined the van, but he did make a note.

"What if"—I framed the question as I asked it—"what if whoever took Autumn was really after me?"

To my surprise, Burton had already thought of that. Yes, I was listening to his thoughts again. He was brooding on the placement of the body, how likely it was that whoever killed her had known the route of our canoes, had wanted us to find her.

"Anything's possible," he said. "All we can do now is conjecture."

Aside from signs of struggle—the broken lamp, the sleeping bag half-turned inside out—the dorm room held no evidence of the presence of anyone aside from Autumn, Bernadette, and me. But the police had found the note Bernadette left for Autumn, and they questioned Chip, her ex-boyfriend. Chip's alibi—that he'd been trying to steal a car on the night in question—didn't impress them much. They'd also questioned Jesse and Autumn's father, both in Sassa and in Georgia, where they'd volunteered to come. At the family's request, I met Mr. Springer and Jesse one afternoon at the brick police station.

Mr. Springer was a middle-aged man, overweight, who perspired heavily and barely spoke. He had Autumn's chin and eyes. Jesse looked different—his head was shaved, and he'd lost weight. His eyes were clear, and every move he made seemed purposeful.

"We know you had nothing to do with it," he told me. "We just want you to tell us what happened."

I told them the same details I'd told the police about Autumn's visit. She hadn't seemed upset so much as depressed about the break-up with Chip. And I mentioned her phone call to me, when she'd told me Jesse was joining the marines. "She sounded very proud of you," I said.

He straightened his shoulders for a moment, nodded as if to say thanks. He and his father hated talking about Autumn's death. It made them feel powerless.

My time as a person of interest ended after the forensics lab found DNA under Autumn's fingernails. The sample they took from me didn't match it.

The last thing Burton said to me was, "Call me if you remember anything else. Meantime, please be careful."

I thought about the night in the tent, the thing outside, the weird noises. If I mentioned any of that, Burton would once again think I was imagining things. But Mãe must have heard what I thought. As we walked to the truck, she checked to be sure I was wearing my cat amulet.

∞

During the week of my interrogations (that's how I've thought of it ever since), I lost my normal sense of taste, smell, sound, and touch, and I saw things without taking in details.

In my philosophy class, the professor had told us about "philosophical zombies": hypothetical creatures who act like humans, but who lack any sense of being alive. They can walk, talk, eat, drink—without any subjective sense of the experience. That week, I felt like a zombie.

My mother rented a motel room near the state police headquarters; she told the Hillhouse administrators that I needed time to re-cover from the shock of Autumn's death. Every day she made sure that I ate and drank tonic, slept (she gave me sleeping pills), and took a walk. The two of us walked around the small town near campus for half an hour every day. No one knew who we were, and no one both-ered us. At night my mother read to me, and as soon as she stopped, I couldn't remember what she read. When she thought I was asleep, she'd telephone someone and talk in a voice so low I couldn't hear her. Curiously, the murmur of her voice in the dark soothed me more than any lullaby or story could have.

When the week was over, I began to think and feel again, in small spurts. Material that I couldn't process when it occurred now began to present itself in the form of questions.

"What about Autumn's funeral?" I asked Mãe as we walked through town. "Was there a memorial service?"

"She was buried two days ago." Mãe kept one hand on my arm, as if to steer me. "And if there's a memorial service, you shouldn't think of attending."

"Why not?"

She sighed, and again I realized how tired she looked. "Ariella, you won't want to come to Sassa for a while. The rumors and accusa-tions are going to be even worse this time."

We walked on. I noticed leaf buds on a tree. In some other world, spring was on its way.

Another question surfaced: "Mãe, what were you doing in Geor-gia when Burton called?"

"I was taking care of family." She looked around us, as if some-one might be listening. "It wasn't a good idea for me to talk to you about it, while the police interviews were going on. But tomorrow, you and I are going away for a week."

She wouldn't tell me more than that.

We drove to campus the next day so that I could pack fresh clothes and more tonic. Part of me was still in zombie mode, taking in sensory data without experiencing it, but bursts of clarity came more often than the day before. "I'm missing so many classes," I said.

"Spring break begins next week," Mãe said. "Later you can make up what you missed. That is, if you're sure you want to come back here."

I couldn't imagine what else I might do.

"You needn't decide now," she said.

The Hillhouse parking lots and grounds were quiet. It seemed that many students had already left for spring break. Our dorm room looked as if no one was living there. The beds were neatly made, the floor swept, desks cleared. I wondered if Autumn had died in this room, or if it had happened later, in the swamp.

I glanced at the spot on the table where my lithophane lamp had been.

"I'm sorry about your lamp," Mãe said.

I shook my head. "It was only a thing." But it had been much more than that, and we both knew it. The lamp had soothed me when I awoke at night, a small child alone.

"We can try to find another one." Her voice, like her face, was tired, disheartened. "I bought the original when I was pregnant with you."

She rarely talked to me about that time, which I'd heard had been painful for her. She'd been ill and unhappy, unsure if having a child was the right thing to do.

I was trying to think of something to say when I saw a small vase of half-dead wildflowers on my desk. Next to it lay a note: "Ari, We miss you." It took me a minute to be sure of the signature. Walker's handwriting was nearly illegible.

I wondered if I'd see him again.

∞

Sitting in the truck next to my mother, I let myself surrender to un-
certainty. The spring air was cool and the long empty stretches of low
country looked familiar: skinny pine trees, scrubby flats, swamp grass
ranging from ash to pale green to emerald. We headed north, passing
a prairie of grass divided by a river. Across the water, the land along
the horizon looked blue.

I dozed, and when I awoke we were passing a trailer park called
Druid Oaks, whose homes were festooned with two-dimensional plywood nutcrackers and reindeer, even though Christmas was months
behind us. A few miles farther down the road, tidy-looking houses
made of brick sat squarely on mowed lots, facing the road. Those
houses held no secrets.

"Are we near Savannah?" I asked.

Mãe nodded.

I'd been in Savannah a year ago, when I was trying to find my
mother.

"Is that where we're going?"

"We're passing through," she said. "How are you feeling, Ari
ella?"

"All right," I said. My appetite was better now. I could taste the
food I ate. Sleeping was still broken. My mind kept wanting to revisit
the scene in the swamp, at the same time afraid to go there.

"She was a friend," I found myself saying. "Not a very close
friend, but someone I cared about. She was a cool person, in her
way—stubborn and brave. She didn't deserve to end up like that."

"No one does." Now both of us were picturing Autumn, re-
duced to a floating mass of dark clothes and hair discarded in shallow water.

"It will be easier for you, over time." My mother's profile cut a stern shape into the moving landscape. "I hope that you're ready to hear what I need to say next. We're going to see your father."

∞

As we drove on, Mãe told me we were headed for a house she had rented on Tybee Island, off the Georgia coast. "It was the safest place I could think of," she said. "Given the circumstances."

After my father left our house in December—"and he was furious, Ariella, furious about what happened to you and furious to see Burton again"—he'd rented a car and begun to search for the man in the Chevy van.

"He told me all this only a week ago," she said. "He'd wanted to be in touch sooner, but he didn't dare risk it. We think the police may be monitoring our calls."

Mãe told the story with digressions and editorial comments, which I'm trying not to repeat here in their entirety. The circumstances were these: two days after he left us, my father had found the man in the Chevy sitting outside our front gate again. The van took off when my father's car approached. My father followed it to the local high school. Eventually, the man persuaded a teenage girl to get into the van. My father followed the van as it traveled across Florida from west to east, ending up at a suburban house in Daytona Beach.

"Close to fifty teenagers were staying at the house," Mãe said. "Raphael watched some being delivered and others picked up. He wanted to follow the pickup vans, to find out where the kids were being taken, but he was running low on serum. So he called me."

By now we were on the outskirts of Savannah, passing strip malls and car lots. I kept an eye out for beige vans. A school bus in the lane ahead of us stopped, and I watched children climb onto the bus. Were any of their lives as complicated as mine? Quite possibly.

"I thought you said our phones might be tapped."

"Raphael disguised his voice." And then my mother smiled, a small wry smile that seemed out of place. "He imitated my sister. He did that in the old days, after she'd done something annoying, and it made her almost bearable."

Then she looked serious again. "So I drove to a motel near Daytona with the serum. He looked tired, but after he took the medicine he seemed utterly exhausted. And after I'd returned his rental car, I came back and found him barely conscious." She stopped the truck at a red light and turned to face me. "Ariella, your father is very ill. Can you deal with that?"

I nodded. What else could I do?

We drove through Savannah, past houses ornate as wedding cakes along Victory Drive, and out onto the Islands Parkway. Still no beige vans. My mother said she'd barely had time to get my father settled into the rental house when Dashay called her, telling her that Burton wanted to interview me.

"We arranged for Dashay to drive up and look after Raphael," she said. "And I came down to meet you." Mãe said that Dashay had found a doctor in Savannah who was one of us. The doctor had examined my father and was running tests.

"What's wrong with him?"

"We don't know yet," Mãe said.

Now we were driving on a two-lane road with marshlands and water on either side. I rolled down the window to smell the salt in the breeze. The main town of Tybee Island was touristy, lined with lurid signs and shabby souvenir shops. My mother said it had been different when she summered there as a child. She and my father first met on the beach when they were children. "All of that seems to have happened a million years ago," she said now.

She turned the car into a small street that dead-ended at the beach and parked the truck. After we got out, she rested her hands on my shoulders. "Remember what I told you," she said. "He doesn't look the way you remember him."

That's when I began to truly be afraid.

Mãe led me down a gravel path to a house on stilts that faced the beach. I heard the low hiss of the ocean not far away. We climbed a somewhat rickety set of steps that led to a dark green door.

Dashay opened the door, talking into a cell phone—a surprise, since she and my mother had never used one, in my experience. "Okay," she said. "I get it. Thank you, Dr. Cho. See you soon." She clicked off the phone and hugged each of us as we came into the house.

I didn't notice anything in the room, except the absence of my father. "Where is he?"

"He's in bed." Dashay gestured to the left. "Wait," she said, but I was already moving.

The windows of the room were open, and the noise of the ocean was louder now. A figure lay beneath a quilt on the double bed, dark hair against a pillow, face turned toward the wall. Next to the bed, an IV pole held two bags, one of clear fluid, one of red. The red one had a tube attached to it that ran under the quilt.

"Father?" I said.

Behind me, Dashay said, "Did you tell her?" and Mãe said, "Yes."

"Father?" I walked closer. He didn't move. I bent over him to see his face, and when I saw it, a wave of vertigo hit me. Someone grabbed me, pulled me backward.

His eyes were half-open, but he didn't seem to see me. His face looked shrunken, shriveled, the skin tight across the bones. He reminded me of Old Joe, lying stiff and still, getting ready to die.

∞

When Dr. Cho arrived that afternoon, I'd recovered enough to frame a dozen questions. What caused my father's condition? What were his chances of survival? I practiced the questions on my mother and Dashay, who didn't have any answers.

Dr. Cho was a tiny woman with long black hair held back by a clip and a serene, oval face. She didn't mince words. "Severe hemolytic anemia," she said. "His red blood cells are breaking down faster than his body can replace them. There's a growing risk of heart failure."

I said, "Is he going to die?"

"He needs a massive transfusion." Her voice was crisp. "The sooner we begin, the better his chances."

Dr. Cho had brought plastic bags of blood with her; as she lifted them out of a portable cooler, they glowed in the afternoon sunlight, their color between maroon and burgundy. She put them in the refrigerator, except for one that she carried into the bedroom.

Mãe, Dashay, and I offered to help, but she said that would come later. We sat at the kitchen table while she worked. There wasn't a sound in the place except for the ocean.

Suddenly I said, "Is he in pain?"

Mãe and Dashay looked at each other. Dashay said, "We don't know. He stopped talking days ago, and his thoughts aren't making much sense."

We sat silently at the table. Dr. Cho came in after an hour or so and switched on the overhead light. "What, is this a funeral?" she said. "Go take a walk on the beach."

"How is he?" Mãe's voice sounded scratchy.

"He's very sick. You know that. His heart rate isn't regular, and I'm going to put him on a respirator tomorrow if his breathing doesn't improve. Now get outside, look at the moon. Then we need to eat some dinner, please." For a small person, her voice carried enormous authority.

We shuffled out of the room, down the steps, and along the path to a ramp that led to the beach. The darkness and the sounds of the ocean swelled around us. The moon was full that night, but we couldn't see it because of cloud cover, and I was glad. I let my face lose its stoic expression, and I felt it contort. Grief felt close to rage, that night, and I didn't want the others to see what I felt.

He can't die, I thought. *He's a vampire. Vampires don't die.*

That night, I wanted all the myths to be true. And for the first time in my life, I wanted to pray.

The song of my cell phone sounded so inappropriate. I sensed Mãe and Dashay flinch at the sound of *Swan Lake.*

The last voice I expected to hear was Walker's. He said he was at home in North Carolina. Then he asked where I was, and I told him. I told him my father was sick, and he said he was sorry. He asked if he could come to help, and when I told him no, he sounded disappointed.

"After break, I'm going to take you on a picnic," he said.

I couldn't imagine it. "That sounds nice," I said.

"We'll eat strawberries, and I'll show you the new tricks I've learned," he said. "When are you coming back?"

"I'm not sure yet." I didn't have the heart to tell him that I might not be coming back at all.

He said, "Ari, I can change a stone into a flower."

Chapter Thirteen

A t some point in the middle of that long night, I awoke, not sure where I was. What oriented me were the smell of the ocean and the odor of blood.

Mortals often say that blood smells metallic. To me it smells like ozone with a hint of copper, and its smell is dark blue.

I pushed myself out of bed and through the blue-tinged air into the kitchen. A night-light burned above the stove. Dr. Cho sat at the table, eating a bowl of the shrimp gumbo Dashay had served earlier that night. For someone who couldn't have weighed more than a hundred pounds, Dr. Cho had an impressive appetite. She'd consumed three bowls of gumbo at dinner. The rest of us ate very little.

She set down her spoon. "Can't sleep?"

I sat in the chair across from hers. "How long will the transfusion take?"

"It will be over by morning. We're transfusing his entire blood system, and it takes a while."

"Will he be okay then?"

"I don't know. If you're asking if he'll be able to talk, I doubt it." She picked up her spoon again. "It will take some time before we know if he's going to be okay."

"What made him sick?"

"I don't know," she said again. "His condition is unusual, but not entirely unprecedented. His immune system has been compromised.

It's clear that he hasn't been taking supplements or eating properly." She took a large mouthful of gumbo.

I didn't know how she could eat when, in the room next door, my father was barely alive.

She smiled, as if she'd heard what I thought. "You can go look in on him if you want."

I wanted to, yet I dreaded the sight of him. So I sat and watched her eat. She finished the bowl with a small sigh of contentment. "That Dashay is some good cook."

"Are you a doctor for vampires only?" I asked.

She took the bowl to the sink and rinsed it. "I treat anyone and everyone," she said, coming back to the table. "But I don't normally make house calls. Your mother said Raphael hates hospitals, and I was glad to make an exception for him. You know, I met him, many years ago at a conference. He was quite the dashing young man. Even I fancied him, but don't tell your mother that."

My instinctive reaction—*He's ours, not yours*—didn't escape her attention. "Don't worry," she said. "I'm happily married now."

I'd never met a married vampire—unless I counted my mother, and I wasn't sure I could.

"Are you married to one of us?" Immediately I regretted asking such a personal question.

"It's okay," she said. "Yes, I am. My partner and I have been together nine years."

"Did you ever think about marrying a mortal?"

"No." She stretched her hands on the wooden table. Although small, they looked strong. "Mortals are for dating, maybe for a fling. But marrying one? Too many problems!" Then she paused, flexed her hands. "Why do you ask? Are you considering it?"

"No, I just wondered." I blocked my thoughts.

"There are options, you know. This new drug protocol they're testing, what's it called? Revité? It's in clinical trials now, but there's already a lot of talk about it in the Vunderworld pages on the Internet."

"What does it do?"

"Allegedly it makes vampires mortal again." She stood up and stretched her arms. "Does that option appeal to you?"

I couldn't answer. The very idea of such a drug was dazzling, terrifying.

"Now I need to go to Raphael," Dr. Cho said.

Long after she left the room, I sat at the oak table in the dim light, tracing its whorls with my fingertips.

∞

When I was twelve, my father and I had read the *Bardo Thodol*, known as the Tibetan Book of the Dead. It's a guide to dying. The book includes chants and rituals to help the deceased come face to face with the Clear Light and experience the visions that ultimately lead to rebirth.

But he and I had never had the time to talk about confronting our own deaths. We'd assumed that, like most vampires, we'd be around forever, provided we took care of ourselves. As a biomedical researcher, my father knew more than most about monitoring one's diet and exposure to sunlight. I'd thought he had it down to an exact science.

So what went wrong? As I sat there, it came clear to me: his condition was my fault. If I hadn't told him about seeing the shadow man, he wouldn't have set off in pursuit, or let himself get sick. Now I didn't know the right words to chant, or even whether he'd want them said.

At daybreak Dashay came into the kitchen, wearing a pale yellow caftan, yawning. She bent over me, looked at me hard. "You should have stayed in bed," she said. "It's all right. Death is not in this house."

My shoulders untensed, and I sat back in my chair.

While Dashay brewed tea, she told me the story of "that snake Bennett." "He's living in Atlanta with a woman he met on the *plane*," she said, inflecting *plane* as if it meant *sewer*.

"How did you track him down?"

"Cecil helped." Her smile mixed self-satisfaction with unease. "He's been very useful."

Thinking of her with Cecil made *me* uncomfortable. "So you went to Atlanta," I said.

"Yes, I did make the trip. And that is one city I have never much cared for. It grew too big way too fast. Every time I go there, I ask myself why I bothered. But I wanted to see that snake with my own eyes. Cecil told me the address. I got there around five o'clock last Thursday, and Bennett, he answered the door himself—a little apartment in a brown building, *nasty*—and there behind him stood this woman, waiting. Ari, let me tell you, this woman I can almost feel sorry for. She's not pretty, she's not ugly. She's just a woman he met on the plane."

"Um, he met her on the rebound?" That was a phrase I'd learned from reading magazines.

"On the *plane*, he met her." Dashay's voice was so loud and so loaded with indignation that I wanted to shush her, fearful that she'd disturb my father. Then I wondered, could he be disturbed? Was he even conscious?

"Bennett, he took two steps back when he saw me, and that woman came two steps forward. 'We have nothing to say to you.'" Dashay imitated the woman's voice, high-pitched and squeaky as the voice of a cartoon mouse.

"'But I have something to say to Bennett,' I told her. And I told him, 'I want to know why you left me.'"

"What did he say?"

"Not one word. He stood there. He had no expression on his face, and when I looked at him, his eyes went right through me. Then that woman shut the door." Dashay poured two cups of tea, spilling some into the saucers. "It's like she put a spell on him."

We sipped our tea, and the sun turned the kitchen walls red, then golden. "I know I must have scared him, back in Jamaica, maybe even before that," Dashay said. "All I wanted was to ask him why."

Dr. Cho opened the door of my father's room and came to the table. "Do I smell Earl Grey?"

Dashay poured her a cup, but she didn't take it at once. "Come and see," she said to me.

From her voice I knew things must be better, but still I hesitated. Then she took my hand and led me into the bedroom.

He lay on his back, his left arm connected to the IV tube, his chest connected by wires to a heart monitor. His eyes were closed, his face gaunt. I didn't want to look.

"See the color in his face?" Dr. Cho whispered.

And it was true—his skin had lost the waxy quality it had the day before. But it still looked yellowish, and it still clung too tightly to his bones.

Then I saw the figure asleep in the chair at the foot of the bed. Mãe was curled into a semicircle, half-covered by an afghan, her long hair hiding her face. Seeing her there strengthened me, somehow.

I looked back at my father. His breathing was even, his hands lay unclenched at his sides. What had I expected—a complete recovery?

∞

I spent my first spring break mostly reading, or walking on the beach with Dashay, eating her spicy cooking, and from time to time looking in on my father, whose illness made me too anxious to linger long.

Dr. Cho came and went, but Mãe stayed near him. She read to him—essays by Ralph Waldo Emerson, mostly—even though we weren't sure he could hear.

"Our strength grows out of our weakness," she read one morning. "The indignation which arms itself with secret forces does not awaken until we are pricked and stung and sorely assailed. A great man is always willing to be little."

(Later, at the school library, I read the rest of the essay, and I realized it was one she'd read to me only a week ago, to try to make me sleep. In times of trouble, Emerson always consoles and inspires.)

Dashay and I put on sunblock and headed for the shore. She was leaving the next day to drop me off at school, then go back to Sassa. This would be our last walk.

The wide white beach at Tybee was full of kite fliers that day, the kites' colors vivid reds and yellows and greens against a Persian-blue sky. Dashay and I wore UVB-blocking sunglasses, but the intensity of the colors registered nonetheless. We had to be careful not to stay out too long, because the colors could overwhelm us, make us sick.

"I'm not cut out to be a doctor," I said.

"No one said you have to be a doctor." Dashay tied her sunhat more securely beneath her chin.

"I don't like being around sickness." It felt good to say that. I wouldn't have dared, back at the cottage.

Above us the kites soared and dipped, hovered and fell, their ribbonlike tails leaving wakes.

"Dashay, do you think he's going to get better?"

Dashay had tipped back her head to watch the kites. "I think everything that can be done for him is being done," she said. "The one I'm worried about is your mother. Nobody's making sure she eats and sleeps."

We turned and headed back. As we walked, I found myself telling Dashay about the night in the swamp with Jacey, hearing the thing outside circle our tent. She listened closely, and when I finished, she said, "Rollin calf."

"What?"

"It's a kind of duppy, you know. A spirit who takes on the form of an animal. Sometimes an obeah man will summon the spirit from the graveyard, make it do his bidding. Other times, the rollin calf settles in at the roots of trees, waiting for some unlucky fool to come along. When he moves, you hear the chain around his neck."

A few weeks ago I would have dismissed the rollin calf as a legend or superstition. But now I was prepared to believe.

"Why didn't it harm us?"

Dashay picked up a small shell and put it in her pocket. "Don't know. You stayed out of his way, and maybe he wasn't coming for you, anyway. There's a saying in Jamaica: 'Duppy know who to frighten and who to tell good night.'"

We left the beach and approached the cottage. Dr. Cho's car, a hybrid model, was parked in its driveway. As we came up the steps, my mother's voice rang out above us: "What are you suggesting? That I tried to kill him?"

The two women stood in the kitchen, and neither looked up when we came in. The air glowed red with their hostility.

"The serum you gave him was tainted." Dr. Cho's voice was quiet, but it had an exaggerated precision to it that I'd never heard before. "I tested it. It's loaded with quinine. Quinine can induce autoimmune hemolytic anemia."

Mãe looked near exhaustion. Slowly, she shook her head. "It's the same tonic he always takes. It's custom-mixed by his assistant—her name is Mary Ellis Root. I called her, and she brought it over on the morning I left for Georgia."

Dr. Cho's eyes and mouth showed her skepticism. "She's a

well-respected hematologist," she said. "She'd never add quinine to a blood supplement. I also found a considerable amount of antidepressant, by the way. Many sera contain some, but rarely as much as this one." She turned to me. "Ari, could I take a sample of the tonic you've been using?"

I looked at Mãe. Her eyes blazed, but she nodded, so I went to my room and brought back a prescription bottle of tonic.

"Thanks." Dr. Cho took the bottle and headed for the door. "I'll let you know what I find."

After she'd left, Dashay and I tried to calm Mãe. "She all but called me a poisoner." Mãe said. She paced the kitchen, then abruptly turned and went into my father's room.

Dashay and I exchanged glances. *Dr. Cho once had a crush on my father,* I thought.

Dashay sighed, and thought, *Maybe that explains some of it.*

The next morning, as we were loading Dashay's Jeep with my things, Dr. Cho's car pulled up. She took a carton out of the car's back seat and carried it to us.

"This is what you should be taking from now on," she said to me. "Discard the other tonic."

Dashay took the carton and slid it into the back of the Jeep.

"What was wrong with the old stuff?" I asked.

"No quinine, thank goodness." Dr. Cho's long hair fell out of its clip and swirled like silk in the ocean breeze. "But enough antidepressant to produce serious side effects. Have you experienced loss of appetite, dizziness, decreased libido?"

From my brief exposure to the works of Sigmund Freud, I knew that the word "libido" meant sexual drive. "Yes to the first two," I said. "I don't know about the last one."

"How much *libido* does a fourteen-year-old usually have?" Dashay asked.

Cho smiled. "Plenty. Remember, she's a vampire. Granted, the formula she's been taking has been popular for years in Sanguinist circles, where celibacy is traditional. But the new thinking about blood supplements is to manage instinctual drives, not suppress them."

"Aren't you a Sanguinist?"

"I'm an independent thinker," she said. "The Sanguinists and Nebulists—those sects were fine in their time. The Colonists are nuts. I don't see the need for any of them now."

I didn't turn around, but I sensed the presence of my mother in the cottage window, watching us.

Dashay stayed outside to talk to the doctor, and I went back to the house. By then my mother had left the window and was sitting next to my father's bed. Her face looked tense, and her hands were clasped in her lap.

"I first met your father outside, on the beach not more than fifty yards from here." She talked without looking at either of us. "Then I didn't see him again for twenty years."

I sat on the floor between them to listen. Near me, the IV stand held a fresh bag of red fluid, dripping slowly through the tube into his arm.

"One night I was going to a party. Or was it a restaurant? I remember I was going to meet someone."

My father moved his head on its pillow. The edge of his face looked paler, less yellow now.

"And there was your father, sitting in a booth at the restaurant. He was alone, and he looked hungry."

My father had told me a different version of this story, in which they met at an outdoor café. But I didn't mention that.

"I recognized him first. I said, 'Aren't you that boy I met on Tybee?'"

My father exhaled—a soft sigh.

"But he didn't remember me. Then I looked into his eyes—Ariella, have you ever seen eyes so green as his?"

"No, ma'am." Dashay had been trying to teach me to say *ma'am* or *sir* when I spoke to elders. Almost always, I forgot.

"He looked up at me, and he said, 'I'm sure I would have remembered meeting someone like you.'"

My father sighed again. His head moved from side to side on the pillow. Was he listening?

"For that woman to suggest I tried to kill him—" Her voice shattered. There's no other word for it, really. It fell into shards, faintly visible as they fell and faded.

Dashay came in, her face wearing a guarded expression. "Almost ready to leave?" she asked me.

"I guess." I had mixed feelings about going away.

My mother stretched her arms toward me, and I went to embrace her. She pressed her face against my hair. "You are my precious child," she said, and I so wished she hadn't, because I began to cry.

"Now there, stop that." Dashay's voice sounded gruff. "Ari, in six weeks your first semester will be over. And you all will be together again, and then you can cry as much as you want."

As we separated, Mãe used her hand to wipe away tears on my cheek. Then she said, "What did the doctor want?"

"She gave Ari some new serum." Dashay's guard was up again. "She said she'll stop back this afternoon to check in, and she's going to find a nurse to keep watch over Raphael."

"We don't need a nurse," Mãe said, but Dashay interrupted her.

"You need sleep," she told Mãe. "If I didn't have to get back to the horses and Grace, I'd stay here and *make* you sleep. The nurse is a good idea."

It was easier to say good-bye to Mãe than to my father. I bent over his head, noticed the one unchanged part of his face—his eyelashes, long and thick and black—then quickly kissed his temple and pulled away. It was the first time I'd ever dared to kiss him.

∞

I spent the first few days back on campus hunting down my professors and making up the assignments I'd missed. The work went fairly quickly, since my dorm room was no longer a beehive. Friends didn't come and go at all hours. Even my roommate had deserted the room.

Bernadette had moved in with Jacey, it seemed. She didn't tell me herself; Jacey did.

"I'm sorry, Ari," Jacey said, playing with one long blond braid. "She says it's too spooky in that room."

It seemed spooky even to me, without Bernadette's threads and shells and feathers. I spent as little time there as I could.

Whenever I saw Bernadette, in class or in the cafeteria, she looked away. The first time I went up to her and said, "How was your break?"

She drew back and turned slightly, as if to minimize her exposure to me. In a low voice, she said, "Please leave me alone."

I hadn't expected that.

Jacey told me a few days later, "It's not you, Ari. She says it's just that people around you tend to die."

If Walker knew about Bernadette's feelings, he never mentioned them. He turned up my first night back. I was walking alone on the path from the cafeteria to the dormitory when a white luminous sphere about a foot in diameter bobbed out of the shrubs alongside the path. The thing hovered, then moved toward me.

Was I startled? Yes, for a moment, before I spied, beneath the sphere, a black cloth suspended in the air by two black-gloved hands.

"Hello, Walker," I said.

"I am a zombie trapped inside this ball." Walker made his voice high, squeaky.

The word *zombie* did startle me. After a few seconds, I said, "Zombies don't sound like that."

He ignored the comment. "If you kiss the ball, the zombie will be freed."

Somehow he made the sphere rise and move toward me. It was a pretty good trick. I couldn't see any strings.

Walker made squeaky zombie sounds.

"Okay," I said. I stepped closer to the ball. "Let's free the zombie." I pursed my lips.

The globe and the cloth both vanished. In the darkness, Walker's lips touched mine.

For seconds, our mouths were disembodied entities doing a dance in midair. His lips were soft as a violet. (Yes, I had kissed more than one flower. It's the best way to practice.)

For seconds, I heard nothing, saw nothing, felt only his lips pressed against mine. Then something inside me sprang into being, as if a small flame ignited, rose, spread through all my nerves and into my lips, and then crossed into his.

The kiss ended. It was still the same night. We stood on the same path—Walker wearing a black hood with holes for his eyes and mouth, I saw now. The sound of faraway laughter made him pull the hood off. His hair was tousled, his eyes reflecting light from the globe. He'd dropped the cloth that had concealed it.

"Amazing," he said. "You are amazing."

I lacked the strength, much less the desire, to contradict him.

∞

After that, we were a couple. Walker and I held hands (clumsily, wearing gloves) between shifts at the recycling center. We walked back from the cafeteria to the dorm with our arms around each other. We studied together, in the lounge—actually studied, eyes on books, each of us savoring the tension that kept us from touching—so that when we did touch, the sensations were indescribably intense.

What I felt was wild. It went deep and made me dizzy—pleasantly so, nothing like the vertigo of before—creating a sweet laziness that bathed me in a sense of well-being, temporarily dulling the wildness. Maybe it was the new tonic I was taking. Maybe I was in love. Whatever it was, I felt charged with life, fully aware of each passing moment.

When our American Politics class met, Walker and I made efforts not to look at each other, with limited success. I caught Bernadette watching us more than once, trying to figure out what was different.

Meanwhile Professor Hogan spoke in her strident yet unconfident way about third parties. "Even though we can argue that the two-party system has become muddled at best, corrupt at worst, most interest groups realize that working within the two parties is the only real path to power?" Her voice rose at the end of sentences, making them sound like questions.

Walker yawned. His teeth were small and even, pearl-like. Bernadette caught me staring at his mouth and wondered how far things had gone between us. When I looked over at her, she turned away.

"In American politics, third parties have sometimes played a corrective role? They've raised issues that the traditional parties avoided because the issues couldn't generate social capital?"

Walker and I glanced at each other. A slow shiver climbed my spine.

"Ariella? Please define social capital for us?" Her large, dark eyes looked hunted, like a deer's.

Professor Hogan didn't like me. Even if I hadn't been able to hear her thoughts, I could have read her feelings in the tone of her voice and her body language. It wasn't anything I'd done or said—what prompted her hostility was that I'd dropped Professor Evans's physics class. She was having an affair with Evans, and they enjoyed talking about wayward students when they were in bed together. Yes, I'd listened to her thoughts.

"Ariella?"

"Social capital is a term for concerns that promote cooperation between two or more individuals."

"Er—yes?" she said. "And can you give us an example?"

I was trying to think of an example when Walker said, "You know, social capital is just words. It's jargon."

Professor Hogan turned her deerlike eyes on him. "It's language used by social scientists like me to describe a behavioral norm?"

"But it's jargon. If you're talking about relationships based on earned trust, why not say trust? If you mean common interests or reciprocal favors, why not say that? To me, *social capital* makes fairly simple things sound complicated."

Virtually every student in the room agreed with Walker. Bernadette looked at him as if he were a hero. I thought so, too—not because he'd come to my rescue and deflected the professor's attention. He'd had the courage to say what I thought, but didn't dare express. I didn't mind abstract terms in my philosophy class—they were appropriate there—but used to describe American politics, they seemed grandiose expressions of a kind of wishful thinking: that politics were governed by scientific principles. The little I'd read about politics suggested that science had nothing to do with it.

The class time ended before the debate could go further. But Professor Hogan had the last word.

"Next month, when we go to the Third-Parties Caucus in Savannah?" she said. "Then you'll see social and political capital in action?"

On the weekend after spring break ended, Walker took me on the picnic he'd promised.

Over the unofficial Hillhouse uniform—jeans and a T-shirt—I threw on a cardigan made of cashmere, lavender pink. Dashay had given it to me during our short-lived Yule celebration. I'd never worn pink before, and the sweater made me self-conscious at first, but the color flattered my complexion, made me seem to blush. Vampires never blush.

We walked to the orchards adjoining campus, Walker carrying a large canvas tote bag. The peach trees were in bloom. The breeze drifted their light pink petals and wafted their faint, sweet perfume, which made the air as exotic as incense.

Watching Walker spread a blanket on the ground made me think of Mysty, carrying a blanket to her last date with Jesse. I felt goose bumps on my arms.

"What's wrong?" He fell onto the blanket, rolled onto his back, propped himself on his elbows—all in one movement.

I rubbed my forehead and tried to clear the memory, let myself live in the moment, savor the sheen of spring in the tree blossoms, the powder-blue sky, the fragrant air. "Such a beautiful day," I said.

"*You're* beautiful." His North Carolina accent made the compliment sound natural, not hokey, the way it looks as I write it down. Words take on new meanings when they're spoken. "When I was growing up I used to dream about meeting someone like you."

I sat cross-legged on the blanket. "What do you mean—someone like me?"

He moved closer to me and lay on his back. "Someone mysterious, and beautiful, and smart. The girls I grew up with, they were all right. Some of them were very pretty. And some were smart, too. But

I kept dreaming about meeting someone special, someone *enigmatic*." He pronounced the word slowly, as if he liked its sound.

"You must have been in love a hundred times." I heard my own voice, and for the first time it reminded me of my mother's Savannah drawl. I was *flirting*, I realized.

"A couple." His silver-blue eyes were the color of topaz. Our encyclopedia at home had plates of gemstones, and I'd studied them, fascinated by their range of colors. I wondered if anyone had ever made photographic plates of human eyes. They seemed even more variegated than gems.

"Five, actually," he said. "Six if you count a blind date. That time I was in love for all of two hours." Suddenly he reached toward me, touched the amulet that hung from my neck. "What's this?"

"An Egyptian cat." I told him cat amulets were linked to the Egyptian goddess Bastet, who transformed herself into a cat with an all-seeing eye in order to protect her father from enemies. "Amulets are designed to protect travelers."

He placed the cat back against my neck. "Enigmatic," he said again. He sat up, reached into the canvas tote, and pulled out a bottle of rosé wine and two glasses.

We sipped the wine, light and floral as the air around us. We ate strawberries and tomato sandwiches wrapped in waxed paper. For dessert we had meringues—stale clouds that melted and vaporized in our mouths. Walker had taken as much care with the food as he did with his magic tricks.

When we'd finished eating, I lay back against the blanket next to him. For a while we both watched the sky. Walker said, "Ever wonder what makes it blue?"

I knew why the sky appeared to be blue—the color was an effect of Rayleigh scattering. Air molecules disperse the blue wavelengths of visible light more effectively than longer wavelengths, such as red. But to say that would have broken the mood.

"It's the same reason the Blue Ridge Mountains look blue," Walker said. "It's called Rayleigh scattering."

"I know about light scattering," I said. "I thought you'd come up with something more poetic."

"What could be more poetic than Rayleigh scattering? Without it, we'd be looking up at black space."

I thought of my telescope—I'd left it back in Sassa—and then my mind leapt to the night Mysty disappeared, to the moment when I blacked out.

"What's the matter?" Walker leaned over me, his face full of concern. He had luminous skin, tinted sand-brown by the sun. I would never have skin like that, I thought. "Are you thinking about that friend of yours?"

I nodded. Then I realized he meant Autumn, not Mysty.

"It's been rough on you." His hand touched my hair, pushed back a strand. My scalp tingled. Then we were kissing.

Wordsworth defined poetry as "the spontaneous overflow of powerful feelings from emotions recollected in tranquillity." I will never be a poet; I can't recollect my emotions in tranquillity, because the moment I think of them, the emotions recur, every bit as strong and overwhelming as they were that day in the peach orchard.

We kissed until our mouths hurt, and then we kissed more. My lips felt swollen. My blood surged, and I heard my heartbeat, loud and fast, against Walker's chest. My eyes were closed, but, when we pulled apart to breathe, I opened them. The first thing I saw was Walker's neck, pale, arced above me as he tipped back his head. I would be lying if I didn't admit to having a sudden strong urge to sink my teeth into his skin.

I flung my hand over my mouth.

He bent forward again, breathing hard. "Ari, Ari, no one on this earth can kiss the way you do."

I didn't say anything. I'd managed to scare myself.

The next morning he slipped a letter under the door of my room. In it, he wrote a poem about kissing. He ended by saying that he would love me forever. I felt elated, frightened, and grateful that the letter didn't use the word "eternity."

∞

In my dorm room that Sunday—a long brown day that pretended Saturday had never been—I used my cell phone to call Dashay. I didn't dare call the cottage, in case the call might be traced. As arranged, we didn't say a word about my father in case someone was listening in.

"How are things?" I asked.

"Things are about the same." Her voice sounded so cold, so detached that it didn't seem hers. "How are you?"

I still felt numb from the picnic, the kissing, the urge to bite. I said, "I am perfectly fine, ma'am."

THREE

Blue Moon Rising

Chapter Fourteen

I wanted to talk to Dashay about hormones. I wanted to talk to Dr. Cho about Revité.

But I couldn't use the phone to talk freely, and I couldn't get away. On the Internet I found some posts about Revité. Apparently the clinical trials were over, and the drug was now available through Vunderworld.

One posting, from the drug's manufacturer, featured a photo of a woman running in a meadow, captioned with a line from a Beatles song: "Get back to where you once belonged." And while part of me did want to go back—to being Ari, the home-schooled girl who cared only about learning and pleasing her father—more of me wanted to go forward. But to what?

Someone wrote: "Revité saved my marriage." The poster said she'd been vamped "against my will, forced into a hideous dependence on human blood and foul-tasting supplements, unable to have a normal life, missing holiday celebrations, regular meals, safe relations with my mortal husband."

I would have blushed, if I could.

"Those soulless nights, lying awake craving blood while he snored," the post went on, "I thought about suicide."

Did vampires commit suicide? I'd never thought of it until now.

"Then I found Revité." The anonymous poster changed tone. "Now I can cook, and shop, and make love like a real woman! And someday soon, I may be a mother."

It all sounded soppy, horribly wrong. Why, then, did I keep reading?

∞

Professor Hogan was envious of me. So was Bernadette, and so were four or five other female students whose thoughts I heard. They could tell Walker was in love with me, and it made them feel unloved by contrast, and bitter.

Walker was not one to hide his feelings. One day he walked into class juggling paper roses, which he laid on the arm of my chair. Another, he sang a silly song he'd made up in which he rhymed *Ari* with *sorry, tamari,* and *Ferrari.* The song made Bernadette and Professor Hogan laugh, after which their envy only grew.

I tried to understand their feelings, but failed. At that point in my life, envy was something I'd experienced rarely, and only in the abstract: I'd envied other girls' normal family lives, for instance. But what Professor Hogan and Bernadette felt went deeper, and it expressed itself in hostility toward me.

When Professor Hogan wrote "Wrong!" in red ink on one of my essays, next to a statement that I knew was true, I tried not to take it to heart. After all, she was in a relationship with a married man who would never be able to publicly acknowledge his feelings as Walker did. She had reason to be envious.

But when Bernadette began telling lies about me, it hurt. In spite of her moving out of the room, some part of me had thought we still were friends. (It embarrasses me now to recall how naïve I was. Is there anything more fickle than friendship among teenage girls?)

Walker was the one who told me about Bernadette. We were sitting under a tree one afternoon; I was reading our politics textbook, and Walker lay with his head on my lap, playing with my hair. He pulled it all forward, so it hung like a curtain over his face; then he separated it into strands, peering through them at me.

"Is it true that you slept around in high school?" he said suddenly.

"What?" I let the book snap shut.

"Bernadette told me that." All I could see was one of his eyes, and it had a strange, hard brightness.

"First of all, I didn't go to high school—I was home-schooled." My voice sounded less indignant than I felt. "And second, I happen to be a virgin." There—I'd said something I'd never imagined saying to anyone.

"Are you really?" He reached up, through my hair, and stroked my cheek.

"That tickles." I brushed his hand away. "Why would she say something like that?"

"She's jealous, I guess." Walker sighed. "You know, she and I, we hung out a few times our first year. I thought it was no big deal, but maybe she still has some feelings for me."

"Maybe she does." Why hadn't I picked up on that sooner? And what did he mean by "hung out"?

"What else did she say?" I asked.

"Just, you know, that I should be careful when I'm around you. That bad things have been happening. You know."

"My friends tend to disappear or die." It was the same thing Jacey had said.

"Forget about her," he said. "She's jealous. Ari, do you love me?"

This conversation was too confusing for me. I didn't know the answer.

"In my family," I said slowly, "when I was growing up, no one used the word *love*. It's not something I've ever said, to anyone."

Walker lifted my hair and sat up, letting it fall past my shoulders, against my back. His eyes had lost the hardness. "I want to be the first one you say it to," he said, his voice close to a whisper.

As he kissed me, I felt the confusion grow.

∞

Professor Hogan bombarded us with reading assignments the week before our field trip. We studied the history of political parties in American politics—how the Republican Party, for instance, emerged in opposition to slavery and became a primary party.

"Today, when someone chooses to vote for a third party, that vote is a rejection of the primary parties?" Professor Hogan said. Her hair was frayed and her skin had broken out, as if the added stress of the field trip was taking a toll. "Third-party voting happens only under extreme conditions, when voters feel so alienated from the positions of the major parties that they're willing to sacrifice their votes for a party that they're sure can't win?"

Walker was folding a scrap of paper into an origami flower. He didn't agree with what she was saying. He thought that people who bothered to vote did believe their party could win.

"Our election laws discourage the growth of third parties?"

Walker flicked the flower onto the arm of my chair.

"And how do they do that, Ariella?"

She almost always called on me, so I paid close attention, even when she was particularly dull. "They make it harder for third parties to obtain funding," I said, careful to keep my tone neutral. "And many states make it more complicated for third-party candidates to get onto the ballot, such as requiring them to submit more names on their petitions."

She nodded, grudgingly. Bernadette shot me a resentful look.

I hadn't had a chance to say anything to her about the lies she told Walker. But I had plenty to say, when the right moment came. For now, I simply stared back at her, until she turned away.

Professor Hogan reminded us that we'd need to be on our best behavior in Savannah. "Please wear something that looks professional?" she said.

It was the first time several of the third parties had decided to hold a regional caucus, to meet both independently and collectively to share strategies for undermining the primary parties. Our group had been given special passes by the Third-Parties Caucus to attend some of the sessions. We wouldn't all go to the same ones, however. At the end of class, Hogan handed out our assignment sheets.

"I got the Green Party." Walker had been hoping for that assignment, and I felt pleased for him. Then I looked at my own sheet.

"What did you get, Walker?" Bernadette touched his arm.

"I'm Green," he said.

She looked disappointed. "I'm Social Democrat," she said.

He'd already turned back to me. "What are you?"

"The Fair Share Party," I read. "Must be one of the new ones."

"Maybe we can switch with someone so we're together," Walker said.

Professor Hogan heard him, of course. "No substitutions?" she said.

As we left the classroom, Walker said, in a low voice, "Can you imagine being in a relationship with her? You'd never know when she actually asked a question."

The philosophical and linguistic implications were intriguing, I thought. "Someone should write a paper about Professor Hogan's voice," I said.

He grinned. "Title? Maybe 'The Sound of Madness'?"

"How about 'The Abuse of Aural Ambiguity'?"

"Or 'Everything's Hypothetical'?"

We kept joking for a while, but part of me thought: What if her continual questioning *was* deliberate? How could you hold a person responsible for what she said when everything she said sounded speculative?

Bernadette came up behind us. "Walker?" she said.

He turned around. When he saw who it was, he slipped his arm across my shoulders. "What do you want, Bernie?" he said. "Want to talk more trash about my girlfriend?"

Everything he'd said was phrased as a question. I appreciated that. There were moments when I thought that yes, I might indeed be in love with Walker Pearson.

∞

Someone wrote once that the best moments in life occur just before you arrive.

Actually, I wrote that, in my journal. But it doesn't sound original. Surely someone else thought it first.

In any case, as our bus rolled and braked and cornered through the squares of downtown Savannah, I felt excited. I'd explored these streets on my own last spring, and now they were familiar to me. There was Colonial Cemetery, and across from it, the brick house where my mother once rented a flat she said was haunted. There was the Marshall House, the first hotel I'd ever stayed in. Up ahead lay the river, and somewhere close by was the café where my parents had met for the first time as adults. I wanted to walk through all of those places, reclaim old memories and make new ones.

Walker squeezed my hand. He had his own plans for our time in Savannah. I tried not to listen to his thoughts, but I didn't try hard.

It's probably a bad idea to listen to the thoughts of someone who loves you. Love makes minds soft and sentimental, prone to even more digressions and lapses of logic than usual. Of course, the average mortal thought process is pretty messy to begin with, continually interrupting itself with observations and expressions of physical need and desire; vampires, by contrast, tend to think in cooler, more linear patterns (though my mother was one notable exception).

Walker was thinking about himself, as most mortals do most of the time. He felt a little sleepy, fairly hungry, and consistently amorous. He had a desire to devour me (his words) and simultaneously revere me. I listened long enough to learn he was planning a romantic evening for us in Savannah; then I felt uneasy about eavesdropping. My mother would have called it meddling, but how could I resist?

I resisted. I didn't want love to turn out to be a mere jumble of feelings.

I turned to look out the bus window. We were passing the rough stone streets that led down to River Street, the place where I'd turned invisible for the first time. My father had given me the metamaterials clothing and shoes that bend light rays, and I'd taught myself the process of absorbing the heat of my body's electrons and deflecting light. The process had been physically tiring, but the experience entirely justified the expense of energy—being invisible was the most fun I'd ever had. Moving through crowded streets as if you're flying, weightless, and free—could anything be better than that?

And yes, I'd packed my special trouser suit, underwear, and shoes for the field trip. After all, they were the most professional-looking clothes I owned.

The conference hotel overlooked the muddy brown river. We clustered in the lobby under a high arched ceiling made of glass and steel. Professor Hogan checked us in and announced the room assignments. I was in room 408, along with Bernadette and a girl called Rhonda.

Bernadette immediately went up to Hogan and talked to her in a low voice.

"No substitutions?" Hogan said.

We all crowded into an elevator, and Walker, Richard, and four other boys got off on the third floor. Walker blew me a kiss as he left.

Bernadette sighed—a sigh of frustration and anger, not sadness. Her thoughts were scattered, but I detected enormous jealousy and fear at the root of her feelings about me. Autumn's murder had been Bernadette's first experience of death, and she hadn't yet come to terms with it. Blaming me was the best she could manage.

In our room, Rhonda talked nonstop while I unpacked, and Bernadette lay on a bed. "You can have the sofa bed," she said to me.

"Let's flip coins." I pulled three dimes out of my backpack.

When we flipped, Bernadette got tails while Rhonda and I got heads. I almost regretted that she was the odd one out, because it gave her one more reason to resent me.

∞

The keynote speaker for the caucus was Neil Cameron, a thirty-year-old U.S. senator from Georgia who had quit the Democrats to join the Fair Share Party. He ignored the podium and walked to the edge of the stage to address us. Walker and I sat in the third row. From the moment he appeared, we couldn't take our eyes off him.

Was Neil Cameron good looking? Every woman in the room would have said so, although he wasn't conventionally handsome. His nose looked as if it might have been broken once, and he was probably five-foot-ten at most. But his dark blue eyes were warm; I'd read the phrase "dancing eyes," but I'd never seen them until that night. His eyes moved from face to face in the audience, lingering long enough to create the impression that he was fascinated by each one. His hair was thick and dark, his hands square and strong looking. As he spoke, his hands did a kind of dance of their own.

"Two days from now, when you leave Savannah, more than fifty species will have become extinct," he said. "Think of it—fifty species never to be seen again. The major causes? Habitat destruction, exploitation, and land development—all actions taken by humans."

He paused and rested his hands on his hips. "We say, it's time for them to stop."

He had a wonderful voice, strong and deep, melodic as my father's, but with rough edges.

Now he leaned forward, and his hands began to move again as his eyes swept the crowd. "By the time you leave Savannah, more than fifty-eight million tons of carbon dioxide emissions will have entered the earth's atmosphere. Each and every year, thirty billion tons of CO_2 emissions are generated by humans—from their power plants, cars, airplanes, and buildings."

Again, he placed his hands on his hips. "We say, it's time for them to stop."

Cameron walked across the stage and back again, spouting statistics about global warming and coral reef destruction, about deforestation and fertilizer runoff, punctuating the statistics with the same line. And by the third repetition, the crowd was chanting it along with him: "We say, it's time for them to stop."

I'd heard the word *charisma*, knew that it came from a Greek word meaning "gift." But the word didn't begin to describe the charm and electricity of Neil Cameron. As he moved about the stage, I thought of a line from "Richard Corey," a poem by Edwin Arlington Robinson: "he glittered when he walked." This man had a magnetic sparkle to him that I couldn't explain, and didn't even try to at the time.

When he stopped walking, Cameron held out both his hands, palms up. "But who are *we*?" he said. "Who are we, and who is *them*?

"I say, America is divided into two groups: insiders and outsiders. And I, my friends, along with every one of you, we're on the outside. We're fundamentally different from the insiders. We care about different things, and we live different lives. They are highly protected. We are not. They have built a system of laws and customs that protects them. We live in a more precarious place. They and their system are killing the earth. We are here to save it. We are here to-night"—he spread his arms wide—"to take the first steps toward defending our home."

The crowd broke into a kind of roar. The sound was electric, pulling us out of our chairs to clap and whistle and wave our arms. Down the row, Bernadette shouted something, and in front of us, Professor Hogan made an odd sound, a high-pitched hoot of approval. Next to her, a woman in a red dress gave her a derisive look, but didn't stop clapping.

Cameron stood silent in the center of the stage beneath a spotlight, watching us, seeming to drink in our approval. Was I the only one to notice that he cast no shadow?

When the noise died, Cameron said, "Thank you," and that made the cheers begin again. Walker looked at me and shook his head. "Wow," he said.

Volunteers came along the aisles, handing out sheets of paper and envelopes for donations. The papers were loyalty oaths: statements that we would support third-party candidates and pledge not to vote for Democrats or Republicans. Like everyone else in the room, I signed my form and passed it back. Later, much later, I'd wonder how Cameron got us all to sign. Nothing he'd said was news, really. But that night, buoyed by the man himself more than anything he said, no one hesitated.

Cameron was the first to leave, the crowd trailing him to a reception set up in an adjoining room. People formed a ragged line, waiting for a chance to speak to him. Walker and I waited, too.

And that's when I saw Mysty.

At a table near us, volunteers had clustered to collect and sort the loyalty oaths. One of them, a girl with dark brown hair, seemed oddly familiar to me. It wasn't her hair or even her face, but the way she stood, her weight on one foot and the other knee bent, and the tilt of her head. *Mysty,* I thought. Yes, her nose was the same. But her eyes were brown, and they had an unfamiliar listlessness.

I moved to get a better look. Her hands were shuffling papers. Her right wrist had no tattoo, but as I grew closer I saw it: a faint pink outline shaped like a rose. It was *her.* She must have had the tattoo removed.

"Mysty?" I said.

She looked up at me, no sign of recognition in her eyes. "My name's Pauline."

"How are you?" I said, feeling stupid.

"I'm okay, how are you?" Her voice lacked a Southern accent now—its inflections and tone were colorless—but its cadence and pitch were unchanged. They belonged to Mysty.

What has happened to you? I wondered, sure that she'd never tell me. I couldn't even listen to her thoughts—all I heard was a soft buzzing, like the sound of a fly in a large vacant room.

∞

When Neil Cameron took my hand to shake, I wanted him to hold it. His touch was cool and smooth, and his hand enveloped mine lightly. Behind me, Walker coughed.

"Ariella," he said, looking at my name badge. "A beautiful name. It means 'God's lion.' Where are you from, Ariella?"

"Florida," I said. I didn't think of saying Saratoga Springs. I felt lucky I could remember the word *Florida.*

His eyes lit up. "Oh, I'm from Florida, too. I was born in Deltona. Do you know where that is?"

I nodded. I wanted to ask him how long he'd been a vampire.

His eyes fixed on mine then, as if he'd heard my thought. I realized that he was still holding my hand.

Walker coughed again, and Cameron let my hand go. "I'll be seeing you soon," he said. His eyes lingered, reluctant to leave my face. Yes, I know it sounds like a romance novel, but that's how it felt.

I moved away, dazzled. Behind me, I heard Walker introduce himself, his voice sounding nervous. And out of the corner of my eye, I saw Mysty and another young woman walk toward the door. I thought they might be heading for a restroom, which I wanted to visit myself, so I followed them. No, that's not entirely truthful. I followed them. I have no idea why.

The two of them walked through the lobby and out the sliding glass doors. Both put on earbuds and turned on MP3 players. I trailed their scent (Mysty wore perfume or lotion with an apple fragrance, while the other girl smelled like cinnamon) across the parking lot and down the sidewalk that bordered the river. Even if I hadn't seen the outline of the tattoo, I knew I was following Mysty. No one else walked the way she did.

We passed restaurants and bars and souvenir shops. Then they turned left and began to make their way up a steep cobblestone street. I'd been here before—this was the place I'd first turned invisible. I saw no reason not to do it again.

The elation of invisibility came instantly the second that I ceased to be seen. I felt I could do anything! No one could watch and judge me now. No one could make me feel like an outsider, because I was no place at all.

Mysty and her friend moved down Abercorn Street through Reynolds and Oglethorpe squares, then turned right. I flitted along behind, happy as a dragonfly about to descend upon its prey.

A few blocks later they reached a cast-iron fence surrounding a four-story brick house; they turned and strode up to its front door. I hung back, in the mossy shade of a live oak tree, watching.

The door was painted black, matching the fence and the shutters, and black lamps with flickering lights inside flanked it. The brick walls were covered in ivy. Eighteen windows faced the street, all heavily curtained, none showing any sign of light.

Someone I couldn't see opened the door. They stepped inside. I waited a few minutes, in case they returned. Then, disappointed, I let myself be visible again and headed for the hotel.

The reception was still under way when I came back. People gathered around tables holding platters of hors d'oeuvres and a punch bowl. Some carried glasses of red liquid that made me feel thirsty. It was a mixed crowd—old and young, men and women. Some were expensively dressed, and others wore jeans. The woman in the red dress stood out in her sophistication. She had dark, wavy hair and she was beautiful, but her expression conveyed habitual scorn. As I watched, she crossed the room and broke into a conversation Neil Cameron was having with an older woman. When her face lost the disdainful look, it was utterly charming.

Some part of me wanted to be like her—effortlessly amusing, worldly, elegant. The girl in the pink sweater longed to become a woman in a red dress.

Walker was nowhere in sight.

I headed for the bar, where I showed my fake ID and bought a glass of Picardo.

A voice behind me said, "Make it two."

I didn't need to turn around. Even if I hadn't recognized his voice, the pleasure I felt told me it belonged to Neil Cameron.

Chapter Fifteen

*I*t was nearly 2 A.M. when I reached my hotel room, but Bernadette and Rhonda were awake, sitting on the carpeted floor, talking. Behind them a TV blared, and every light in the room was on. They were drunk.

They smiled bleary smiles at me—the first time Bernadette had smiled at me in months. "Did you try the punch, Ari?" she said. "It was fan-tab-u-lous."

"Fantabalous." Rhonda stretched her arms over her head and waved her hands.

"Fanta*bul*ous."

Both of them giggled.

Someone pounded on the door. I looked at them, and they didn't move. I went to the door and put my eye to its peephole. Walker stood there, blue eyes vivid against the beige walls and beige carpet. But he wasn't my Walker. He looked a little crazy—his eyes were heavy lidded, almost shut, and his mouth hung open.

I didn't want to let him in. But I opened the door.

"Ari," he said, "hey, Ari. What the hell?" He didn't say it in an angry way. His voice drawled.

Yes, he was drunk, too.

"I was looking for you." Walker sounded almost maudlin now. "I looked and I looked, and then I saw you, talking to that guy Cameron." He took a deep breath. "Now don't get me wrong, I can see why you'd be talking to a guy like that. But I, I . . ." He lost his train of thought.

"Were you drinking punch?"

He smiled at me, a lopsided grin.

I wondered, *What did they put in the punch?*

"Walker, go back to your room." I spoke clearly and slowly. "We can talk in the morning, after you've had some sleep."

He stood there for a minute, shifting his weight from foot to foot. *My skinny boyfriend,* I thought. Even drunk, he was cute.

"I'll walk you there." I went back inside to grab my key and I told the others where I was going, although I'm not sure why I bothered. They were laughing again, more loudly now, their heads tipped back.

When I led Walker back to the third floor, he said, "Aw."

When we reached the door, he said, "Aw. You are so nice." He leaned forward and might have fallen if I hadn't braced his shoulders, propped him against the wall. I knocked on the door, and Richard opened it. He, at least, was sober.

"Another drunk?" he asked. "Great. Now we have a pair."

He pulled Walker into the room. I said good night and went back to the elevator. But instead of going up, I went down.

The reception room was empty now. What had I expected? I went to the corner where I'd stood next to Neil Cameron for more than two hours, making polite conversation with him and his supporters, savoring every second of his presence. I didn't remember much of what we'd said (I remember saying that I liked his suit, and he said it was made of bamboo fiber; he asked what my parents did in Florida, and I said something I can't remember), but I recalled vividly what I felt each time his eyes swept across my face.

Was this what love felt like? I wished I could call my mother or Dashay to ask. But Mãe was out of reach, and it was too late to wake up Dashay.

I slowly went back to the elevator, back to room 408.

∞

When I slid into my seat at the Fair Share caucus next morning, Richard looked surprised to see me. "I assumed you'd be in bed like everyone else, sleeping it off."

I'd just left Bernadette and Rhonda fast asleep in our room. "What happened last night?"

"First there was punch at the reception," he said. "Don't ask me what was in it. I don't drink. Then everyone got together in one of the student rooms, and I guess they drank more, and who knows what else they did. I didn't go."

"Neither did I." I looked the room over, but Cameron wasn't there. Neither was the woman in the red dress. I was wearing my trouser suit again, but I'd taken time that morning to put on mascara and tinted sunblock. Richard would never have said it, but he thought I looked pretty.

The seminar leader that morning reviewed the history of the Fair Share party, which had been born two years previously after efforts to tighten state environmental protection laws failed in several states. Richard listened skeptically. *Those laws failed for good reasons,* he thought. Tuning in to his mind was like entering an antiseptically clean, brightly lit restaurant. There was nothing to tempt one's appetite.

The first priority of the Fair Sharers was to give the party greater national visibility, the speaker said. "By the time the presidential primaries are held next year, we need to be a household word," she said. "Luckily, we have a candidate who will make sure that happens."

"Who's the candidate?" I whispered to Richard.

"Probably that guy we heard last night," he said, doodling an American flag in the margins of his notebook. "Cameron. Might as well call himself a socialist. That's what he talked like."

In Richard's way of thinking, the environment existed as an industrial resource, plain and simple. It would renew itself, he figured. That was *nature's way.* I thought for a second how out of place he must feel here and at Hillhouse, where the majority cared passionately about environmental conservation. But Richard didn't mind being an outsider—in fact, he relished it. He felt confident that he was superior to the rest of us.

"That speech last night was a lesson in how to lie with statistics," he said.

Someone shushed him, and the speaker turned toward us. "But we'll need the support of each and every one of you if our message is to reach the American people."

Richard said, "Fat chance."

The man sitting next to him said, "Why are you here?"

"Did you ever hear the expression 'Know your enemy'?"

I pretended that I was somewhere else. Usually, when I did that, my mind went to Jamaica, a place I knew only from Dashay's descriptions. I thought the words *Montego Bay,* and off I went: white sand, turquoise water, no Richard.

We spent the rest of the day, apart from a lunch break, sitting in that hotel conference room. We learned how a fledgling political party organizes and finds its place in the public eye. The audience comprised students and volunteers of all ages. Our speakers were hardheaded, but their addresses were designed to be optimistic. Thanks to grassroots efforts and community-building, the Fair Share Party would get its national reputation. Cameron would appeal to more voters than the primary party candidates. The media would be reluctant at first, but would buy in after the primary elections showed that FSP could win.

Midway through the afternoon, Richard said to me, "I'm leaving. This is a waste of time. No real decisions are being made here—they happen late at night in smoke-filled rooms, same way they always did."

I wasn't sure what he meant, but I was glad to see him go. I remembered my father's words that politics were ephemera—transitory events that recurred in cyclical patterns, hardly worth one's interest. By the end of the day, I half agreed with him, and I wondered if Richard could be right.

From time to time, images from the night before visited me, made me look around the room again in case Cameron had come in. I must confess, I didn't think once about Walker.

But when I got back to room 408, he was there, sitting on the sofa that opened into Bernadette's bed, while Bernadette sat on my bed and Rhonda lay across the other one. Their eyes looked glazed, and they all smiled at me. *Drunk again?* I wondered.

Walker patted the sofa seat next to his. "Ari, Ari," he said. "I missed you."

I sat down. Trying to pick up their thoughts brought me such a jumble that I gave up. "Are you all going to the reception tonight?" That was the next thing on the agenda. On the following day, we'd have morning seminar sessions, then lunch, then head back to Hillhouse.

"Love receptions," Rhonda said. "Just love them."

"Okay," I said. "What are you all on?"

They smiled at me.

"What substance are you imbibing?"

Bernadette took a small plastic bottle off the nightstand and tossed it to me. I opened it and saw little pills stamped with *V*s. *Sugar pills?* Looking around me, I didn't think so.

"Try one." Walker put his arm around me, but I shrugged it off.

"Thanks, but no," I said. "It might interfere with my lupus medication."

∞

That night Walker, as planned, took me out to dinner. This was a real "date"—I wore a blue silk dress, and Walker had put on a jacket and tie.

As we came down Broughton Street, I said to him, "I didn't think that you used drugs."

"I don't." He seemed completely happy, moving along next to me, taking in the sights. "V is more of a mood enhancer, you know? One of the guys at the party last night had a bunch of it."

I felt disappointed and confused, cheated out of what I should have been feeling on the night of a date.

"I don't see what harm it does," Walker said. "But if it bugs you that much, I won't take any more."

"Don't take any more." Whatever was in those pills made Walker someone else, to me. Yet part of me questioned: Easygoing, affable, uncritical—what was wrong with being that way? How do we distinguish genuine feelings from ones induced by substances? And why do we value the "real" ones more?

I said, "There's the Marshall House. That's the first hotel I stayed in by myself."

Walker looked up at the black wrought iron that supported and trimmed the hotel balcony. "Cool," he said.

Through the burgundy-draped windows, the hotel lobby looked the same—black-and-white diamond-patterned floors lit by glass bowl-shaped ceiling fixtures. The restaurant next door had its candles lit; they made the deep green walls glow.

Then I saw him. Sitting at the bar, his back to us, was a tall blond man in a black suit, drinking from a dark red glass.

Malcolm. I stopped moving. Walker sauntered on a few steps, then turned.

"What's the matter?"

I didn't say a word.

"Ari, you look like you saw a ghost."

But he wasn't a ghost. As I looked, he raised the glass as if toasting someone. Had he seen my wavering reflection in the mirror over the bar?

"Let's go in." My voice sounded matter-of-fact, but my blood was racing. The last time I'd seen him was in Sarasota. *This man set the fire that nearly killed us,* I thought. *This man made my father and my mother vampires. He killed my best friend.*

Walker followed me into the bar, thinking I wanted to have a drink. But I wanted answers. Why had he singled my family out? Was he somehow responsible for my father's illness, too? No matter what the answers were, in my heart I craved revenge.

As we walked in, Malcolm didn't act surprised at all to see me.

"Ms. Montero," he said, rising from his seat and extending his hand.

I didn't have a plan for this meeting. I took his hand, shook it, let it go. His hand was cold. His face had a kind of arrogant handsomeness—an aristocratic nose, pale eyes, blond hair parted on the left side.

"I'm Malcolm Lynch," he said to Walker, shaking his hand. Walker introduced himself. *I should have done that,* I thought, but my mind was full of other matters. How could I say anything in front of Walker?

"What are you doing in Savannah?" I said. He looked as fit as the last time I'd seen him.

He shook his head slightly, as if I'd been rude, but he seemed to find it amusing nonetheless. "Do sit down," he said. "Join me for a drink."

Walker slid onto a stool. I said, "No."

They looked at me—Walker's surprise genuine, Malcolm's feigned.

"We're on our way to dinner," I said. "And then we have to attend a reception." I wasn't ready to face Malcolm after all, with Walker there. I added, "Perhaps we can meet at a later time."

"By all means." Malcolm's smile crinkled the skin around his eyes. "We have some catching up to do." He reached into his jacket, pulled out a case made of engraved metal—platinum, probably—opened it, extracted a card. I took it without reading it, slid it into my purse.

"Good-bye," I said.

"Good evening." He nodded at both of us, then smiled again as he watched us leave.

Outside, Walker said, "That was weird. Who was that guy? Why didn't you want to stay?"

"He's an old acquaintance of my family." I pushed my hair back, tried to calm down.

"And why are you talking all formal-like?"

"I don't know." We turned a corner and there was the restaurant: an old house painted pink.

"I'm sorry," I said. "Seeing him was a bit of a shock. I'll explain why, someday. Don't let it spoil our dinner."

What spoiled our dinner was Walker. He was restless, constantly moving in his seat, his eyes darting around the crowded room. He had trouble figuring out what to order, and later he barely touched his food. An older couple at the table next to ours kept looking over at us, wondering what was wrong.

It was a relief to return to the hotel, to change back into my trouser suit and go to the reception. There were no speeches tonight, just food and drinks and a band. The band was playing a pop song when I walked in, and some people were dancing.

Walker had already visited the punch bowl. He pulled me onto the dance floor and began to flail his arms and move erratically. When the song ended, I steered him to a seat near the refreshments table.

I leaned against the wall nearby, watching the crowd, taking in the kaleidoscope of colors and scents and patterns, knowing that Walker wasn't noticing much of it, if any. He slumped back in his chair, eyes half-shut, smiling inanely.

And so, when Neil Cameron asked me to dance, I went with him gladly. We danced a fast song, then a slow one; from the first moment we danced together, we fit. I stole glances at his face, his profile and deep-set eyes.

"You dance the way a cat moves," he said. "Grace without effort."

"Are you flirting with me?"

"A little," he said. "Is that all right?"

"I guess so." It was more than all right. Multicolored adjectives filled my head—pearl-colored *wonderful,* garnet-red *divine,* sapphire *enchanting,* all words I'd normally never use. I felt grateful that Mãe had taught me to dance—but this was nothing like our tentative steps across the airport's tiled floor. In my mind Cameron and I were not slow-dancing—we were spinning, soaring out across a night sky.

He smiled at me, and I remembered too late to block my thoughts. Suddenly I felt clumsy, naïve.

But near the end of that dance, something strange happened, something I couldn't put a name to at the time. A wave of intense energy rose up in me and passed to him. The feeling was akin to what I'd felt when I'd first kissed Walker, but its magnitude was far greater. Mãe told me some time later that I'd experienced what the French call a *coup de foudre*—a term variously translated as "lightning flash," "bolt from the blue," or "love at first sight." To this day I'm not sure which term best applied.

Cameron stopped dancing, stared at me, and I looked back into his dark blue eyes. "Like star sapphires," I heard my voice say, but he didn't seem to hear.

Then the music stopped, and we moved apart. Three FSP supporters came up and took Cameron away, but he looked at me over his shoulder, mouthed the word *later*. I took a deep breath and looked around the room.

And there he was again; Malcolm sat at the bar, head tipped back, laughing. I glanced away, pretending I hadn't seen him.

But when Malcolm left the reception a few minutes later, I decided to follow him. Cameron stood at the bar, surrounded by admirers. Walker leaned over the punch bowl, refilling a glass. I didn't bother to tell anyone I was leaving.

Malcolm walked with long strides, his black trench coat flapping out in the wind. I turned invisible and began to run to catch up. When I was within half a block of him, I resumed walking, all the while wondering how to make him tell me what I needed to know. Finally I hit on a plan. The last time I'd seen him in Sarasota, he'd been trying to persuade my father to join him in researching and developing a new kind of synthetic blood. I could pretend to be interested in the research, offer to be a go-between to entice my father. The plan might work, I thought—unless Malcolm knew that my father was too sick to work. Unless Malcolm was the one who'd made him sick.

The route varied, but the destination was the same as the night before: we ended up at the vine-covered house near Oglethorpe Square. The small lamps on either side of its door glimmered. Malcolm strode inside before I had time to approach him. No, to be honest, during the last few minutes I fell back, uncertain and afraid. My strategy suddenly seemed silly to me. How could I hope to fool him?

I stood under the live oak tree, beneath its curtain of Spanish moss, waiting for an idea. Two teenage girls, both with earphones plugged into music players, walked down York Street toward me. They passed so close to me that I could smell the body lotion they wore: lemon on one, vanilla on the other. When they walked up the path to the house, I was close behind, and when they opened the door, I stepped inside just after them.

The girls moved through the dimly lit entranceway and headed up a curving flight of stairs. I paused long enough to get a sense of where I was—a long corridor loomed ahead, with several doors opening off it—then followed them. At the top of the staircase, another corridor began. They were halfway down it, opening a door.

After they went inside, I moved quietly down the corridor. They'd left the door ajar, and I could see rows of cots inside, twenty of them or more, neatly made up. The girls removed their earphones and began to undress.

I retraced my steps, looking into two other rooms whose doors were open. One was too dark to see inside, but in the other, five teenage boys were lying on cots. They were awake, but no one was talking.

The building was some sort of dormitory, I thought. I walked down the stairs. The lighting was too dim to see many details of the artwork on the walls, but one appeared to be a print of the painting that had hung on a wall of our house in Saratoga Springs: a still life featuring a tulip, an hourglass, and a human skull, called *Memento Mori*. When we'd cleaned out the storage unit, Mãe had given it away, saying she found it depressing.

As I moved in near-darkness through the downstairs corridor, I made out a large living room, a dining room with five long tables and scores of chairs, and a room with walls of bookshelves. On impulse, I went inside.

The only light in the room came from the streetlights outside, filtered by heavy drapes. I lifted one a few inches, and in the brighter light I saw a map of the continental United States on one wall, with circles drawn on it and pins stuck in clusters. One cluster, I noticed, was around Homosassa Springs; a smaller one was in southern Georgia. Savannah was marked with a circle, as were Daytona Beach, Washington, New York, Chicago, Los Angeles, and dozens of other cities.

Papers and small cards were stacked on a library table next to a filing cabinet. I folded back the drape and tucked it behind a hook attached to the window frame, then went to the table. The cards were blank. Next to them were sheets of paper—the loyalty oaths we'd signed the night before.

I was pulling open a drawer of the filing cabinet when I sensed movement behind me. I turned, and froze.

Malcolm shut the door behind him and locked it with a key he slid into a pocket. "Come out, come out, whoever you are." He half sang the words.

He moved toward me. The light from the streetlamp glinted on his blond hair. He walked slowly, but with assurance, as if he could see me. I took a few steps to my right.

Malcolm altered his course a few steps to his left. "What's the matter, cat got your tongue?"

I veered right, nearly falling over a set of library steps. With each move I made, he moved directly in front of me. I stepped backward, toward the bookshelf.

"You know the old saying." He was less than two feet away now. Then he lunged forward. "Curiosity killed"—his right hand grabbed my amulet and pulled hard—"the *cat*."

I strained to pull away, but he was much stronger than me. The silk cord bit into my neck, making me lose concentration. I felt myself turning visible again.

Malcolm looked down at the replica of Bastet, then at me. There was no surprise in his face. "How nice of you to drop by," he said. He let go of my amulet.

I rubbed the back of my neck.

"Shall we have our little talk?" he said.

Two sofas faced each other in the room's center. He sat on one. I didn't move. I thought how stupid I'd been not to realize the amulet would be visible. It had become part of me, so familiar I rarely noticed it.

"Don't berate yourself unnecessarily." Malcolm leaned back, utterly relaxed. "The house has an extensive security system. Even if you'd been entirely invisible, the infrared sensors would have detected your presence."

Immediately I blocked my thoughts.

"That's more like it." He folded his arms across his chest. "We seem to do better as enemies than as friends, don't we? A pity, really." His voice had a slight English accent that he'd probably acquired when he and my father were postdoctoral students at Cambridge University. "But I am your friend, Ariella, more than you know."

I said, "Right. And you're my father's friend, too. That's why you tried to kill us."

"*Kill* you?" He sighed. "Quite the opposite. I've saved both your lives, more than once."

When we'd met in Sarasota, he'd told me about rescuing me when I was a child. He said he'd carried me out of range when the house in Saratoga Springs caught fire. My first memory was of that fire, but not of my rescuer.

Now he was thinking of a different fire, and he let me listen to his thoughts: that night in Sarasota, as the hurricane spiraled toward us, he came to the condominium my father rented (in a building called, preposterously, Xanadu). He intended to try to talk business with my father one last time before giving up on their research collaboration. In the parking lot he saw Dennis, my father's former assistant, unloading a canister—some chemical necessary for research, he initially thought. But Dennis's thoughts were full of guilt and confusion.

Dennis carried the canister into the elevator and Malcolm followed, making himself invisible. When Dennis entered the condo unit, Malcolm also entered, stepping around the canister and taking a seat in the kitchen.

"Raphael was asleep, and so were you," he said. "I checked. But when I came back to the kitchen, I smelled smoke. Dennis had opened the canister and ignited the vapors. I asked him what in hell he was trying to do, and he kept saying he had no choice. From his gabbling, I think he thought I was God; since he couldn't see me, he imagined that some immortal being had come to reckon with him. I hit him, mostly to make him shut up. Meanwhile the flames shot up and the smoke grew thick. It smelled of carbon monoxide.

"I turned my attention to putting out the fire. There was no extinguisher. I filled a pot at the kitchen sink and poured it on the canister, to keep it from exploding. That's when your father came into the kitchen, coughing. I don't think he even saw me."

By this time, I was sitting on the sofa, opposite him. He paused to take a breath. Every word he spoke sounded sincere, unrehearsed.

"And then?" I asked.

"I don't remember." He rubbed his eyes. "I woke up alone in the EMT ambulance. I knew I didn't want to be *there*. When they stopped, I let myself out."

"But weren't you hurt?" I could see only his silhouette now, and the gleam of his hair.

"Yes, I'd inhaled a lot of smoke. But I'm strong. I bounce back quickly. Your father, with his diet of tonics and cow's blood and artificial supplements . . ." He shook his head. "He was more vulnerable. There's no substitute for the real thing."

I didn't want to think about Malcolm's dietary habits. "What happened to Dennis?"

"Apparently he left while I was trying to put out the fire. He must have, because when I tried the door, it was locked from the outside."

I had complete access to his thoughts now. Unless he was a remarkable liar, capable of lying to himself as well as me, he was telling me the truth. Yet part of me held back. He still was the one who'd killed my best friend.

"I killed her to protect you and your father." His voice was almost a whisper. "She knew that you're vampires, and she planned to expose you. Why can't you believe that?"

I put up my hand. Once a story has a villain, it's very hard to recast him as a friend, almost as hard as it would be to make him into a hero. "Tell me some other time," I said. "I don't think I can take any more tonight."

He leaned forward, and the light from the window lit one side of his face: narrowed eye, long nose, one corner of his thin mouth. "But you said you wanted answers. Don't you want to know what's going on here?" He waved in the direction of the wall map. "Don't you want to know what *that's* all about?"

"Could we turn on a light?" The sight of his half-face made me nervous.

He switched on a table lamp, and the room sprang into being: bookshelves, fireplace, furniture. Now he had three dimensions, too. He was just a man, I realized—just a vampire, I corrected myself. He wasn't a demon, or a monster.

"Okay." I looked across at him. "What's *this* all about?"

He stood up, went to a corner cabinet, came back with a bottle and tumblers. He poured two glasses of Picardo and handed me one. I hesitated, then I took it. We drank.

He said, "Welcome to the Society of N."

∞

The house near Oglethorpe Square was a regional outpost of the Nebulists, Malcolm said. "I assume that you know who we are?"

I remembered Mãe's hand-drawn chart. "I know a few things," I said. "My mother explained the differences among the vampire sects."

"She probably got them wrong."

I began to protest.

"Sara never did understand the differences." Malcolm pushed his hair from his forehead. "Neither did Raphael. No doubt they put the Sanguinist spin on whatever they told you. They typecast us. They say they're the ones who care about preserving resources, about sustaining the earth, but they don't do much to make it happen."

"They try—"

"They aren't prepared to make it happen." Malcolm had none of my father's inhibitions about interruptions. "But we are."

"I didn't know that Nebulists *cared*." From what my father and mother had said, I'd gathered the Nebulists were self-centered, ruthless, amoral. And I let Malcolm hear that thought.

He smiled, and for the first time I thought him handsome. "Our caring takes the form of action," he said. "Ari, can you imagine a world without humans? Think for a moment. Everywhere humans go, they leave waste. They pollute the soil and the atmosphere, the ocean and the rain. They cut down trees and murder whole species of animals. I'm speaking in the simplest terms possible, but there are other, more sophisticated analyses.

"The truth is, if humans were wiped out tomorrow, the world would be a better place. Within perhaps twenty thousand years, everything made by man would be gone. The hideous houses, the factories and nuclear reactors, the skyscrapers and schools—all would crumble into dust. The air, water, and land would cleanse themselves. Species would rebound. All of that would happen on its own—and happen even sooner, if we vampires helped the re-covery process."

His speech seemed as compelling as Cameron's, at first. "So what are you proposing?" I asked. "Exterminating the human race?"

"Of course not." His tone was mildly amused, not shocked. I thought, *But you wouldn't rule extermination out.*

He heard that thought. "You're putting the Sanguinist spin on it again. Once, I admit, the Nebulists were proponents of such a plan. But we've evolved, as all intelligent beings do. Now we advocate a form of enlightened coexistence." Malcolm swirled his glass, and the Picardo gleamed ruby red as the lamplight caught it. "You will agree that things can't go on as they are?"

I nodded, slowly. All I'd seen and heard and read about environ-mental damage made clear the need for dramatic change.

"Then it's apparent to you that even enlightened humans aren't doing enough to reverse the damage to the ecosystem. Buying a hy-brid car or low-energy lightbulbs is all very well, but hardly a means of eliminating the problem."

"So what are you proposing?"

He clasped his hands over one knee. "We're proposing more meaningful modifications of human behavior that will actually make a difference. Imagine humans who act sensibly, mindful of the long-range consequences of their behavior. Imagine humans who care beyond their immediate needs and desires or gratification, who live frugally and respectfully."

I shook my head. "You can't make that happen."

"We're already making it happen." He gestured toward the map on the wall. "Each circle you see there is a seedling community. The program began five years ago. Eventually there will be more circles, and they will overlap and cover the entire continental U.S. If you went to our outposts in Europe, Asia, and Africa, you'd see similar maps."

I looked at the map and at the pins stuck in it, and I didn't understand.

Malcolm explained it for me. The pins represented potential "recruits," people identified by scouts as likely candidates for behavior modification. They were brought to regional sorting centers where they underwent a series of tests. Those who succeeded became candidates, and they were given "makeovers."

"In essence, the Nebulists offer our candidates a fresh start, a new life," he said. "Some eventually return to their home communities, but most move on. Some go to big cities—we have a number in DC, working as lobbyists and interns and aides. Others attend universities or enter the military. But first they go through supervised training at centers like this one."

I thought of Mysty. "Is that what happened—"

"—to your friend from Homosassa? Yes, she was recruited last year. Her appearance was altered to enable her fresh start. She's coming along very nicely, from what I hear. I don't take part in the actual modification process, you know. I'm just a consultant. When my visit here is over, I'll be heading back to England."

I didn't much care about his travel plans. "When you say 'modification,' do you mean brainwashing?"

"Such an outdated term." He looked disappointed. "Particularly when you consider the research that proves that free will is an illusion. The human brain essentially is programmed by DNA, and human action is causally determined. The brain is already *washed,* to use your quaint terminology.

"What we do is a form of reeducation. We wipe the slate clean. Our candidates are chosen because they're ripe for reform—they've proven, to varying extents, dysfunctional in their communities. Most of them are unhappy with themselves and their lives. What makes them wayward is what identifies them as likely future leaders, oddly enough. They simply need to be rescued from their old identities and old habits."

From what I'd seen of Mysty and the residents of the dormitory upstairs, they'd been turned into zombies. And not philosophical zombies—more like the duppies Dashay had described.

Again, he heard my thought, and he seemed pleased. "Ah yes, duppies, the Jamaican undead. Another quaint term. Although I confess it would produce a nice name for our project: the Duppification of America?" He smiled. "No, our ambassadors—that's our name for the successful candidates—are very much alive."

"Are they on drugs?"

"Most Americans are on drugs. Alcohol, mood enhancers, sedatives—all designed to promote illogical thinking and impulsive action. If a drug promotes logic and rational behavior, can that be a bad thing?"

"Is there such a drug?"

"Of course." Malcolm stood up and went to the door. He unlocked it and left the room.

I considered running away. But I stayed. I wanted to hear the rest.

Malcolm came back, carrying a leather bag shaped like a doctor's satchel. He set it on the library table, opened it, and pulled out a vial.

"This is Amrita," he said. "We named it for a Hindu term meaning 'water of life.' Short of becoming a vampire, it's the best chance humans have for long-term survival. It strengthens the immune system, promotes strong bones, enhances digestion, and improves psychological health by stabilizing moods."

It all sounded beneficial, but I had reservations. Then a question sprang in my mind: "What happened to Autumn?"

He raised his eyebrows. "Who's that?"

"Mysty's friend. Another girl who disappeared."

"I can check the files. What's her last name?"

While Malcolm was at the file cabinet, I looked around me, trying to dispel my anxiety. Why was he telling *me* all of this? The room's walls, painted cinnabar red, seemed to be closing in on me.

He pulled out a card. "Autumn Springer. Her parents must have quite a sense of humor. Yes, she was recruited, but not in Homosassa Springs. The recruiter trailed her to Georgia." He looked up at me. "The recruiter was Sal Valentine. I've met him. He's very persistent."

"She was murdered," I said. "Her body was found in the Okefenokee Swamp."

He glanced back at the card. "All it says here was that she proved resistant and was dismissed as a candidate. That can happen, you know. The scouts try to identify recruits who want to change, but sometimes they make mistakes."

"And the *mistakes* are killed?"

"I truly don't know the circumstances, Ari." Malcolm replaced the card and shut the file drawer. "Next time I see Sal, I'll ask, if you like. He's due to bring in three people tomorrow."

Sal Valentine. Now my harbinger had a name. "He tried to recruit me, too," I said.

Malcolm frowned. He riffled through another drawer in the cabinet. "Yes, you're here. You were identified as a candidate last December. Well, sometimes mistakes are made. The scouts leave written instructions, and they mark recruits—usually with a small scratch on the forearm or leg. But the recruiters don't always follow instructions. They're thugs, most of them."

I thought of Mysty's mother scratching me, back in December; but that had been an accident. Hadn't it? I put my hands on my forehead, trying to calm myself. "Are you going to kill me?"

"Kill you?" He walked to the sofa, sat down next to me. "My

dear Ari, no. I've devoted so much time already to keeping you alive. You're one of my favorite freaks."

"I'm a *freak*?"

"You're an aberration of nature." His voice was like plum-colored velvet. "You're one of only a few living half-breeds, as far as we know, and as such you're of significant interest and value to biomedical research. We don't want anything to happen to you."

"If you're not going to kill me, why are you telling me all of this?" I stared into his pale eyes. "What if I tell someone?"

He gazed back at me, his expression insulted but unalarmed. "Tell the world. No one will believe you. And in any case, our operations are set up so that we can disappear and relocate them in literally seconds." He leaned his head back against the sofa cushion. "No, I don't think you'll do anything like that. I rather think you're likely to join us."

I moved as far away from him as I could, without leaving the sofa.

"Perhaps you're not ready yet." He sounded sad. "But I respect your intelligence. The stuffy ways of the Sanguinists can't suit someone like you. My only concern is that you seem to have fallen in love—it shows in your eyes, you know. Is it with that young man who accompanied you earlier?"

I blocked my thoughts and didn't answer.

"Well, even if it is, you have choices," he said. "Haven't you heard about Revité?"

I nodded. He gestured toward his satchel. "If that's the way you want to go, I have some and I'll give it to you. You can revert to a mortal state and live a conventionally mortal life. I wouldn't advise the change—it would be a loss in terms of our research, and I think you'd be bored to death—but no one can force you to remain one of us. Vampires, unlike humans, do have free will. And believe it or not, I'd like to see you happy."

I pressed my hands against my forehead again. He'd told me too much, too fast.

"How's your father?" he asked abruptly.

I saw no point in lying to him now. "Not well." It was the first time I'd thought of my father today, and the thought made me feel guilty. "He needed time to recover from the fire, and then he took some tainted serum. Something that had quinine in it. You weren't responsible for that?"

His shock seemed genuine. "I'd never do anything to hurt Raphael. He's my oldest friend."

"That's how he thought of Dennis," I said, "and look what he tried to do." I still couldn't quite believe that Dennis had set the fire.

Malcolm nodded, slowly. "I agree. Dennis isn't the malicious sort. But maybe he was only the agent."

"What?"

His face was solemn. "Have you considered the possibility that your father's real nemesis isn't me, or Dennis, but someone else?"

"Who?"

I thought the name just before he said it: *Root.*

"But she's taken care of him since before I was born." Throughout my childhood, Root had been there, working with my father to make the tonics and sera that sustained not only us, but a network of vampires. "Why would she turn on him?"

Malcolm sighed. "Why indeed. Well, I suppose that I could be wrong."

"Yes." But my mind had already seized the idea and begun to embellish it. I'd always hated Root. It was almost too easy to cast her as the new villain.

Chapter Sixteen

With mock courtesy, Malcolm offered to walk me back to the hotel. I declined his invitation. We both knew that I could take care of myself.

As I walked down the steps, I thought of one last question. I turned around. "What were you doing tonight at the hotel?"

He stood in the doorway, looking down at me. "We have some ambassadors working at the caucus," he said. "I thought I'd check in and see them in action. We take an active interest in politics, you know. It's one more way we can try to shape the future."

He said good night again and closed the door.

As I passed the cast-iron fence that surrounded the house, I had a view of the courtyard behind it. Parked in a row were three beige Chevrolet vans. The sight of them made me want to run, but I kept my pace steady.

The cool night air outside smelled faintly of the horses who pulled carriages carrying tourists through the streets. After the stuffy air of the house, the smell was welcome, triggering memories of home. And the scent also brought me a story that Mãe had told me on one of our road trips.

When she and my father first lived together in Savannah, she went through a box of his old letters and photographs without his permission. She was curious, she said.

In the box she found a photograph of a beautiful young woman with wavy blond hair and "the face of an angel," Mãe said. Instantly, she was jealous.

For the next few weeks she never mentioned the photo to my father. But the woman's face was often in her mind, and it made her feel deeply bitter and angry. She despised this woman, whose name she didn't even know.

Mãe knew her feelings weren't rational, but she indulged them anyway. They began to poison her love for my father. Every time she looked at him, she pictured him with *her*.

Finally, one night she broke down and told him what she'd done. He seemed displeased, but not surprised, and she wanted him to react more emotionally than that. So she got the photo and tore it up in front of him.

He said, "What a pity. That's the only photograph I had of my cousin Anna."

Mãe felt stupid and ashamed, but more than that she was disappointed. She'd invested so much energy into creating a rival. And for weeks after that, the image of the blond woman would come to her, make her begin to seethe again before she realized her feelings were completely unjustified.

"Hatred easily becomes a habit," she'd said.

Her story told me how stupid I'd been to hate Malcolm. I'd created a myth about him, about his manipulations and misdeeds, and I'd carried a mental image of him with me, taking pleasure in loathing it. Now I had to let that image go.

When I'd left the house near Oglethorpe Square, he'd asked me to give his regards to my father. "One day, I hope that he and I will work together again," he said. "And perhaps you'll work alongside us."

I'd said only, "Good night." Yet for the first time I sensed his true feelings for my father: immense respect and deep, genuine affection. Whatever he'd done, he'd done for what he thought were good reasons.

The cold air and exercise began to clear the fog in my brain. But I felt tired, too tired to think about Root. Whatever she might have done, for whatever reasons—I'd come to terms with all of that tomorrow.

It was close to midnight by the time I reached the hotel. The lobby was still busy; delegates and tourists sat at the lobby bar, and a few Hillhouse students sprawled along a sofa watching sports on a large-screen TV. One of them waved to me. I waved back, but walked on toward the elevator. I'd had enough conversation for one day.

As I unlocked the door of room 408, I expected to find my roommates awake, probably drunk again. But the room was quiet, lit only by the lamp next to Rhonda's bed. Her bed was empty. I made out two forms in the other bed, two heads on the pillows, and my first thought was: *Bernadette and Rhonda? In my bed?*

I came into the room, shutting the door quietly. But it wasn't Rhonda in bed with Bernadette, I saw now. It was Walker. *It was Walker.*

Maybe I made a noise. Bernadette stirred, turned her head, rested her chin on Walker's shoulder. I couldn't tell if her eyes were open.

For the second time that night, I wanted to run. Instead I made myself walk to the closet, pull out my knapsack, stuff my things inside. Before I left, I couldn't resist taking a last look at the bed, at Bernadette's profile against Walker's neck. She seemed to be smiling in her sleep.

∞

That night I slept—or tried to—on a sofa outside one of the second-floor meeting rooms. I don't recall how much I did sleep; I remember long hours staring at the taupe-colored shade of a squat brown ceramic lamp on the table next to me, trying not to think, trying not to feel.

Finally I gave up. I found a chair by the plate-glass windows overlooking the river and watched the dirty water lighten as the sun rose in a place I couldn't see. I'd succeeded in making myself feel numb, but every two minutes or so the numbness gave way to a sensation like goose bumps along the inside of my skin. Gradually the goose bumps became sharper, like pinpricks, and threatened to intensify into stabs.

I went back down to the lobby and asked for stationery and a pen at the front desk. After writing a note to Professor Hogan (saying simply that I had to leave for personal reasons), I sealed it and handed it to the clerk.

Briefly I thought about going back to the house near Oglethorpe Square, asking Malcolm to let me stay there. I'd fit right in with the other zombies now.

But what I really wanted was to go home.

Florida was miles and miles away, but Tybee Island lay perhaps fifteen miles to the southeast. I put on a thick layer of sunblock, strapped on my backpack, and prepared myself for a good long walk.

∞

I'm forever surprised and impressed by the kindness of strangers. So many times, when I've felt ready to give up, they've made the small gestures that sustained me.

That day I lost direction twice. The first time I stopped at a gas station to ask about street names. The clerk looked at my backpack and said, "You walking?"

After he told me the best route, he insisted that I take a free bottle of water.

The second time, as I trudged along the shoulder of Route 80, a woman in a yellow two-seat convertible pulled over on the road's other side. "Where're you headed?" she shouted across to me.

So I arrived at the cottage on Tybee Beach in fine style, sitting in the convertible's passenger seat, the car radio blaring rock and roll. "You be careful now," the woman said as I climbed out. When I thanked her, she said, "Whatever it is, you'll get over it."

My face must have told her much more than I'd said.

As I stood in the bright sunlight, knocking on the cottage's front door, I felt a wave of lethargy pass through me. What was I doing here? I could have stayed where I was. So what if Walker slept with Bernadette? Was it really such a big deal?

Mãe opened the door. She looked more haggard than she had the last time I'd seen her. But she threw her arms around me, almost as if she'd expected to see me. When we pulled apart, she said, "Today he's worse. Yesterday he seemed much stronger. He even said a few words. But today he's taken a turn."

She led me into the kitchen, past the table, cluttered with cups and plates, into my father's room. His face was turned toward the wall, but his arm, still attached to an IV tube, looked thinner and frailer to me.

I felt someone watching me and instinctively looked to the left, straight into the eyes of Mary Ellis Root. She sat in a chair at the foot of his bed, an open journal in her lap. Her dark eyes gleamed at me.

When we didn't greet each other, Mãe said, "Mary Ellis came by yesterday. She's been reading to Raphael, trying to catch him up on some research."

I wanted to run away. Instead, I came closer to Root, careful to block my thoughts, keeping my eyes on hers. The gleam in her left eye seemed to contract, to flicker.

Root said, "Aren't you supposed to be at school?" Her voice was gruff, yet oily.

"I'm taking a break."

The light in her eye moved again, enough to convince me.

"You look hungry, Ariella." Mãe's voice sounded sweet and warm. "Come and take a look at what we have in the fridge."

I didn't want to leave Root alone with my father. But I needed to talk to Mãe, so I went. In the kitchen, I took her arm, pulled her down the hall, into the small bathroom. I shut the door.

"We have to call Dashay," I said. "She can help us deal with this. I think Root may be the one who made Father sick."

Mãe's eyes were wide. They looked weary, but I saw no suspicious gleam.

"Please, Mãe. Call her now and ask her to come. Tell her there's a sasa waiting for her."

"Ariella, what are you talking about?"

"I'm sure I'm right," I said, although I wasn't. *"Please."*

She looked at my face, my eyes, and shook her head. Then she said, "Very well."

While my mother went to use the telephone in her room, I went back to my father's bedside. His face was still turned to the wall, and Root apparently hadn't moved. She seemed to be reading the journal in her lap. I pulled a chair between her and my father and sat in it.

"Remember that pill I asked you to test?" I said. "The one called V?"

She raised her head. The mole on her chin had sprouted new hairs—four of them, about an inch long, dark and bristly.

"What about it?" she said.

"You made a big mistake," I said. "That was no sugar pill."

The light in her left eye intensified. "Are you telling *me* what was in that pill?"

"I'm telling you," I said, wondering what it was I was trying to tell her, wondering why my thoughts were so scattered. I shook my head, pressed my hands to my temples. Inside my brain, I heard a kind of buzz.

Mãe came in and put her arms on my shoulders. "You're tired," she said, her voice soft. "Go on now, have a snack, and then take a nap in my bed. I'll stay here and keep Mary Ellis company."

The confidence in her voice told me she'd talked to Dashay. I left the room without saying another word.

Her bed smelled of lavender and chamomile, and its cotton sheets were worn soft as flannel. I fell asleep almost before I took my shoes off.

∞

Someone was standing in the bedroom doorway, watching me sleep.

I heard my voice say, "Mama?" As far as I knew, I'd never said the word before. Perhaps as a baby I'd said it, hoping that she who had never been there before would suddenly manifest herself, respond to me.

"Not your mama."

My eyes opened. Dashay sat on the edge of the bed, her brown eyes steady on mine. She stroked my forehead with both hands and pushed back my hair. "You're all right," she said. "Broke your heart, looks like. First time always hurts the worst."

She lifted her hands and sat back. "Now you better wake up. I just had a look in at your old friend Ms. Root. We have some work to do there, you and me."

I sat up and reached for the water bottle next to my bed. But Dashay pushed my hand away from the plastic bottle.

"Where'd you get that?"

I told her about the kindness of the gas station attendant.

She read the label: "Orion Springs. Bottled in Miami." Then she moved the bottle out of my reach. "He may have been kind, all right.

But I've been hearing stories about bottled water from Miami. I'll tell you some later. Meantime, you stay away from that stuff." She held the bottle up to the light. It was a third empty. "You feel funny?" she asked me.

I laughed, and it wasn't a happy sound. The spectrum of all I'd felt in the last day fanned through me.

She lifted a patchwork tote bag from the floor and rummaged though it. She lifted out a glass bottle and handed it to me. "Drink this. It's from the springs back home."

I took a long drink from the bottle, felt the cool water flow down my throat, into my veins. My thoughts began to form clearly again. From the window came the crash of the ocean; the tide must have been coming in. I breathed deeply and drank again. When the bottle was two-thirds empty, I said to her, "I hope you brought more."

"Local water's okay." Dashay set down her bag. "At least, it tasted fine last time I was here. But yes, I did bring some more. So you finish what you have there. Wake up, get your thoughts straight. Then we need to go to work."

I drank the rest of the bottle. "Mãe's still with my father?" I asked.

"She is." Dashay wore a green-and-black batik-print dress that made a pool of freshness in the room. "Along with that Root, who's sitting in her chair like a sphinx, all full of secrets she's not telling. You know what she's up to?"

I told her about meeting Malcolm, about the moment when he and I arrived at the conclusion that Root was responsible for the fire in Sarasota. "She could have put Dennis up to it. And she could be the one who made my father sick," I said. "After all, she had the opportunities. She's the one who made his blood supplements."

"Why would she all of a sudden want to hurt Raphael?" Dashay said.

"I don't know."

She sighed. "And what happened to you? Why are you here, looking like somebody killed your best friend?"

She and I winced simultaneously.

"Ari, I'm sorry," she said.

I shook my head. I couldn't put what I felt into words, but I let her sense the depth and weight of my feelings: about losing Kathleen, and Mysty, and Autumn, and about finding Bernadette and Walker together.

After a while she said, "Didn't I tell you? Love is misery." She looked into my eyes again. "You haven't had a thing to eat, since when? Come on and help me doctor Ms. Root. Then we'll do some serious cooking."

∞

Ms. Root did not want to be doctored.

She sat, squat and impervious as a beetle, on the upholstered chair at the foot of my father's bed. Her posture told us she was not about to go anywhere.

Dashay and my mother both tried to hypnotize her. If the problem hadn't been serious, the spectacle would have been funny.

Dashay sat on the end of the bed, close to the blanket that covered my father's feet. I wondered if he heard any part of what we were saying. If he did, he showed no sign of consciousness.

"Mary Ellis, I drove up here to talk to you." Dashay's voice was singsong, deepened by an emphatic Jamaican lilt. "I came here, all this way, to talk to you. I can see your eyes, now can you see mine?"

Root smiled—the sort of smile others call a smirk. I've never liked that word.

"Look at me." Mãe moved in front of Dashay and bent over Root. "Mary Ellis, you need to take some deep breaths. In and out, deep breaths. Now your eyes are tired, and they want to close. Let them close."

Root laughed, a sound like gargling dirty water.

Dashay and Mãe alternated their efforts. I watched, agonized, sure they had no chance at putting her under. Then I noticed a half-full glass of Picardo on the small table next to Root's chair.

"I'm going to the bathroom," I said. No one seemed to notice.

In the bathroom's medicine cabinet I found a pill bottle with my mother's name on it: sleeping pills prescribed by Dr. Cho. I took six of them into the kitchen and ground them up with the bottom of a spoon. Then I used the spoon to push them into a glass. I added two healthy shots of Picardo and stirred. Next, I poured three more glasses and set them all on a tray, careful to keep the unadulterated ones on the left.

With the tray in my arms, I went back to my father's room.

"I'd find this annoying if it wasn't completely ludicrous." Root took the glass I handed her and gulped from it.

After I passed around the other glasses, I sat on the floor below the window. A sip of Picardo further cleared my head. Dashay had been right—something was in that water.

Mãe walked back and forth across the room. "You've been with our family for a long time. Raphael so admired your work, and we always thought you were our loyal friend."

"But friends don't try to poison their research partners." Dashay leaned forward from her seat on the bed, peering at Root's eyes. She sat back again. "Friends don't set fires."

They were playing good cop, bad cop. It wasn't working.

Root watched them with undisguised contempt. "What have you ever done for him?" she said to my mother. "You deserted him. You didn't take care of your own baby—the child you tricked him into having." She took another drink from the glass.

Mãe's face contorted. She wasn't strong enough to hear this.

"Yes, I know about that." Root's voice was smug. "I know about all of it."

I tried to tune in to her thoughts, but heard only the usual static.

"You know nothing." Dashay's voice was like a hiss. "You think you know, and all you know is lies."

Root tipped her head to one side. "When it comes to lies, you're the expert here. You lied to your family back in Jamaica, you lied to that poor half-breed Bennett. And when they realized you were lying, they all abandoned you."

Dashay flinched.

I thought, *Bennett is half-human, like me?*

Root must have heard my thought. She turned to me. "Yes, another half-breed like you. Another child that in the end, no one wanted. A constant embarrassment to humans and vampires alike. You'll never be accepted by them, and you'll never truly be one of us."

My eyes went to my father, instinctively expecting him to defend me. But he never moved.

No one spoke. She'd managed to wound each of us, and her satisfaction was evident. She sat back in her chair and finished the glass of Picardo.

Dashay sat on the bed, her shoulders slumped. Mãe leaned against the wall near me, her eyes closed. I kept my eyes on Root. And the second her eyes began to glaze, I said, "Dashay. Now."

Dashay raised her head. Root's eyelids had begun to droop, but she tried to open them wider as Dashay moved toward her.

"I see you now." Dashay's voice crooned, as if she were talking to a baby. "Oh, you're so pretty. So ugly, ugly as sin. What a beauty you are. What a cretin. No mother could love you. My little beauty. Come out now, come to me."

Her voice deepened, then rose. I put my hands over my ears. Mãe sat next to me, put her arm around my shoulders.

Was it ten minutes or an hour later that we saw the first sign of it? None of us could remember, afterward. But we all watched as a trickle of black fluid emerged from the corner of Root's left eye. The trickle thickened, coagulated, and became a kind of blob that oozed out onto her cheek. Dashay crooned and beckoned and cupped her hands, waiting to receive it.

I didn't see the last part—Dashay bent over Root, hiding her face. Then Dashay spun around, and I uncovered my ears.

"Quick, Sara. Get me a plastic bag." Dashay's hands pressed together. Between them I saw the sasa: black and slimy looking, an amorphous shape against her fingers.

Mãe ran out and came back with a bag. She held it open while Dashay slid the thing inside and zipped it shut. "Want to see?" she asked me. There was a weird pride in her voice, as if she were a midwife instead of an exorcist.

"I can see from here." I wanted to see, but I didn't want to get too close. The sasa looked like black gelatin, marked by one pink ring—the mouth that must have attached itself to Root.

"Ugly," Mãe said, her voice low.

Root lay back in the chair, her eyes closed, the bristles on her chin aimed at the ceiling.

"Never saw one so big." Dashay held the bag by its top edge. "Never had to work so hard to get one out."

"Get it out of here," Mãe said.

While Dashay disposed of the sasa outside, Mãe and I looked at each other. We felt exhausted.

I pointed at Root. "What are we going to do with her?"

My mother took a deep breath. "We're going to wait until she opens her eyes. Then, we're going to hypnotize her."

∞

Her demon gone, Root wasn't hard to put under. The lingering effects of the sedative helped.

Dashay returned, after washing her hands for five minutes. She sat next to me, and we watched Mãe interrogate Root.

"Why did you do it?" Her voice was low and even. "Why did you try to kill Raphael?"

"I never tried to kill him." Root's eyes were open wide now, but they had a dazed expression. For a moment I thought of Old Joe, and I wondered where he might be now.

Mãe consulted the list of questions we'd written out moments before. "Did you ask Dennis to start the fire at Xanadu?"

"Xanadu." She sighed. "Dennis set the canister in the wrong place. I told him where to put it. He set the fire in the kitchen instead. Stupid."

"Where was he supposed to put it?"

"In the doorway of the child's room." She said it without any emotion.

Dashay reached for my hand.

"So the fire was meant to kill Ariella?" My mother's voice sounded strained, as if she were struggling to keep it calm.

"Of course. You can't think it was meant for Raphael?" Root's face seemed to lose shape, suddenly; it spread into sadness. "I didn't aim to hurt Raphael. I was after his attention. It was high time! All those years I worked with him, and he considered me like a—like an appliance. Something he used to produce the results he wanted."

Mãe glanced back at us, shook her head, then turned to Root again.

"So you made Dennis start a fire to get Raphael's attention?" she asked.

"And to kill the child. A half-breed shouldn't have survived a fire like that, and she wouldn't have, if it had been set properly. I should have done it myself." Root nodded vigorously. "I should have known better than to count on Dennis. All he cared about was becoming a vampire. He never paid attention to details."

"That was the deal?" Mãe sounded authoritative again. "Dennis would become a vampire?"

"I said I'd make him a vampire."

So she was *one of us,* I thought.

"But he botched it. I told him that, once we left the unit. 'All deals are off,' I told him, and you should have seen him then!" She grinned. Without question, she was the ugliest person I'd ever seen.

"As for Raphael, I gave him just enough quinine to make him realize he needed new tonic, that he needed me around to make it. I hadn't seen him in months. No one told me how ill he was. I kept asking. Finally, Dashay told me he was here."

Dashay was thinking that she should have kept her mouth shut. But I disagreed. If she had, we'd likely never have found out about Root's sasa and her obsession with my father. Were they linked?

"So I drove up yesterday. And he didn't seem too bad. He talked, and he looked as if he were on the mend." Her eyes moved slowly from side to side as she talked, as if she were watching a metronome or a Ping-Pong match.

"Yes, he did look better." Mãe's voice was so low I could barely hear it. "Mary Ellis, did you do something to him?"

"I gave him a shot."

We all stared at her.

"You gave him an injection?" Mãe's voice sounded hoarse. "What was in the shot?"

"A little quinine," Root said. "Not enough to do him real harm. Just enough to keep him still, enough to make him realize how much he needs me. In a few days I'll bring him back again. I'll save his life." She nodded, sure of her plan.

Mãe turned to us. "Dashay," she whispered. "Call Dr. Cho. Tell her we need her *now*."

When Dashay had left the room, Mãe said to me, "Anything else?"

"Ask about the V drug," I whispered.

She looked down at her list. "Mary Ellis, Ariella gave you a pill to analyze, a pill called Vallanium. What's in the pill?"

"Vallanium is an addictive depressant, a semisynthetic opiate." Her voice was crisp, as if she were reciting from memory. "It has the potential to permanently alter brain structure. Two capsules daily create a mild euphoria, but over time the drug disrupts normal brain activities. It renders users incapable of reading or logical analysis. Cessation of use causes severe withdrawal symptoms."

I thought of Walker, and I shivered.

"You seem to know a lot about it," Mãe said.

"I should." Root looked pleased. "I helped develop that drug. We sold the patent to a group in Miami."

"Ask her about Amrita," I whispered.

This one wasn't on Mãe's list. "Um, what about Amrita?"

"It's an antidepressant. One of the so-called lifestyle drugs, derived from jimson weed. It alters the brain, inhibiting certain neurotransmitters and enhancing others, producing selective amnesia. Amrita interferes with DNA replication and RNA transcription by alkylation and cross-linking the strands of DNA. It renders users sterile."

Sterile? Malcolm hadn't said anything about that.

"Did you make that one, too?" Mãe said.

"No. Amrita was created by a Nebulist research team in Britain."

"Are you a Nebulist?"

Her face contorted. "I don't belong to a sect. If I had to choose one, I'd lean toward the Colonists. They know how to keep humans in their place, and they don't tolerate half-breeds." Even though she was hypnotized, her eyes seemed to veer in my direction.

"Then why did you make Vallanium?"

Root shot back, "To see if I could. You won't understand that. *You* are not a scientist."

Mãe sent me the thought, *Enough?*

Too much, I thought.

Mãe recited the standard litany: When Root awakened, she wouldn't remember being hypnotized or drugged. She wouldn't remember a thing she'd said. And she would never again try to harm our family or anyone else.

It was a tall order, I thought. Why not ask her to find a cure for cancer?

Mãe heard me and sent me admonishment: *This is no time to be sassy.*

While Dashay and I made dinner, I asked her, "Did you drown the sasa in the ocean?"

"No, in the rain barrel out back." She spooned pesto over the angel's-hair pasta. "Then I buried it. You don't *need* to bury them—they're harmless once they're dead—but this one was so very nasty that I didn't want to leave it lying around."

We ate dinner in my father's room, balancing plates on our laps. We didn't want to leave him alone.

Root had come out of her trance, and she sat, calm as a Buddha, twirling pasta onto a fork. She had no idea what she'd put us through. She didn't even remember what she'd done to my father. Her demon gone, she was the familiar churlish woman I'd known since my childhood. I wanted to slap her.

I sent Dashay the thought: *Why do we have to feed her?*

Dashay sent back: *Try to act normal.*

Root glowered at us.

We didn't talk much at first, but the food revived us. Mãe wanted to know what I was studying, and I told her about the Third-Parties Caucus. "There's one candidate who may run for president," I said. "Have you heard of Neil Cameron?"

Mãe and Dashay hadn't.

Root said, "His name is familiar. He's the senator from Georgia, right?"

I didn't want to have a conversation with her, but I made myself nod.

"He's a vampire." She sucked the pasta from her fork and began to twirl another forkful as she chewed. I'd never seen anyone consume pasta as powerfully as Root did.

She inhaled another mouthful, chewed, and swallowed. "He'll never make it," she said.

"Why not?" I must have spoken more passionately than I'd intended, because Dashay and my mother stopped eating to watch me.

"Eventually his true nature will come out." Root patted a napkin across her thick lips. "Some reporter will see him drinking blood, or one of his donors will talk to the press."

"Maybe he takes tonic instead."

Root shook her head, as if she knew better.

"What if he decides to run as a vampire candidate?" I hadn't thought much about it until now. "What if he doesn't hide who he is?"

"Then he'd be an idiot." Root took a swig of Picardo. "Only he's not. I met him once. He's an old soul, probably a hundred and fifty years old by now. He knows better than to come out of the box.

"Americans will never elect a vampire." Root belched—an awful noise that reminded me of the furnace in the basement of our house in Saratoga Springs.

A hundred and fifty years old, I thought. *That means a hundred-thirty-six-year age gap.*

Dr. Cho strutted into the room and said, "What sort of circus is this?"

Chapter Seventeen

D r. Cho shooed us out of my father's room so that she could tend to him. She looked angry, as if she blamed us for his relapse—and later, when we told her about Root's part in it, she seemed skeptical.

We didn't tell her about the sasa. We didn't think she'd believe in such things.

Root was ready to leave. She said that she'd be back the next day.

"No." Mãe's voice was clear and firm. "Once Raphael is ready to work again, we'll let you know."

Root stared at Mãe as if she'd never seen her before. Then, muttering something we couldn't hear, she left.

Dashay nearly fell into a kitchen chair. "Sweet mother of life, what a night."

I sat next to her. Mãe poured us glasses of cold spring water from the bottles Dashay had stored in the refrigerator. Then she took a chair across from mine. We sat and listened to the ocean, felt the breeze from the open window, rubbed our eyes. I wanted to scream.

Instead I broke the silence. "We didn't ask Root what's in the bottled water. I bet she'd know."

Mãe looked confused until Dashay explained her theory. "Go fetch the bottle the nice nice man gave to you," she said to me. "We can ask Dr. Cho to have it analyzed."

"Better give her a sample of our tap water, too. And some of that water you brought from home." Mãe stretched her arms behind her and shook the tension out of them. "First the bees are tainted. Now the water. What's going on?"

"I don't know for sure," Dashay said, "but it looks to me as if someone's out to take control of nature. Manipulate it, use it. I don't know why. But I think Bennett is one of the victims."

Then she confessed: the week before, she'd driven to Atlanta again. "This time I didn't even bother going to his place," she said. "I knew that woman would be there. So I called him up, told him the Internal Revenue folks needed to meet with him."

Mãe explained it for me. "Vampires have to be careful to file tax returns. Otherwise the government comes after us, takes away our property, may even put us in jail."

"Bennett came downtown to the federal office building, and I was waiting." Dashay sighed. "I put on a pretty dress and all, think-ing he'd see me and realize what a dog he'd been. It didn't work. I touched his arm and I looked into his eyes. I admitted I'd been the one who called him, not the tax man. I told him we needed to talk. All that time he looked right through me. Finally he said, 'So I don't need to meet with the IRS?' And then he bolted right out of there, back to that woman he met on the plane."

"So you think maybe he drank the water?"

"Of course he drank the water!" Dashay slammed down her own glass. "What else do you do on a plane? Unless you're smart, like me, and don't ever take what strangers hand you."

Mãe and I each thought she was being—*a little crazy,* Mãe thought; *somewhat irrational,* I thought. But who knew? She'd been right about the sasa.

"Did Bennett have a sasa in his eyes?" Mãe asked.

Dashay shook her head, making her long green glass earrings bounce. "When I looked into his eyes, I saw nothing. You understand? I couldn't even hypnotize him. Nobody was home. But he was carrying a bottle with him, and you know what it said on the label? Orion Springs."

"I don't understand why you even went to see him." Normally I wouldn't have made such a comment, but tonight was not normal. "I thought you were with Burton these days."

Dashay didn't seem offended. "Cecil takes me out to dinner," she said. "Sometimes we drive down to Tampa and go dancing, have a bite at this little supper club we go to. There's no harm in that."

"Why can't we be like geese and mate for life?" I said.

They seemed stunned. Then they made weird noises, my mother and her best friend, noises that mixed amazement and sympathy and laughter. And I was *not* trying to be funny.

Dr. Cho came out of the bedroom, closing the door quietly behind her. "Glad you're having fun," she said. "Well, I think he'll be all right. Now do you think you can keep him stable and not let anyone give him injections?"

"Root has been banned." Mãe spoke again in her hardheaded voice, so different from her usual Savannah drawl. "We'll keep watch."

Dr. Cho turned to me. "What are you doing here?"

"I came home for the weekend."

"But it's *Wednesday*."

"I was on a field trip in Savannah," I said. "I dropped by to see how things were going."

"That's fine," she said, "but don't you have schoolwork to do?"

It was none of her business, really. But she was right. I had a paper due early the following week: an analysis of what we'd seen at the caucus. I had a working thesis for the paper, and even a tentative title: "Situating Outsiders in Contemporary Culture." The paper I really wanted to write would have a different title: "Eternal Outsiders: Vampires as Outlaws in the Mortal World."

"Yes, I have schoolwork to do." I'd hoped to have a few days on Tybee to lick my wounds—a cliché of which I'm fond. But maybe it was better for me to go back than wallow in emotions.

Dr. Cho nodded briskly. "I'll take you back tomorrow, if you like. I have a few calls to make near Hillhouse."

My mother made soft sounds of protest, but Dashay said, "Ari needs to finish things up. You wouldn't want her to flunk out in her first semester."

After the doctor left, my mind began to sift through the implications of what Root had told us.

"Mãe," I said, "what are we going to do?" Then I felt guilty for asking, because she looked so tired.

She bent over the table, her hands clasped. "Do?"

"About the drugs. So many people are taking V. And the kids taking Amrita—I'll bet they don't know it's making them sterile."

Dashay said, "Well, we'd better find out who's distributing the drugs and make them stop."

She knew as well as we did how difficult such a task would be.

"I can't come up with an answer tonight, Ariella." Mãe pushed back her chair. "Raphael needs me now. Once we get him on his feet again, then we can think about saving the world."

I nodded. But the weight of what we'd learned sat on my chest all night.

∞

The next morning, I looked in on my parents—my father breathing deeply, his eyes closed, my mother huddled in the same chair Root had occupied the night before. I kissed both of them. In the kitchen I hugged Dashay good-bye.

"Be careful," she said. "Don't worry too much. We'll figure this thing out."

Then I climbed into Dr. Cho's hybrid car and buckled my seat belt. She looked across at me, her black hair loose over her shoulders. "Do you know how to drive?"

I said no.

Some mother she's got, Dr. Cho thought.

"I never asked to learn," I said. "I'm only fourteen."

"Fourteen going on forty." She started the car and, on the way out of town, pulled into a church parking lot. There she gave me my first driving lesson.

My initial nervousness gave way to elation as the car moved around the lot, braking and turning. When she told me it was time to stop, I said, "Please, one more lap."

"You're a natural," she said. "You should ask your parents about getting a license."

We changed places, and she drove us off the island.

"Is my father ever going to be himself again?" I tried to keep emotion out of my voice, but it wasn't entirely possible.

"He'll be better than his old self. Just you wait." She drove as fluidly as Mãe, but with more emphatic stops and starts. "Now that he's off that old formula and onto mine, he'll have a full emotional range. His feelings have been suppressed for years, thanks to that Root woman." She shook her head. "What was *that* about, anyway?"

"She loved him," I said. "And she hated my mother and me for being in the way."

"How melodramatic."

"It was more than melodrama." I didn't know how much to tell her. "Last night Dashay removed a thing from her eye."

"What sort of thing?"

I described the sasa, not using the word.

"And she extracted it how?"

Once again, I felt as if I were being interrogated. "I couldn't see it all."

"Sounds as if it might have been a tumor." She was angry. "No job for an amateur."

"But Dashay's done it before." I was probably making things worse, I realized, but I kept talking. "She has the ability to see these things in the eye."

"Sounds as if she's practicing iridology."

"What's that?"

"It's an alternative medical practice," she said. "The theory is that defects in the iris indicate tendencies toward particular illnesses. Iridologists use elaborate maps of the iris, linking locations to certain organs and glands. It's largely bogus, of course. But even traditional Western medicine acknowledges that the eyes can be indicators of diseases."

"Dr. Cho, I appreciate you talking to me about these things," I said. "But my head is kind of full right now."

She gave me a quick, curious look. "Is the serum I gave you working out?"

"I seem to have more energy," I said. "That is, when I'm not sleep-deprived. And I feel things very deeply."

"Aren't those good signs?"

"I guess." Feeling deeply wasn't much fun, I thought.

"Better to feel than not," she said. The car moved onto the Islands Expressway.

"I guess. I wouldn't want to be a zombie, like Mysty."

Then I realized: she didn't know about Mysty, or the house near Oglethorpe Square. As we drove, I told her about the recruiting, and the "makeovers," and the use of Amrita. While I was at it, I told her about V, too. It turned out she'd heard about that drug.

"I see kids at the clinic who use V," she said. "But this Amrita stuff sounds really serious. Making people sterile without their consent—do you know how bad that is?"

"What can we do about it?"

"We need to talk to the authorities." She said it decisively.

My heart sank. I'd had enough of the police and the FBI.

"No, Ari." She turned to me and smiled. "I mean the *vampire* authorities."

∞

As someone who'd spent several months studying politics, I'd thought I had a basic understanding of how governance systems worked. But Dr. Cho showed me that I didn't know much.

Vampires don't have police. We don't have a separate government or court system. But we do have a group that arbitrates and advises: the Council on Vampire Ethics, or COVE. Known generally as the Council, it comprises ten members selected by a group of former members. Members serve ten-year terms. Some represent sects and others are independent. They range in age from forty to one thousand years.

"The age thing is a little skewed, you might say," Dr. Cho said. "Why not have younger representatives? But younger vampires tend to focus on learning how to live, not how to make judgments about others. And in the end, age isn't important, anyway. Wisdom and experience are what count."

I thought of Cameron, and I wondered how important his age might prove to be.

"So the Council has the power to make the Nebulists stop their ambassador program?"

"Not power in the sense you mean it. They don't try to force anyone to do anything." Cho braked hard and made a decisive turn off the main road.

"I hope that you're past the good-versus-evil battleground way of thinking about conflict," she said. "It's archaic. Resolving problems demands delicate negotiations that are premised on mutual respect. If the Council considers an issue and takes a position on it, their judgment is communicated throughout the vampire world. It carries enormous influence. It has the clout of tradition behind it."

We were entering the Hillhouse campus now. I stopped thinking about big issues and turned to my own problems. How would I face Walker? What would I say to Bernadette? I suddenly wished the drive weren't over. I wanted to tell the doctor my sorrows.

Dr. Cho stopped the car abruptly. "Ari, go and write your papers. Don't worry about the Nebulists now. I'll contact the Council and report all you've said. Okay?"

"Thank you." I felt relieved knowing that someone was doing something to help Mysty and the others.

"And I'll let you know the second I get the lab reports on the water samples." She got out of the car as I did and walked around it to give me a hug. "Meantime, better not drink the water here, either. Stick to Picardo. It's safer."

❧

I expected awkwardness. I even anticipated an ugly scene. What I didn't expect was to find Bernadette back in our room, sitting on the carpet, sewing.

"Oh, hey, where've you been?" Her eyes had the now familiar glazed look.

"I had some personal business," I began, but she wasn't listening. In her head she was humming a tuneless little song—dah dah *dah* dah, dah dah *dah* dah, dah dah *dah* dah.

"What are you doing here?" I said.

"Me? Oh, I moved back." She finished a line of stitches and bit off the thread with her teeth. "There," she said, admiring her sewing. "Walker's sleeve is good as new."

"I thought you moved in with Jacey." The mention of Walker brought back the image of the two of them in my hotel bed.

"It didn't work out." Her tone was nonchalant. She stood up and threw the shirt toward a chair. It fell on the floor. She giggled.

I looked at the calendar over my desk. Three weeks until the last class, and then exam week. Afterward I'd go back to Tybee. My father would be well again—better than well—and I'd tell him everything, everything that had happened, and he'd make sense of it all. He'd know what to do. And my mother would be able to rest, and the three of us would—

"Ari, Ari, we're going to happy hour at the Anchor downtown. Come with!" Bernadette stood up and danced across the carpet, tripping over her feet, collapsing onto her bed.

The Anchor was a townies' bar that served Hillhouse students grudgingly, knowing that most of their IDs were fake. "No thanks," I said. "I have a paper to write."

After she left, the room filled with golden stillness. I picked up the clothes she'd discarded on my bed and desk and tossed them onto her bed. Then I opened my laptop, sat down, and wrote the first half of my American Politics paper.

On the way to dinner that night, I saw Jacey. Her hair was unbraided, and it spread over her shoulders like a cape.

She came up to me, looked hard at my eyes, touched my arm as if to be sure I was real. "Thank goodness," she said. "Ari, when you didn't come back with the others, I thought you'd been disappeared. Like your friend."

"I went to visit my family."

We took quick short steps down the incline that led to the cafeteria. I tried not to see the shrubs where, less than a month before, Walker had first kissed me. But I did see them, and I remembered.

"Thank goodness," Jacey said again. "The others came back all weird—except for Richard, and he was weird before, but in a different way. Walker and Bernie and Rhonda, they're high all the time."

"I noticed."

We jumped over the low stone fence that bordered the paved path below us. No one followed the paths at Hillhouse; everyone devised shortcuts through the landscape.

"Walker doesn't do Walker things anymore. You know, magic tricks and juggling and singing and playing guitar. He acts all spaced out."

I missed my old Walker, suddenly.

"Rooming with Bernie drove me crazy." Jacey had to take two steps for every one of mine. "It was hard enough before, when she acted depressed and critical and mean. Now she's Ms. Mellow. What she says doesn't make sense. She seems to get worse every day."

I stopped walking and faced her—looked down into her face, more accurately. "Jacey, will you trust me if I tell you something?"

"I trust you," she said. "You were the only one brave enough to spend the night with me in the swamp."

"I think that what's going on with Bernadette and the others is just as strange as what happened that night."

Her eyes narrowed, and she made them even smaller as I spoke.

"They're taking stuff that makes them pseudo-mellow. Have you heard of V?"

"Half the campus is on V," she said. "Bernie offered me some two days ago."

"Did you try it?"

"I can't handle drugs," she said. "I tried to smoke pot once and I gagged."

"Anybody you care about, tell them not to take it." But even as I said it, I doubted anyone would listen to her.

We entered the student union. The stairs to the cafeteria were crowded. Jacey and I made our way downstairs and went through the line, setting plates on our trays. At the end of the line, she pulled a glass out of a rack and a bottle of Orion Springs water from a bowl of ice.

I grabbed the bottle, put it back, and set the glass under the milk dispenser instead. "Don't drink the water," I whispered. "Trust me."

We were seated at a long table, eating, when I realized: *How do I know the milk is safe?*

∞

As I wrote my assignments and went to class, part of my mind focused on class work. The other part watched students around me disengaging from academic life. Few went to class. The library was deserted.

The duppification of America. Malcolm's phrase began to haunt me. I couldn't tell if I was a paranoiac or a prophet, and I hoped I wasn't either.

Even Professor Hogan had changed. Her voice and posturings were less brittle now, although her tone continued to rise at the end of each phrase. She'd been born to ask questions, it seemed.

"Where's your paper, Walker?" She'd worn the same skirt to class for a week.

"I'm, you know, working on it." Walker didn't shave anymore, but the stubble on his face wasn't yet a beard. He grinned at Professor Hogan, and she said, "Whatever?"

Then Walker said to me, "How's it going?" His blue eyes were glassy.

"It's going," I said. This version of Walker didn't attract me in the least.

The professor called on two more students, then seemed to lose her train of thought. "Make sure you've all registered to vote?" she said.

Another activity I was too young for, I thought. Unless I used my fake ID to register. Unless I lied again.

Dr. Cho called my cell phone a day or so later. The Sassa spring water was pure. The Tybee tap water contained chlorine and the usual trace elements. "Nothing to worry about," she said.

But the bottled water was loaded with the same opiates found in V.

"How can that be?" I said. "Isn't the quality of bottled water monitored?"

"Yes, the FDA is supposed to monitor it."

Is the Food and Drug Administration doing its job? I began to feel like a conspiracy theorist, or like Autumn, who'd found the existence of UFOs more credible than the government's claims to the contrary.

"Orion Springs is a fairly new company, based in Miami," Dr. Cho said. "Council is aware of the situation. They may call you to give testimony."

"Where are they, anyway?" I asked.

"They move around." Her voice sounded clipped, as if she were busy. "Have you talked to your mother? Your father is recovering nicely. He took his first walk on the beach yesterday."

"That's good news." I still felt wary about calling Mãe. But if someone *was* monitoring my phone, they certainly heard an earful that night.

When the call ended, I made a vow to talk to Bernadette about taking V, although I doubted it would do any good.

But Bernadette didn't come home that night. I went out into the main lounge area, littered with students. She wasn't there, either.

Richard and his girlfriend (she wasn't in any of my classes, and I never did learn her name) sat in front of a television set, watching a hockey game. He waved me over.

"Jacey says you're telling people not to drink water," he said.

"Bottled water can be risky," I said carefully.

"Bottled water, tap water—it's all risky." He leaned forward, his fuzzy hair catching the light from the TV. "Who knows what the government puts in our water? The Social Ecologists Club has been on to that issue for more than a year. You ought to come to our next meeting."

"I'm not much of a joiner," I said, and excused myself.

I walked through the corridors on all three floors of the dorm, looking into the rooms with open doors. Then I gave up on Bernadette. Why should I care where she spent the night? So long as she showed up eventually. So long as she didn't completely disappear.

Chapter Eighteen

The next two weeks passed before I knew where I was or what I was doing. Our professors suddenly elevated their expectations and demands. When I thought I couldn't read or write another word, I read another book and wrote another paper.

This, it turned out, was the Hillhouse tradition: low pressure on students all semester coupled with certainty that their self-motivation would drive them to produce first-rate results by semester's end.

The tradition took some getting used to. Three first-year students and two sophomores gave up and went home to recover from stress. Most of the juniors and seniors knew enough to stock up on caffeine and pills that kept them awake; they strode among us with bloodshot eyes and cynical sneers, like battle-hardened veterans.

But while some of us—such as Jacey, Richard, and me—virtually lived in the library and spent hour after hour at the computer keyboard when we weren't in class or at our work assignments, a large number of the others blissfully self-medicated themselves against academic achievement. I was tired of the sight of Bernadette—yes, she did come back—wandering in and out of our room at all hours, sometimes with Walker in tow, sometimes with another boy or a couple of girls. She'd given up regular hygiene habits, and I could literally smell her before she came in. Sometimes I found a T-shirt or underwear that belonged to me, balled up on the floor, carrying the same smell. I washed the T-shirt, but I threw the underwear away.

Walker didn't smell yet, probably because he liked to walk in the rain. Still, when I stood near him during our shifts at the recycling center, I noticed how straggly his hair and beard had become. He talked to me sometimes, a kind of stream-of-consciousness ramble. I felt sorry for him. After a while, I tried to avoid him.

Those two weeks were the period when the campus split into two groups, defined by use of the drug Vallanium. The younger students seemed more prone to take it, maybe because they tended to be less self-assured, struggling for a sense of identity. But I was struggling, too. If I'd tried the drug, I might have been one of them; since I hadn't, I had a clear-eyed view of its effects, and the sight was not attractive.

Early one morning I awoke with a start. Someone was in the room, rustling papers at my desk. I switched on the light that re-placed my lithophane lamp—an ugly ceramic lamp I'd rescued from the recycling center.

Bernadette was leaning over my desk.

"What are you doing?"

"Looking for your politics paper." She blinked, adjusting to the light. "I'm stuck. Reading yours might help me."

"You want to copy my paper?"

"Just a little bit." She smiled at me.

I slid out of bed and went to the desk. "You have no right to go through my things."

"Whatever." She yawned again and went back to her bed.

"And stop taking my clothes." I tried to keep the anger out of my voice, but it came through. "You already took Walker. Isn't that enough?"

She pulled blankets up to her chin. "You don't have to be so up-pity about it. Anyway, I didn't take Walker. You can sleep with him, too, anytime."

I gave up.

I stacked the papers on my desk and left the room with them and a blanket in my arms. Tomorrow I'd lock them in a suitcase. Better yet, maybe I'd find a new roommate.

Jacey found me sleeping in the lounge the next morning. When I told her what happened, she said I should hide my work in her room. "You can move in with me, if you want," she said.

Later that day, I moved my things into Jacey's room.

∽

Once I turned in my papers and classes ended, some of the pressure decreased. Still ahead were exams in philosophy and literature, but I didn't need to prepare for them. I knew the material already.

Now I had time to catch up with laundry, talk to Dashay on the phone, and even, one Friday afternoon, collect my mail—something I rarely bothered to do, since no one wrote to me. The wall of metal mailboxes was in the student center basement, near the cafeteria. I turned the combination lock. Under some fliers advertising events long passed, I found a small blue envelope, with my name and address written in sharp strokes of black ink.

A small blue card inside was engraved with the initials NC in indigo blue. The handwriting read: "I'm going sailing this Saturday. If you'd like to come along, call the number below. A car will pick you up and bring you out to St. Simon's, where I keep the boat. Hope you can make it. Neil."

I'd never been sailing, or to St. Simon's Island—part of a chain of islands off the Georgia coast that included Tybee. What would I wear? I didn't know how to handle a rudder or tie special knots. What if I made a fool of myself? My head filled with anxious thoughts and questions, along with the certainty that no matter what, I was going to see Cameron again.

Jacey wasn't in the dorm room, so I took my cell phone from

my backpack and called the number on the card. After two rings, a woman's voice said, "You've reached voice mail for the home of Neil Cameron. Please leave a message after the tone."

I left my name and number, and hung up. Then I went to the closet and looked at my options. I looked best in the blue silk dress, but one didn't wear dresses to go sailing, did one? Jeans and a T-shirt weren't special enough. He'd already seen my trouser suit, but perhaps he wouldn't remember it—

My cell phone played the familiar notes from *Swan Lake,* and I grabbed it. "Hello?"

A man's voice said he was returning my call. It wasn't Cameron's.

"I was responding to Neil Cameron's invitation to go sailing," I said.

"Excuse me?"

"He sent me a note," I said. "He told me to call this number if I wanted to go sailing tomorrow."

"Neil's in DC." I heard static and noise that sounded like papers rustling. "Wait a sec. That invitation was for last weekend, when he was out at St. Simon's. Looks like you missed the boat."

Mortified is a word I rarely use, because it means "gangrenous" as well as "embarrassed." But that day, I said, "I'm mortified," without reservation.

"Don't be," the voice said. "I'll tell Neil you called."

When Jacey came back late that afternoon and found me lying in bed, fully clothed, staring at the ceiling, she said, "Oh, rocks. Did you fail an exam?"

"I missed the chance to do something really special," I said.

She grinned. "Is that all?"

I quoted the Whittier line: "For of all sad words of tongue or pen, the saddest are these: 'It might have been!'" I threw my arm over my eyes so that I couldn't see her laughing.

Then I quoted Longfellow: "Ships that pass in the night, and speak each other in passing, / Only a signal shown and a distant voice in the darkness; / So on the ocean of life, we pass and speak one another, / Only a look and a voice, then darkness again and a silence."

"Ari, stop." Her voice was serious now. "That's too depressing."

"So is my life." I wallowed in the deep pink pleasure of self-pity.

"Now you sound like Bernadette," she said.

That was enough to make me sit up.

"Come on," she said. "Grab a sweater. I've got just the remedy for you. We're going to All-Mart."

I'd never been to an All-Mart, and I had no desire to go. "Aren't we supposed to boycott places like that?"

"Yes!" she said. "They mistreat the environment. They exploit workers. But we're not going to buy anything. We're going to take notes!"

I didn't move. "I didn't think they had All-Marts around here."

"There's one near Waycross."

Waycross was at least forty-five miles away, near the entrance to the Okefenokee Swamp.

"I'll drive," Jacey said. "It will be fun. A real road trip!"

I supposed I had nothing better to do.

∞

In her car, Jacey told me about the minicourse she was taking called Corporate Ethics. "It's kind of theoretical," she said. "For my final paper, I want to make it real. If we're lucky, we'll see some All-Mart abuse in action."

Her car was old and battered looking. I wished it were mine.

We passed gas stations and vacant lots for sale, a Baptist church, a sign that read PRENATAL CARE CEMETERY, and several roadside shrines featuring crosses that bore the names of highway accident victims. Most of the shrines were festooned with artificial flowers and wreaths, and one was attached to four helium-filled balloons. We rode on concrete bridges over brown rivers. The marquee of a used car lot read GIVE GOD THE GLORY.

I clutched my cell phone, willing it to ring. When it didn't, I reminded myself that service was spotty in this part of southeastern Georgia.

Jacey sat on two cushions to let her see past the steering wheel. She talked most of the way.

"Tonight we get a full moon," she said.

"Then it must be a blue moon." The moon had been full early this month, when I'd first been to Tybee Island.

"Really? What shade of blue?" Jacey's enthusiasm never annoyed me. It was refreshingly genuine, in contrast with the attitudes of most Hillhouse students.

"Not literally blue," I said. "It's a term for the second full moon within a month."

"We heard about blue moons last year in my folklore class." Jacey pulled into the All-Mart parking lot. "That's when the moon talks to people who've been unlucky in love."

"Do you really believe that?"

She parked the car and we got out. "I'd like to believe it. I'd like to hear what it would say to me."

I realized that never once had I seen Jacey with a boyfriend—or girlfriend, for that matter. I'd been so wrapped up in myself that I never wondered if she was happy.

"Thanks for driving," I was saying, when I noticed the van: beige, Chevrolet, bald man at the wheel. I felt the words freeze as I spoke them. I saw only the back of the driver's head, but it looked like Sal Valentine's. I wondered if he'd followed us.

The van had parked along the curb outside the store entrance. A girl smoking a cigarette leaned against the passenger door, talking to the driver inside.

As we approached the store, I told Jacey to go in without me. "I'll catch up in a minute," I said.

She looked surprised, but she kept walking.

I came closer to the van. "Excuse me," I said, loud enough to make other shoppers turn around.

The girl turned. She had short red hair, and she looked about fifteen.

"Get away from here." I pitched my voice lower now, but I made each word as emphatic as I could. "This guy is trouble. He abducts girls. He killed a friend of mine. Get away *now*."

She didn't move. She didn't even blink. She took a drag on the cigarette, and that's when I noticed her eyes. They looked lifeless as a store mannequin's.

It was too late. She'd already been recruited.

I felt Sal's eyes fix on me, felt their heat reach my face. I turned and ran into All-Mart.

The place smelled of burnt popcorn and overcooked frankfurters. The shoppers moved in slow shuffles, pushing carts, some carts with babies in them. Most of the babies were crying, and their din blended with music blared from overhead speakers.

At first I didn't see Jacey; she wasn't easy to find in a crowd. Then I spotted her leaning against a jewelry counter, taking notes. With her long hair in braids and her plaid shirt and denim overalls, she looked like a child, if you didn't notice the notebook and pen in her hands. They made her seem older, somehow.

I headed toward her, but before I reached the counter, I looked back, over my shoulder. The girl with red hair was coming after me.

She seemed to be in no hurry. She smoked as she walked. Some part of me thought, *Isn't smoking illegal in stores?*

I changed course, headed down an aisle past greeting cards and craft supplies. The store spread out in all directions, and I didn't see any place that wasn't brightly lit and fully exposed. The speakers in the ceiling played an instrumental song that I recognized from a music box my mother owned. The song was called "Stardust."

The girl with red hair rounded the corner, past racks of yarn and plastic packages of knitting needles. She seemed to be moving faster now.

I wove between shoppers, turned into the appliance section, accidentally shoved a large woman reaching for a toaster oven.

"Hey!" Her voice echoed after me.

The aisles were numbered on signs suspended from the ceiling, but I didn't have time to look up. Then I found myself back at the jewelry counter, Jacey still leaning against it, writing in her notebook.

"There you are," she said.

I grabbed her arm and tugged her toward the entrance. "Jacey, go home," I said. "Get out of here. Don't talk to anybody. Don't wait for me."

"What?" She lurched along with me, her pen in one hand, notebook in the other. "What are you doing?"

She didn't weigh much, and she was easy to drag.

"Remember what happened to my friend Autumn?" I said. "Bernie was right—people around me get killed. Get out of here now. Don't look at anyone in the parking lot. Just go."

She kept trying to interrupt me. Then her eyes grew wide. She'd seen something. I whirled around. The girl with the cigarette stood in front of us, her face without expression. She blew smoke into my face.

Jacey pulled free of my grasp and bolted out of the store. I held my ground. "What do you want with me?" I said.

Beneath her cap of red hair, her eyes never blinked. She inhaled deeply and exhaled toward my eyes. I coughed and looked around for help.

The store greeter, an older man with a potbelly, stood by the line of shopping carts. I called to him: "Sir, please—"

Then she lunged at me, holding the cigarette lit-end outward. It singed the hair on my arm. On her second attempt, the cigarette reached my skin.

The pain made me flinch, shrink back. I heard myself say something incoherent. Then I turned and wove back through the crowd again, past jewelry, past appliances, past sewing supplies, and into women's fashions. That's where I decided to turn invisible.

I wasn't wearing my special suit, but when I passed the T-shirts and jeans pinned to a display board, I saw a chance. I kicked my backpack beneath the wooden pedestal where the board was mounted, climbed onto it, and stretched out my arms. *Like a scarecrow*, I thought. Now, instead of three outfits on display, there were four—the last a little grungier than the rest, accessorized by an amulet in the shape of a cat.

She walked by the display a few seconds later, looking from side to side, scanning like an automaton, holding the cigarette's red end outward, ready to strike. She passed so close to me that I smelled the lotion she wore: a mixture of pineapple and coconut cream. I tried not to inhale, in case it was toxic. I looked down at her, wishing I was someone else, someone capable of fighting back.

∞

All-Mart stays open late on Saturdays. At ten fifty P.M. the loudspeaker announced that the store was about to close.

For more than two hours I'd held my invisible mannequin pose. My neck and arms ached. One foot had gone to sleep, and the cigarette burn on my forearm throbbed and stung. I'd heard more instrumental versions of popular songs from the 1970s and '80s than I can bear to recall; for years afterward, I couldn't stand to listen to that music. Chemically engineered scents worn by shoppers and store clerks mixed with the stench of burnt popcorn, making me light-headed, close to nauseous.

My eyes felt heavy, and I may have briefly dozed. What woke me up was the sight of a dark-haired man pushing a cart filled with junk food. I could have sworn he was Elvis—the Darling of the Chemistry Department, the Once and Future King. He passed me, mumbling to himself, and disappeared down another aisle.

Earlier I'd wondered if I should spend the night in the place. But even if ten cigarette girls and shadow men were waiting, I had to get out. As I turned visible again, I hoped that no one was monitoring the security cameras too closely that night.

Outside, the parking lot gaped, nearly empty. No van. No Jacey's car, either—which came as a big relief. If Sal had grabbed her, I thought, her car would still be there.

It would be a long walk back to campus. My cell phone didn't work. Jacey had been right—the moon was full, rising over the flat landscape like a searchlight beam. I thought about taking off my clothes and turning invisible again, but the air was cold enough to persuade me otherwise. I walked along the road's shoulder, not bothering to look for beige vans. *Let them come for me,* I thought.

When I saw the sign ahead for the Okefenokee Swamp Park, it seemed as good a place as any to spend the night.

The park was closed, but the fence was easy to scale. Tupelo trees glistened silver in the moonlight, and the shallow water beneath them seemed bottomless. I made my way to the docks where we'd launched our canoes.

I'd had some vague idea about borrowing a boat and paddling out to the island where the cabin was. But I felt too tired to go a step farther. I wrapped my sweater around me and lay on a bench attached to the dock. There was no sign of Old Joe, and I said a silent prayer that somewhere, he was well—that somewhere he was, at least, alive.

I wish I could write that the blue moon talked to me that night. High above, it stared down silently, a blank, impervious eye. I crossed my arms and stared back, too exhausted to sleep. I thought of all the things that might be out there in the night—snakes, duppies, a rollin calf, Sal Valentine—and I sent out a thought to them all: *Come and get me. This is your chance. I'm too tired to care.*

But no one, nothing, came. I heard only rustles, barks, and splashes, along with the groans of tree frogs and river frogs, communicating in a language I would never understand. The carpet of stars overhead held no discernible patterns; try as I might, I couldn't find constellations, only stellar clutter.

Left out—the feeling I most feared—is all I felt that night. I remembered an Emerson essay I'd read at the school library:

Where do we find ourselves? In a series of which we do not know the extremes. . . . We wake and find ourselves on a stair; there are stairs below us, which we seem to have ascended; there are stairs above us, many a one, which go upward out of sight. . . . Ghostlike, we glide through nature, and should not know our place again.

Eventually I dozed. When morning came, I shook myself awake, stood up, and stretched. My arm had stopped stinging; the burn had healed. In its place, beneath the skin, a white scar had formed in the shape of a star.

The walk back to school took hours. About halfway there my cell phone began the chirp that signaled a message. I played that message twenty times before I reached Hillhouse.

Ari, it said. Cameron's voice was eloquent even through the static. *I heard you missed the boat. Not to worry. There will be other, better times.*

At that time, that year, his message was enough to keep me moving, heading back to where I might belong.

∞

On the last day of exam week, Dashay came to collect me and my things. My first semester of college was officially over. I wouldn't find out my grades for two weeks, but I knew I'd done well.

All around us, parents and students hauled boxes and suitcases and trash bags to their cars and vans. I didn't have so much; it took fewer than twenty minutes to load Mãe's truck.

Dashay sat behind the steering wheel, watching a student try to repack the contents of a box she'd dropped. She picked up a sweater, stared at it, and threw it back on the ground. Then she picked up the same sweater, stared at it, and put it in the box.

"A lot of these kids are messed up," Dashay said. "I saw boys on the stairs walking like robots."

"They're taking V." I buckled my seat belt. "Maybe when they get home, they'll go back to normal?" *I sound like Professor Hogan*, I thought. "I mean, provided they stay away from dealers and Orion Springs water."

"Could be." Dashay started the engine. "But watching them go through withdrawal—that won't be a pretty sight for Mom and Dad."

On the drive to Tybee, Dashay told me about life back in Homosassa Springs. The horses and Grace were fine, but they missed my mother and me.

"I miss them, too," I said. "When are we going back?"

"I don't know." Dashay drove faster than Mãe did, cutting in and out of traffic when the mood took her. "I think the plan is to stay on

Tybee for a while. The weather's just beginning to warm up, Sara said."

As we drove out onto the island, past the green marshes and blue inlets of the Low Country, I felt a slow surge of excitement.

The cottage looked the same—weather battered but solid except for the stairs, which had some broken and rotting steps. Dashay knocked, then tried the door. "Locked," she said.

She called the cottage number on her cell phone. We heard the phone ringing beyond the door. No one answered.

I felt my excitement die. In its place came familiar anxiety.

Then Dashay turned away from the cottage, toward the beach. She grinned. "Look."

I spun around. Past the patches of sea grass and palm trees, two people walked along the shoreline: a woman with long auburn hair streaming behind her, a tall man wearing a windbreaker.

I tore down the steps, hearing Dashay laughing behind me.

Then I stopped short. The couple was holding hands.

"What's the matter?" Dashay came up to join me. "Ah, I see. You don't want to interrupt the lovebirds."

"Is that what they are?"

My father's face was visible now, his familiar face—composed, strong, healthy again. His head tipped back to study the clouds.

"Don't worry, Ari," Dashay said. "There's room for you, too."

I hung back a moment longer. Then I ran across the sand to join them.

Epilogue

*T*he full text of my testimony before the Council on Vampire Ethics should be available online, so I'm not including that part of the story here. Most vampires are aware of the hearings and their aftermath. The few humans who find them will no doubt dismiss them as fiction.

In any case, the COVE investigation came too late. By the time the Council sent out a research team, there were no opiates in bottled water—at least, none in the samples tested. Orion Springs abruptly went out of business.

As for V, the panel dismissed it as just another "street drug," far less dangerous than crack cocaine or heroin. When investigators went to the house near Oglethorpe Square, they found it empty.

I wasn't surprised. Although the Council is meant to be impartial, two of its members were avowed Nebulists. One of them noticed the scar on my arm and said, "I see you've been marked as an interferer."

Across America and across the world, people continue to disappear, as do honeybees. Scientists are working on ways of limiting and preventing future colony collapse. No one, as far as I know, is researching whether the viruses involved might have been deliberately spread, and if so, who might be spreading them.

I've come to think that rather than a strength, it's the curse of vampires that humans will not believe in them. We've spent the better part of the last hundred years assimilating into the society of mortals, thinking that assimilation would grant us invisibility and survival.

But full *integration* into American society requires agreeing, to some extent, with the social compacts that society holds dear. And I've reached the conclusion that, while vampires may assimilate, it's unlikely that we can ever integrate—unless society evolves and vampires take a visible role in it.

Meanwhile, I dedicate this book to mortals, and I leave them these questions: Are you comfortable with the values your society holds dear? When's the last time you looked deep into your own eyes? Do you know the limitations of your vision?

Acknowledgments

As I wrote this book, some generous people helped address my research questions. I send thanks to Deputy Billy Kruthers of the Hillsboro County Sheriff's Department, Dr. George Everett, and Dr. Amy Ward. Their knowledge and insights were invaluable.

Sheila Forsyth, Clare Hubbard, Kate Hubbard, Mary Johnson, Nancy Pate, Adam Perry, Tison Pugh, and Pat Rushin read and commented on various drafts. Mary Pat Hyland, Rick McCoy, and Sharon Wissert offered moral support. Robley Wilson read the manuscript several times and coped, as ever, with my metamorphosis into a writing zombie. I'm lucky to have you all in my life.

Eternal thanks to Marcy Posner and Denise Roy for their expertise, friendship, and guidance. Thanks also to Rebecca Davis and Leah Wasielewski at Simon & Schuster for their wisdom and support.

To all of the readers who've sent feedback to www.susanhubbard.com: you're the best! As is Fuchsia McInerney, who designed the page, and Caethua, who provided the music for myspace.com/thesocietyofs.

Finally, I want to commend Save the Manatee Club (www.savethemanatee.org) and the Homosassa Springs Wildlife State Park (http://www.hswsp.com) for trying to keep the real Florida from disappearing.